DAMIEN

BY OSCAR DONALD ERICKSON

to

Joan and Peter

with

fondest regards.

Produced by:

FriesenPress
Suite 300 – 852 Fort Street
Victoria, BC, Canada V8W 1H8

www.friesenpress.com

Distributed to the trade by The Ingram Book Company

PROLOGUE

The young man held her hand gently as they walked along the path. It was spring and the sense of urgent growth surrounded them. He felt her hand's softness turn caressingly into his own as he led her off the main path onto a much smaller one that began to disappear among trees and then into a mossy area. There he turned to her and pressed his lips into hers, at first gently until, sensing her eagerness, he slipped his tongue far into her mouth, feeling her tongue curl up and slide over it. They folded into the ground, her fingers opening her blouse to lift the flimsy bra over her breasts and then pulling his shirt off and sliding his pants down effortlessly. She cried out in the urgency of her passion, feeling him slide slowly and deeply into her. That was when, her left hand pressing wildly into the ground, she felt a thick stickiness that made her lift her hand in shock to see the blood covering it, and beyond her upraised hand the young naked woman in the tree above with dead eyes staring down at her.

PART ONE

CHAPTER ONE

Damien woke in the middle of the night. He was crying. In his dream he had as his pet a beautiful humming-bird. It would fly close to his head and then in a moment was out of sight roaming the corridors of air. He called the hummingbird Zynta. He had no idea how or where he got the name, except that the first three letters made the sound "zinnn," reminding him of the sound the wings made, though he couldn't follow the wings themselves in their magic control of the air. What Damien could make out were the vibrant colors of the bird's minute body, especially as it hovered so close to his head. To him this tiny creature was a miracle of nature.

One night all this changed. His dream was dark, filled with the squirming forms of beings who in some way threatened his existence. One of these came closer and closer, its eyes like slate, then the slate color burning into an olive glow. He was sure the creature sought to enter him, and he struck out, grabbing what seemed to be its head, and crushed it. There was a horrible soundlessness and then only darkness. But there was something left in his hand.

Now fully awake he switched on his light. In his hand, crushed, lay a tiny hummingbird, so like his dream Zynta that he almost believed she had become real.

Damien wept for a long time.

When he finally arose he buried the remains of Zynta in a pot of yellow orchids—themselves, like Zynta, triumphs of color.

★★★

Sitting at the small white table in the solarium, Arnold poured himself a cup of coffee and waited for Damien. The soft light, warmed by the concrete mass of the wall behind him, washed out the contours of pots and plants and lounge chairs, seeming to absorb them into nothingness, and himself into a trance-like mood. Constructed away back in 1988, the solarium featured double-glazed iron-free glass at the 46° angle which was optimal for La Jolla, and overlooked a large swimming pool. After the car accident which partially paralyzed him when he was sixty-seven, Arnold liked to ride his motorized wheelchair over from the main house. He'd turn on a composition by Ravel or Berg and take a dip in the solar aquarium, as he called it, emerging renewed.

Damien came upon his father, his face tilted up to the radiance, and his large grey-green eyes closed. With his fine skin and white hair charged with pellucid light, Arnold looked like an incarnation of a Druid priest. Or a brilliant scientist. The two weren't so far apart, Damien thought. His father was a geneticist who had made a fortune through his scientific discoveries. Yet, he just wasn't happy and Damien wasn't sure why. He knew his father's health was uncertain, especially since the accident.

Arnold opened his eyes and regarded Damien, "I'm glad to see you passed all your university exams, Damien, though I expected higher percentages."

"My lowest mark was 78%, Father."

He had once called Arnold "Dad," but was corrected, "Father" being the proper British term.

"I expect nothing less than 85%, Damien. I know you have it in you. You've got the brains."

"I got 94% in calculus."

"Good. But it doesn't come as any surprise."

Damien shrugged. "You always find fault with me."

"Maybe I expect too much."

"Maybe."

There was a long pause as Arnold lifted a pair of binoculars to watch a distant bird.

"Have you decided on your specialty, Damien?"

"Not yet," Damien said. "Do I have to?"

"Of course not. But I trust it will be in the sciences."

"Actually, I was thinking of Law."

"What?" Arnold lowered his binoculars.

"Law. You can do anything then."

Damien had never heard his father snort, but he snorted now.

"What's wrong with Law?"

"It's a profession for dimwits. You got that idea from your girlfriend's father, didn't you? What's her name?"

"Kate Reid."

"Her father's a lawyer, isn't he?"

"Was a lawyer. Now a judge."

There was a long silence. And then: "Are you serious about this Kate Reid?"

"Not really," he said. "She's got a boyfriend already." While this was true, it wasn't the entire truth, and he knew it. He wanted her. And he believed she wanted him.

"So her father wants you to be a lawyer, is that it? And then he will be happy if you marry his daughter."

"Come on, Father."

"It happens, more often than you think."

Damien did not know what to say.

"It's not good enough for you, Damien. I want you to be a scientist."

"Like you."

"Yes, like me." There was a pause. "Or unlike me… but a scientist. You have the brains for it. Please, do not throw that away. Please." He grasped the young man's arm. "I need you, Damien. I need you to carry on the work."

★★★

Waiting for Arnold in the lab, Tom poured himself a cup of coffee, and took a sip as he leafed through the lab results he needed to show Arnold. Damn! There was a key page missing. He riffled back and forth looking for it, then checked the drawer where he had stored it and, not finding it there, began to search through the other drawers, dislodging all manner of lab paraphernalia as he went. Then he paused, looking at an unlabeled file of notes in Arnold's handwriting poking out from beneath a stack of scientific papers. Curious, he pulled it out and glanced at it, intending to see that it got properly filed. What he saw, though, compelled him to continue reading. He had no idea that Arnold had been so far ahead in his genetic research back in the early 90s.

The intercom buzzed loudly, jerking Tom back to the present, and he hastily gathered up Arnold's papers, tried to mop up the coffee ring on the inside of the folder, and shoved everything back where he'd found it, thinking that he'd ask Arnold about it soon.

The intercom buzzed again and Tom answered. Eden Hearn, Arnold's secretary and nurse, explained that Arnold was feeling unwell.

"How unwell?"

"He's got a slight fever, and he complained that he didn't sleep much last night." Her voice sounded strained.

"Is something troubling him, Eden?"

There was a pause. "I don't know. But yesterday he had a fight with Damien. That might have made him worse."

"A fight?"

"He was shouting."

"And Damien?"

"I didn't hear him." Her voice immediately took on that special protective tone she used when she talked about Damien. "I know Damien shouldn't worry his father … but he's just a boy." Though the boy was twenty.

"Maybe I'd better come over."

"Arnold said he wouldn't see anybody; he took a pill and went to sleep." Her voice became business-like. "Do you know a Mr. Peter Keyes, President of the American Laboratories Association?" Without waiting for an answer, she went on: "He wanted to talk to Arnold, but I said you'd have to clear that first. I told him you were in charge of the lab." Tom knew she was aware that that wasn't completely true. "He asked me about you."

Tom pretended nonchalance. "Oh? What'd he ask?"

"Who you were, your credentials, you know—where you got your PhD and how long you'd been in charge. He said he wanted to talk to you, too." She paused. "I told him you were too busy right now."

Tom switched off the intercom thinking that the title Nurse-secretary did little to describe Eden Hearn. She'd been with Arnold since 1991 and had looked after Damien like a mother. But there was more to it. Eden was still plumply attractive now at 41, so Arnold would certainly have responded to the 22 year old, who was also very good at massage. She became his mistress in all but title, which remained always Nurse-secretary.

DAMIEN

Since Arnold wasn't going to show, Tom decided to return to his comfortable bungalow around the corner to talk to his wife Thea. He found Thea in her studio, a splash of reddish-brown clay on her cheek, her clay-covered hands molding a new sculpture. When she saw him, she gave the sculpture a pat, turned to wash her hands, and took off her clay-spattered lab coat. Dressed in a thin white one piece garment that contrasted with her brown skin, black hair and eyes, she walked barefoot toward him with an animal grace.

Thea's Mayan beauty reminded Tom of Tikal, the Mayan temple city in the Petén jungle of Guatemala which Tom and Arnold had explored on a data collection trip in 2005, the first year of his employment with Arnold. He had been fascinated by the sense of dynamic power expressed by the stepped pyramids surrounding the central plaza area. They followed a path through the jungle, passing here and there pyramid sites shrouded in foliage. At last, they came to a temple stretching up through the vined greenery, and found a rope ladder which they climbed with difficulty, while monkeys hurled themselves from branch to branch. Finally, they emerged high up on the side of the pyramid and found themselves looking out over the jungle mass at a far-off temple emerging out of a sea of greenery.

Later, they climbed down the precarious little ladder and made their way back to the great central plaza which was anchored on one side by the Temple of the Jaguar, the tallest of the buildings. Since they had spent much of that day searching for signs of jaguars, Tom had asked Arnold why he was so interested in them, when they were unrelated to their research. Arnold explained that his father had been a zoologist specializing in the leopards of the Kruger National Park in South Africa. The jaguar, Arnold went on, is a close cousin to the leopard, so close that many people cannot tell them apart, and it is revered by the Maya as godlike.

Arnold had arranged to meet his old flame, Ahmal, in the plaza. While waiting, they crossed the plaza to climb the Temple of the Masks, whose feminine identity complemented the virile Jaguar Temple. From the top, Arnold saw Ahmal far down near a sacrificial slab of stone stained with ancient human blood, and they quickly descended.

Ahmal was a small woman, somewhere in her forties, with black eyes like the teen-age girl beside her. Her black hair was braided in strange whorls. She looked distinctly Mayan, with sloping forehead, nose and chin. Her slim body moved with elegance.

"So, you are here," she said in a cultivated voice, surprising Tom.

Arnold embraced Ahmal, but looked at the girl. "You must be Thea." Arnold said, almost wonderingly, gazing at her.

Ahmal nodded. "Yes, this is the daughter you've been supporting all these years, Arnold. Thea, this is your father."

Thea smiled uncertainly at Arnold, who smiled warmly back at her. "I'm glad to meet you, Thea—at long last." He looked at her searchingly. "I hope you will be happy living at my place while studying at UCSD."

Thea glanced at Tom, reminding Arnold to add: "Ahmal and Thea, this is Tom Delaney, who runs my lab for me."

Tom looked with some astonishment from Arnold to Thea to Ahmal. Arnold had never mentioned his daughter, and now it seemed she was coming to live with them.

Of course, Tom knew little about Arnold's private life beyond what he had researched before accepting employment with him. All he really knew was that Arnold was born in England, grew up in in South Africa, and was sent back to England for school at Harrow, eventually graduating from Cambridge as a molecular biologist with top honors. After a few years at a UK laboratory, Arnold developed some patents related to bio-engineering that had important medical applications, and profited handsomely. Two years later he was offered a partnership at a small but renowned lab near La Jolla, just north of San Diego, near U.C.S.D, which became his own when his elderly partner died.

When Tom had completed his first class degree in molecular genetics at Stanford, his Professor, Jeremy Parkins, had offered to recommend him for a Technical Assistant's job with Arnold Head, who ought, Jeremy said, to have received a Nobel Prize for his work in genetics. Tom had leapt at the chance but, in the six years since, Tom often had cause to wonder why he had not made a few discreet enquiries first, such as into Arnold's methods of working, his goals, and exactly what he expected of Tom. Arnold was prone to bouts of ill temper when Tom didn't master something instantly. As they got to know one another, their personal relationship warmed a little, though Arnold always retained a certain aloofness.

That first meeting with Thea six years ago had sealed his fate, though, Tom thought wryly. Deeply attracted to Thea, Tom found himself uninterested in any opportunities that took him away from her. When Tom met her on that trip, Thea had been only 18, seven years younger than he was, and Arnold's daughter, and none of that mattered to Tom, who fell head over heels in love.

A year later in San Diego, six months after Arnold's accident, Tom and Thea were married, and settled down in a bungalow provided by Arnold near his house. Tom knew that adapting to the North American way of life was challenging for Thea at first, since she had spent her childhood in a Mayan village in the Guatemalan jungle, and her high school years at a private school in Mexico City. Her honours thesis in Anthropology at UCSD had certainly kept her busy, which helped. What Tom loved about her, though, was her gentle sensitivity, and her way of seeing that was so different from his. Though she was a brilliant scholar, it was in her sculpting pastime that her true nature shone, it seemed to Tom.

Thinking of this, Tom enfolded Thea in his arms, burying his nose in her hair.

"You've come back early," she said.

"Arnold isn't well. Eden says he had a fight with Damien yesterday."

"Eden admitted that, did she?"

"Why wouldn't she?" Tom asked, reminded of the friction between Eden and Thea. It arose out of the very thing that fascinated Tom about Thea: her hiddenness, her way of looking at you as if she heard more than you said, her way of answering your deeper, unspoken question. This clearly irritated Eden no end because she was, or thought she was, upfront about everything, a straight shooter. Tom believed Eden resented the fact that Damien obviously liked Thea and talked to her at every opportunity. Eden had always considered Damien her boy; after all, she was mainly responsible for bringing him up

"You know how Eden sees only perfection in Damien. It's rare for her to admit any problem, and you know she has too much influence over my father." Thea said.

"But no one controls Arnold."

"I said influence, Tom."

"Do you think something's wrong with the boy?"

"Not wrong, exactly, but there's something not quite right either."

"Well, what is it, Thea? He's tops in athletics and his studies."

DAMIEN

"I know that." She looked away and out the window at the large eucalyptus tree growing there. "I don't like to say."

"Please do, Thea."

She turned to face him. "He likes girls too much."

"What?" he laughed. "He's a healthy young man!"

"No, it's more than that. He likes girls too much."

"At twenty? If he wasn't interested in sex there'd be something wrong with him. Of course he likes girls."

She was silent, looking away.

"What do you mean—too much?"

She shook her head. "Perhaps I'm mistaken."

He waited. He'd come to respect her intuition.

"Perhaps it's mostly the other way around: girls are too attracted to him."

He thought about this. "But you don't know any of his girlfriends."

"You weren't at the pool yesterday. Three of Damien's friends were there, a boy and two girls. One of the girls could hardly leave Damien alone, even when he dove into the pool, though he distanced himself easily. But afterwards, when he climbed out, she was onto him. She lay beside him, kissed his shoulder, ran her hand down his back…"

"Well, he's a good looking guy…"

"He's more than good looking. There are a lot of good looking young men. But he has…a strange force in him. I know it. I feel it myself. I bet you do, too."

Tom thought about this." What do you mean by strange force?"

"Just that."

He could only shake his head, feeling vaguely troubled.

★★★

Kate and Damien were enjoying one of their regular runs along Mission Bay, when she stopped running.

"That sea is too inviting," she said. "I've just got to have a dip." She tore off her T-shirt and shorts and made a quick dash to the ocean. Not to be outdone, Damien stripped to his underwear and followed her in. After diving into the waves like porpoises, they dried out on the sandy beach. Awhile later, Kate sat up and brushed off the dry sand, then lay down on her tummy, murmuring to Damien, "Would you brush the sand off my back?" He readily complied, aware of the olive sheen of her skin and the subtle curves. She giggled a little under his touch.

"You have nice hands," she said. "Now let me do you."

By the time she finished removing the sand from his back, he had a massive erection, and quickly turned away from her when he stood up to brush his own chest and stomach.

"Why are you turning your back on me?" she asked.

"Um…" he muttered.

"Let's see you," she said softly, putting her hand on his shoulder, and turning him around. "My, my," she muttered, looking down at him. "What are we going to do with that?"

She led Damien toward a cabin not far away.

Unearthing the key from the fourth plant pot to the left, she opened the front door, explaining that this was her family's mostly unused old place. Inside were two double beds on either side of the room, with a small kitchen area and bathroom at one end. She gently pushed him down on one of the beds, and disappeared into the bathroom, emerging a few minutes later, naked and holding up a condom. In a moment she had stripped off his swimsuit, and stared down at him.

"I'll bet the other girls are after you."

Looking up at her, he smiled and said, "I want you."

"Well, keep it that way. At least for awhile. I want you all to myself."

She came down on him then, slowly, but he swung her over on her back, to enter a dark void in which he plunged. It was a world in which there was no Damien—only the shrieks of birdlike creatures swinging from the limbs of trees that curved and twisted like giant snakes… then a vast roar and nothing.

She lay beside him, trembling, head twisted to one side.

"My god," she breathed. "Oh fuck."

He turned to look at her, saw the gashes in her neck, and gingerly touched the edge of one, wonderingly.

"You did that," she said.

"Oh god… I'm sorry."

"You should be. That's going too far."

"Yes. I know." But he noticed the bedding under her was soaked with her juices.

"I know," she said. "I've never had anything like that. That's too much." She paused, and looked at him uncertainly.

"Do you remember scratching me?"

"Um… no."

"Like when you beat up those bullies in high school, right? I heard you didn't remember that, either."

"Which ones?"

"That day with Freddie."

"How do you know about that?"

"Everyone knew. Those bullies were wrecked."

Damien did remember now. In grade 9, Freddie Lyall, a rather thin brainy little fellow, had started walking home from school with him, even though they had nothing much to say to one another. Damien didn't mind because he felt sorry for Freddie, who was always getting bullied.

One day Freddie had not quite caught up with Damien when three classmates began pushing him around, calling him teacher's pet. Damien turned and quietly told them to shove off, but they paid no attention, Damien being a new kid at the school. The leader, Joe Brandeis, told Damien to get lost and fast. Instead, Damien delivered a lightning punch to Joe's belly, and the boy crumpled to the ground to the amazement of his friends, for Joe had proven himself to be an expert kickboxer. They glanced at one another and closed in on Damien. The one behind Damien moved first, encircling Damien's neck with his arm, only to find himself flung over Damien's shoulder and smashed into his pal who was moving in on Damien from the front. Damien stared down at the three of them sprawled on the ground.

"You guys leave Freddie alone, okay? He's my friend."

Freddie and Damien walked on together.

"Those guys were bullying Freddie," Damien said defensively to Kate.

"But you didn't have to beat them up like that to make them stop. You go too far." Kate was clearly uncomfortable.

"I'm really sorry about those scratches, Kate. I didn't mean to do that."

"I think you should go now," Kate said quietly.

DAMIEN

CHAPTER TWO

The news media had gone wild about the naked 22 year old female found dead in a tree near the university campus. They had no success in getting interviews with the co-discoverers of the body, Jack Rudolph and Peggy Laplante. In serious shock, the girl was in hospital, deeply sedated. The young man had been questioned by the police and was answering no calls. Now the media were on to Sam Schumacker, FBI, who had already had enough of them.

It was only the second day of investigation, but local police had called in Sam's task force due to the extraordinary nature of the crime and the surprisingly small amount of evidence. After being photographed extensively using a crane, the body had been taken down. Crime pathologists determined that death had come as a result of a severed jugular. But the form of the ragged wound ruled out the use of a knife or other sharp instrument. Unbelievably, it suggested that the jugular had been torn out by teeth, so the lab was analyzing the form of the bite and traces of saliva. There was no evidence of rape. Her shoulder bag was recovered from the bushes below. It had been unopened, which ruled out theft as a motive, and her wallet established her identity. Her name was Catherine Turner and she came from a small town in Vermont. She was in her graduate year in Psychology and her dormitory roommate,

Sarah Trent, soon identified her. Financially supported by her parents, Catherine had complemented her studies with triathlon and photography. She had no regular boyfriend but enjoyed partying.

Local police had sealed the area and canvassed nearby university buildings for anyone who might have seen Catherine the night before, with inconclusive results. Catherine's parents had offered a substantial reward for information and a team of officers was sifting the avalanche of calls. Apparently, a bunch of frat boys had got drunk and thought it funny to report false leads, which did not help. Other officers were researching similar crimes elsewhere to rule out the possibility of a serial killer. It all amounted to a mass of information that didn't seem to lead anywhere. Forensics had nothing beyond the neck wound and the bruises incurred in hoisting the body into the tree. Not even a decent footprint. And the lab was taking too damn long with what little physical evidence it had, even though Sam had put a rush on it. He wanted the DNA from that saliva ASAP.

Sam was accustomed to getting quick results, but this case had him stumped. And the press would not leave him alone, for this could be no ordinary madman who would tear a woman's throat open with his teeth, then carry her into a tree. The media gobbled up every tidbit it could find and then made up a few of its own. Hysterical headlines screamed, "Vampire Tree Murder."

"Did the vampire intend to return and eat portions of her body?" asked one rag.

Another tabloid even recommended that the police should have left the body where it was, and kept watch to see if the madman would return to his kill.

It didn't help that Halloween was in a week.

Sam could not believe the bullshit spilling from the media. Yet he could not ignore it either, or the pressure from his superiors. Crazy as it seemed, Sam Schumacker had to at least investigate whether a madman believing he was a vampire could have been responsible for the heinous murder. His team contacted mental institutions, hospitals, and psychiatrists asking whether they knew or had heard of anyone having this form of delusion, and the answer was universally no. Of course, Sam still couldn't rule out the possibility that such a deluded person might have escaped official notice until now.

Mulling over the facts of the case, he drove home that second night. He picked up a take-out meal of anchovies, salad and chips, the last of which his wife Naomi wouldn't have approved. Wishing she were home with him instead of away visiting her sister, Sam opened a Budweiser and sat down to eat. His cell phone rang and for a moment he tried to ignore it, but of course couldn't, nuisance call or no.

"It's Peter Gregory, Sam. Remember me?"

Of course Sam remembered Peter, having worked with him on a couple of cross-border cases up in Washington State, one involving drugs, and the other, human trafficking. Peter had solved more major crimes than anyone else in the Royal Canadian Mounted Police.

"Peter! Great to hear from you… Got a problem?"

"When don't I have one?"

"Heard you left the Mounties, Peter. Got fed up?"

"You could say that, Sam. It was mainly the Beaver."

"Who's the Beaver? Oh yeah—your Superintendent."

"Yeah, my Super of the wood-chewing voice. He left me to do all the work, and then took the credit when I brought the guy in. Ever heard of that?" Peter forbore mentioning that the Beaver not only tried to take credit for Peter's success but also actively impeded Peter's investigations at times. Peter had finally realized that not only was the Beaver jealous, he actually believed that a "half-breed" like Peter should not have such talent.

"It's not unheard of. So what are you doing for a living?" Sam asked.

"I've gone private and that's why I'm phoning you. A wealthy client in Vancouver has a daughter who's missing. Problem is, he's never received a ransom note. My guess is she's not been kidnapped but captured."

"Go on, Peter."

"An informant tells me she was probably taken by Cass Milette who then sold her to a new gang called The Slavers. Too bad these guys keep popping up, eh?"

"Yeah. Our human trafficking sting only shut things down for a while."

"I know my chances of finding this girl, Sam, are slim, but I can't not try. Fortunately, the client is willing to pay what it'll cost. Thought maybe you could help me get on the right track. I need to come down there because The Slavers are centered in California."

Sam saw a possible break in the clouds.

"Peter, I'll tell you when you get here, but I'm on a bitch of a case myself. So you help me and I'll help you."

"It's a deal Sam."

"When you hear the facts of my case, you won't thank me. A 22 year old woman found dead 20 feet up a tree, her throat ripped open—by teeth, it looks like, no evidence of sexual assault, no theft, inconclusive footprints, and no witnesses so far."

"Not the 'Vampire Tree Murder'?"

"It's in the Canadian press too!"

"Uh huh. I'll phone you from the airport tomorrow, Sam."

Sam hung up and slung down some beer. He felt a smidgen better, knowing that Peter was coming.

In the two cross-border cases they'd worked on together, Sam had discovered unusual abilities in the younger man. Sam remembered that the drug trafficking case had implicated a particular gang of Hell's Angels. The police were getting their information from a gang member, but they couldn't seem to nail the gang itself. The case had stymied the police for some time until Peter figured out that their informant had to be playing a double role, giving the police tidbits—enough to make them think they were on track—while informing the gang on the police investigation. As a result the joint U.S.-Canada force, led by Peter Gregory and Sam Schumacker, was able to leave their informant with no choice but to cooperate fully. They cracked the case and jailed seven members of the Hell's Angels. Sam had never been able to get Peter to explain how he'd discovered the informant's double dealing when he had no real evidence of such complicity.

Then came the human trafficking case, which involved a Canadian and a US gang working together. Girls brought in from Asia by Kim Sung's gang were forced into prostitution in Vancouver, and then shipped across the border to serve big city pimps, mainly in Seattle, San Francisco, and Los Angeles. Sam decided to send a female police officer undercover as a prostitute. Anne Derringer volunteered to work under the name of Brandi. Three weeks into the sting, she was found seriously injured in a sleeping bag at the Church of the Nativity on Main Street. Ten days later she was able to explain that she'd been tortured until she'd confess anything, and did, sure she would get a bullet through her head, and no longer caring. To her surprise she was spared. Sam and Peter knew why. It was a message to the police to lay off the undercover tricks. Anne Derringer slowly recovered, but within three months resigned from the police force.

So there they were with nothing to go on. Peter came up with a diabolical scheme to infiltrate the gangs by exploiting their basic mistrust of each other. Kim Sung's Vancouver gang depended upon Juan Perez' Latin-American Mafia to distribute the girls in the US, but Peter found a way to persuade Kim Sung that Juan's Mafia was cheating him out of his share of the profits. When Kim Sung began to look around for an alternate US distributor, he found Bau Chi, a police informer with credible Mafia credentials. Then it was only a matter of time before Schumacher and Peter had the evidence to break the prostitution ring, free the 27 girls currently in circulation, and send Kim Sung and Juan Perez for a nice long stay in their respective countries' penitentiaries.

Sam had to acknowledge to himself that, in both cases, although they were joint operations in which the RCMP and the FBI were credited with success, the successful strategies were entirely Peter Gregory's. He was the mastermind.

Yet it wasn't Peter who received the credit on the Canadian side. It was the Beaver, his superintendent and nemesis.

Sam was looking forward to seeing Peter tackle the "Vampire Tree Murder" case.

CHAPTER THREE

It was a superbly cooked seafood dinner on the terrace by the pool, which was lit from underneath. Danielle would have loved the scene except that Damien was not there yet. She'd been enjoying reconnecting with Eden, but she was also looking forward to seeing Damien for the first time in five years. They'd been great friends from 10-14 years of age, then her family had moved away and they'd lost touch.

Arnold and Tom and Eden and Thea had given up on the young man and were digging into the crab salad. They'd had a couple of drinks and Arnold switched on a piece by Telemann, and then a type of music that was strange to Danielle's ears. She looked over at Thea and saw that the young woman was totally absorbed in the music. Despite the beauty of the setting, Danielle noticed that Eden seemed annoyed by Thea's absorption in the music and Arnold was distracted. Tom seemed to be the only one holding up the conversation.

Then Eden glanced over at Danielle.

"I hope you are being careful, Danielle," she said.

Danielle frowned, puzzled.

"Haven't you heard about the body they found in the tree out at the University?" Eden asked, surprised.

Danielle had just returned from a trip to San Francisco and hadn't heard.

"Just two days ago in a treed area out there. They've never had a murder like it. She was a student."

"They said her throat was torn open, not cut," Tom added. "The papers are calling it the 'Vampire Tree Murder.'" He shook his head. "The whole thing makes no sense."

"So be careful, Danielle. Be very careful," Eden added unnecessarily.

"Hi." Damien approached them, nicely dressed in slacks and a cream short-sleeved shirt that contrasted with his tanned skin. "Danielle, I didn't know you were in town."

Danielle had forgotten the vividness of his yellow eyes and that lock of dark hair that always fell over his forehead.

"Hi Damien," Danielle said a little breathlessly, surprising herself. Quickly recovering her composure, Danielle went on, "Eden has just been warning me about being careful at the university. Do you know anything about it?"

"Not really. Catherine was in my Chemistry class, though," Damien said, shifting uneasily. "I can't believe what happened to her!"

"You'd better dig in before we eat everything," Arnold said with a small smile.

"Did you know her well?" Tom asked as Eden handed Damien a plate.

"Not that well. We were lab partners on and off."

"Where've you been, Damien?" Eden asked. "In somebody else's pool?"

"As a matter of fact, that's just where I was," Damien answered. "My swimming coach was clocking six of us for the one hundred. There's a race at the end of the month. He made me swim it three times."

"With what result?" Arnold asked.

"I've been chosen to represent the team in the one hundred."

Eden beamed. "That's wonderful."

"Great." Tom added. "But you'd better grab some food as your Dad says, or there'll be nothing left."

Danielle was stunned at her visceral response to Damien. She'd always liked him, but she couldn't believe how attractive he'd become. So she avoided looking at him and focused on her plate and on Arnold.

"I'd forgotten that you have an English accent." she said quietly to Arnold beside her.

"Not surprising," Arnold said, "since I'm English."

"I thought you were African. Damien told me you were brought up in Africa."

"In my earliest years, yes. Not long after my birth in England my parents took me to South Africa. My father had a research grant to study leopard populations in Kruger National Park."

Arnold raised his plate as Eden ladled out more crab. He was a small man, not more than 5'6" and, despite his wheelchair dependence, had no fat on him. When he lifted his plate up, Danielle noticed the thinness of his arms. It was his head that made him so distinctive: a noble head, such as she had seen on copies of Roman statuary, with a strong jaw and imposing forehead. His eyes intrigued her. They were dark green and had a piercing quality somewhat like, yet unlike, Damien's eyes, which were more yellow than green—eyes she had never seen on anyone else.

"I remained in Africa until I was 13 and then was shipped off to private school in England, Harrow as a matter of fact."

"Did you like it there?"

"It was horrible."

"That's a very strong statement, Dr. Head."

"Please call me Arnold. It's time now. I have to get used to you as a young woman, not as the kid who played with Damien years ago."

He paused, looking into the distance, and she felt warmed by his words.

"You see, my childhood in Africa was wonderful. I'll go so far as to say magical. My father was off on expeditions into remote areas most of the time for he had been made Senior Park Warden by the government in Pretoria. I sometimes went with him, but not often because we lived outside Durban on a large property, and along with two other boys I had a private tutor who taught Latin and Greek and, believe it or not, pretty good mathematics, well beyond Euclid, though my real interest was always biology, particularly animal life. Most of the time I and my friends were left alone to do our homework and roam around the veldt on horseback. It was an ideal existence."

Eden came to him bearing a full plate of prawns in a special sauce.

"Would you like some wine, Arnold?" she asked.

"More white would be fine, Eden."

"But not so ideal at Harrow?" Danielle persisted.

"Not so, indeed. You see I was always small and physically unskilled, with the exception of riding. So my schoolmates looked down upon me, as indeed they did anyone who did not measure up in sports. And I wasn't used to the rough and tumble skills which I suppose you acquire at prep school which I never attended. They not only made fun of me, the prefects beat me regularly, and so did the senior boys. You see, I was different and therefore fair game. They had various ways to make my life miserable. I think what I went through… well, I remember reading about the poet Shelley, also a much abused lad, considering what he suffered at school… it was sheer hell."

"My God..." Danielle muttered, "How did you manage to get through it?"

"I created my own world based on my studies. I made myself excel in academics. It was my revenge, and I succeeded. I got top marks at Harrow and a scholarship to Cambridge."

"It's amazing," Danielle exclaimed. "You're amazing to have found such strength."

He looked at her. "It was amazing, I agree, but it was also at great cost. It meant loneliness... isolation... hard things to manage." His voice changed a little, becoming slightly hoarse, "to this day."

★★★

Later that night, after the dinner things were cleared away, and Eden and Arnold had gone up the path to the main house, accompanied by Tom, no doubt to plan the next day's lab work, Danielle looked around for Damien, and finally saw him at the far end of the pool. He and Thea were sitting on two chairs in deep conversation. She walked down to them, and they abruptly stopped talking.

"Hi guys, are you into something deep?" She knew they were. Thea was wearing a filmy silk top and pants and looked up in a way that bothered Danielle, but she couldn't say why. She wondered if it was Thea's deep black eyes.

"I think I'll be running along now," Danielle said, "I've got an exam coming up."

Damien stood up. "The evening's young. What about a swim?"

"I didn't bring my swim suit."

"Don't need one, you know that." Of course she knew that. They'd been swimming in the pool without suits since childhood. But she was no longer a child.

DAMIEN

Still he was challenging her, and she wasn't going to back down.

"Okay," she said softly, "how about you, Thea?"

"No, Tom will be expecting me. But thanks for asking." Thea glided quickly out the side gate that led to their bungalow. Watching her, Danielle thought she might get to know and like Thea.

Danielle and Damien stripped quickly. Danielle felt a sudden change in the air as Damien looked at her before he abruptly turned and dove in. They swam several lengths, Damien slicing ahead. Danielle found herself less interested in her own swimming than in the beauty of his strokes, his muscular shoulders, lean body and slim hips. Watching his smooth economy of movement, she remembered climbing trees with him when they were small. She'd been an expert scaler of the enormous weeping willow next to the pond in her parents' front yard. It had been her favorite place to hide and spy on the neighbors. That was actually how she'd met Damien, because he knew instantly that she was in that tree, as if he'd smelled her or something. When he challenged her for spying, she'd challenged him to come up and stop her, since everyone else she knew never could make it past that first lower branch. She couldn't believe it when Damien practically flew up the tree and perched nonchalantly above her. Not only that, but he developed the habit of napping in the crotch of the tree and leaping out to surprise her when she least expected it. That was the start of many such pranks that they perpetrated upon unsuspecting neighbors, knocking on doors, running across roofs and the like. She remembered the big sweaty guy on the corner who'd gotten so apoplectic that he'd chased her right out of his yard, and only Damien's distracting him had given her the chance to escape his meaty clutches.

She couldn't believe herself now; she who was usually so coolly in control could not stop staring at him. And with those powerful shoulders he outdistanced her easily—at least in the pool.

By the time she had swum ten lengths, Danielle felt that she had settled down and was determinedly calm when she found herself beside him at the end of the pool. All she had to do was think of 10 year old Damien and she'd be fine.

They smiled at one another.

"I'll bet you won't tell me what you and Thea were in such deep conversation about."

"I don't mind. It was about Guatemala. I'm going down there soon."

"To Guatemala? When?"

"Between terms. You see, I've never known my mother."

"But I understood you were an orphan."

"That doesn't mean I don't have a mother."

"Someone from Guatemala?"

"That's what Thea thinks."

"How would she know?"

"I can't answer that completely. But you see, Thea is half Guatemalan and my father is her father. Only he's not my biological father."

"So she thinks maybe he adopted you in Guatemala?"

"I guess."

He turned in the pool, sliding past her and for a moment she felt his body, so familiar but definitely not that of a 10 year old.

"Let's climb out," he said.

So they did, Danielle looking up at his nakedness as he climbed ahead of her.

He reached down to help her up, so that she stood facing him, only a few inches away. He looked down.

DAMIEN

"You're really beautiful," he said wonderingly.

And he kissed her, softly at first, but then he groaned, and thrust his tongue deep. She pushed away.

"No!" she cried. "I'm… I'm…" but she was unable to finish, grabbed her towel, and wrapped herself in it.

He reached for his own towel and spread his hands. "I'm sorry. I just can't believe how attracted I am to you. It's like I know you so well and yet not at all. When did you become so damn beautiful?"

She looked at him—at those yellow eyes—and trembled.

For the first time in her life, in her desire for him, she was truly afraid, not of him but of herself.

CHAPTER FOUR

Sam picked up Peter Gregory at the San Diego airport at 1:30 PM, selecting him from afar by his limp, acquired in the far north. Peter was booked into a hotel only a few blocks from where several historic ships lay at dock, including a former Soviet submarine. Sam ordered a beer in the hotel lounge while Peter checked in.

"Which do we start with, Sam, my case or yours?" Peter said when he joined him.

Sam laughed and ordered a beer for Peter. "You never did waste words, my boy."

Peter smiled. "I don't have much time for small talk. But of course you're an exception, Sam."

Sam was suddenly serious. "I'm in a real mess, Peter, and I honestly don't think you can help me, but I'm going to ask you to try."

Sam then outlined the facts surrounding the murder of the young woman found in the tree: the findings so far, and his frustrations with the way the media's rampant speculations had generated so many false leads. Ironically, their theory about a madman with a vampire delusion probably best fit the facts.

"So you're saying the facts suggest an impossible crime?" asked Peter.

Sam shrugged helplessly.

"There's really no evidence that a crane or rope pulley or other mechanical device could have been used to put her in the tree?"

"Quite the opposite. The markings on the body and the ground indicate that she was gripped and hauled over to the tree and up into it. The tree is scuffed as if by shoes, but the markings are too indistinct to take a viable sample," Sam replied.

"And no skin fragments from the hands of the climber on the bark?"

"None. Which is weird. We think he either had gloves or the presence of mind to wrap his hands."

"So who buries their dead in trees?"

"Damned if I know."

"Well I have heard of certain aboriginal tribes that place their dead in trees." Peter commented.

"Well now, we haven't looked into that. You would come up with that, wouldn't you?" Sam grinned at Peter. "Still doesn't deal with the torn jugular and how she got into the tree, though."

"So we have a madman with superhuman strength— or maybe hopped on steroids—who favors ancient burial practices or thinks he's a vampire or both." Peter observed.

"That's about it."

"And to have avoided the authorities, such a person would have to be either highly intelligent and capable of appearing normal or protected by somebody." Peter mused. "Shall we visit the site?" he asked as they finished their beer.

Shortly after 3:00 in the afternoon they arrived at the homicide site, still ribboned off. Sam pointed out where the assault occurred and where the body was found in the tree and its height from the ground. They stood several feet away, near a large pond on which a duck swam with her fluffy brood.

Signaling Sam to stay back, Peter walked slowly from the tree to the site of the assault, then crawled painstakingly back along the same path, his face only a few inches above the earth. In his entire career, Sam had never seen anything like it—a professional criminal investigator wriggling along the ground. But he said nothing, just watched as Peter approached the tree trunk and slowly rose upright, carefully studying the tree.

"We've already traced all that, Peter," Sam said. "Her throat was torn open right here, about a foot and a half beyond where I'm standing, and then she was dragged across to the tree, along the route you just followed."

Joining him, Peter said, "I know."

"So what were you doing? You risked contaminating the scene."

"But I didn't." Peter paused, looking thoughtfully at the tree.

Sam was really irritated and began to wonder if perhaps he'd made a mistake bringing Peter in.

"Sorry Sam. I've seen enough for now. Can we head back?"

As they walked slowly back to the car, Sam remembered that he'd been similarly frustrated with Peter before. Working with Peter meant accepting some of his oddities. Sam started thinking about that, and as they climbed into the car it struck him.

"Did you smell something? Is that what you were doing?"

Peter looked at him. "You're kidding me, right?"

Sam looked away, coloring a little.

"All the same, how would you feel about a visit to the zoo?" Peter went on.

DAMIEN

"The zoo?"

"I just need a few minutes there, with a big cat."

"Why?"

"Just a hunch. Not even a theory worth discussing yet."

Sam sighed mightily, "Okay, we'll try the zoo. You'd better hope the press doesn't get wind of this! I can't believe I'm going along with it."

"As you pointed out, Sam, nothing about this crime makes sense."

The Director of the San Diego Zoo was naturally surprised at their request. Nor did Sam go out of his way to explain it. Peter did ask if any big cats like tigers or leopards had escaped in the San Diego area, and was rewarded with a treatise on management of big cats.

When the leopard had been tranquilized, Peter went over to it. He knelt down and buried his nose in the animal's fur, changing position to nuzzle various parts of the animal's body. This procedure lasted nearly five minutes, according to Sam's watch. He knew what his colleagues in the FBI would make of this... that Sam was as crazy as the young half-breed in there. The zookeeper caught Sam's eye, and Sam could only shrug and roll his eyes.

At last Peter emerged. They thanked the zookeeper, and left, neither saying a thing.

As they drove away, Peter finally spoke. "I guess you didn't see me."

"What? I saw you sniffing all over that poor damned animal, that's all."

"And I cut away a few tufts of its fur." He held out his hand to show Sam, who scowled angrily.

"I'm sure that must be a felony, Peter."

They looked at each other. Peter smirked, Sam chuckled and then they laughed and laughed.

When they got to Peter's hotel, Sam looked expectantly at Peter.

"I'm going to need some time to ponder all this, Sam," Peter said.

"Any preliminary thoughts for us to chew on?" Sam asked.

"Well, since you've already investigated known madmen, I would put some resources into looking for two things: a freakishly strong individual and any link to tree-burial practices."

CHAPTER FIVE

Tom was frustrated with the results of his experiment. On one hand it showed that rat intelligence could be improved by a minor genetic manipulation; on the other hand, the genetic change seemed to make them frantic, running from goal to goal as though possessed. He took a short video of this phenomenon, made some notes, and decided to return to his bungalow, hoping to see Thea and have a spot of lunch, though it was only about 10:45 a.m. He'd leave the video on and return to the lab about 1:30 to see if the rats had calmed down. That afternoon he would randomly select a few rats for brain scans, using a new method of measuring neuronal activity, to look for the link between the genetic change and the rats' behaviour.

On the way home, he wondered about Arnold. Today, Arnold had not made an appearance at the lab before his UCSD luncheon. Such no-shows were happening more and more frequently. And, increasingly, Arnold had been asking to be left alone in the lab when he did come in. Usually they worked companionably, both on their own projects and in collaboration, so this was a marked change that concerned Tom.

When Tom opened his front door, he was surprised to hear Eden's voice raised in anger. He stopped, listening.

"You say I don't like you, but that's not the point. The fact is, Thea, I am the only mother Damien has ever known. And I know he's just fine. Better than fine, actually. And that's why I'm telling you to lay off him! Do you hear me, Thea?"

Thea spoke in a much lower tone, and Tom had to strain to hear.

"You're wrong about my interest in Damien."

"Let's not beat around the bush, Thea. You like the boy in a way that's not good for him, or for you. I've seen you together. He's really only a boy, but you're not that much older. And I can see it in his eyes. You fascinate him. It's not healthy, and if it goes on I'm going to tell your husband and Arnold too if I have to. I will!"

"Get out Eden," Thea said with a deadly calm Tom recognized. "You are just a jealous misguided bitch. Get out."

Tom heard the back door open.

"Out," Thea repeated.

"You're not going to get away with this," Tom heard Eden say, a little more distantly, and then the door slammed. For a moment Tom waited, then reopened the front door and let himself out, closing it soundlessly behind him. He walked slowly back to the lab, stood motionless for a few minutes, then sat down numbly at his desk.

Eden was wrong—wasn't she? Except, Damien was not only handsome, but also very brainy. Tom remembered Thea's comment about Damien being unusually attractive. That had bothered him, but then at some level Tom had to admit he too recognized that Damien was somehow different, exceptional even. Though Tom hadn't heard the whole argument, he was aware of the attraction between them, and it might become a dangerous situation. Tom knew himself well enough to realize that he could not tolerate an affair. Besides, Eden would surely tell Arnold, and that could blow everything apart just when his work at Arnold's lab was beginning to show results—important results—for his career. He knew it would be difficult to find another position which would offer the same latitude to pursue his own research. And just being associated with Dr. Arnold Head conferred a certain prestige.

Automatically, he started doodling, something he did when he was troubled by a problem. Curious, geometric shapes. He would have to clear things up with Thea, that was for sure. Would she cease to have these private sessions with Damien, in which she seemed so fascinated with what the boy had to say? Tom had been thinking that the two were like brother and sister together, but now he wasn't so sure.

He stood up and walked around the lab, then back again. Perhaps he should talk to Arnold first, before Eden got to him. But of course Arnold would exonerate Damien and blame Thea—then what would Tom do? But perhaps he was wrong about this. Eden had mentioned that Arnold had been giving Damien hell about something or other just the other day. Tom stopped wandering near the drawers. Why? Then he remembered that file he'd found and put away so hastily.

He pulled open the drawer and found the unlabeled file again. It was full of twenty year old notes in which Arnold described a new method he'd worked out for cloning animals, as well as some other instructions that Tom skipped through. As he paged through the notes, Tom's eye was riveted by the following, "And what animal will I clone? Myself."

DAMIEN

★★★

Peter rubbed his eyes and looked away from the computer screen, out the hotel window at the wan light leaking from the hotel into the darkness of the lane. He was glad of the hotel's Business Centre and its internet access, but it was a dingy little room and he'd spent too long in it. And he wasn't getting anywhere, it seemed. He'd been researching all the ways that someone could have enhanced their strength to the point that they could carry a body that heavy that far up into a tree, and it just didn't seem possible—yet. He thought ruefully of the television show he'd loved as a boy, "The Six Million Dollar Man," about a man whose bionic implants gave him super speed and strength and x-ray vision, making him an incredibly efficient secret agent.

His phone rang and Sam was on the line.

"We got the lab results back."

"And?"

"Well there's one really weird thing, which is why it took them so long. The DNA from the saliva has anomalous elements."

"What do you mean?" Peter asked.

"Well, it's not exactly like other human saliva, but the lab couldn't figure out where the unusual DNA came from."

"Huh." Peter felt a frisson of excitement.

"Have you had any luck with the aboriginal burial angle, Sam?"

"Not so far, but you wouldn't believe the practices some people get up to."

"You mean like spending tens of thousands of dollars on a box to put in the ground to rot?"

Sam grunted.

"Bye, Sam," Peter said, yawning.

Peter switched on the TV and scrolled through a canned-laughter sitcom, a leopard with its kill on a nature program, a steamy soap opera and more of the same before shutting the machine off in disgust and sliding under the antiseptic hotel sheets, staring at the shadowed stucco ceiling.

★★★

Peter awoke the next morning chasing the tendrils of a dream about a cougar that morphed into a leopard that wasn't exactly a leopard, but the answer faded in the daylight. He could still smell it in his mind, though. It reminded him of a case on Vancouver Island in British Columbia. A forestry guy had been mauled by a cougar near his fire-watching tower. Peter was dealing with the aftermath when the cougar had returned and he'd had no choice but to shoot the animal. It was an old cougar with diseased gums, but still dangerous for all that. Peter had never forgotten the smell of that big cat, not unlike the faint whiff that he'd caught at the tree-murder site yesterday—but that didn't make any sense. He faded back into slumber, thinking of the human enhancement research he'd been reading about the night before and wondering still about the strength needed to get that girl into the tree. The tree. He sat up suddenly. That nature program last night. The leopard took its kill up into the tree, and the gazelle's weight must have been similar to that girl's. Peter threw off his sheets, pulled on his jeans and a t-shirt and bolted for the computer room. Was it possible?

★★★

Tom was stunned. Could Arnold actually have done it? The method was revolutionary and worthy of a Nobel

Prize if it had worked, particularly since it was so far ahead of the technology at the time.

He heard the lab door open and rapidly turned to face it, expecting Arnold. But Thea stood there.

"Hello Tom. Were you expecting Arnold?"

She came towards him, seeming to glide rather than walk, and stopped a few feet away.

"You heard us didn't you? You were in the hall."

Tom couldn't believe she'd heard him; he had entered so silently.

"Yes, I heard."

"And what do you think, Tom?"

"I think maybe… you're attracted to Damien, but it's not just that."

"Because Eden said so?" Her look was searching.

He had to have her answer. "Is it true, Thea?"

"It's not that simple, Tom, not by a long way." She spoke softly but firmly.

"Please explain."

"I feel strongly attracted to him, yes—but I'm not in love with him. I am fascinated by him, Tom, and very much troubled."

"Why troubled?"

There was silence for a long moment.

"He's not an ordinary… human being."

"What exactly do you mean?" Tom asked, his anger growing.

She stepped forward and put her hand on his arm. All at once he saw the look of genuine concern in her eyes.

"Tom," she said. "I'm really worried."

He waited, feeling her sense of urgency.

"I told you he has a sort of… dynamic power he's holding in, but it's… it's… more than human."

"I don't understand, Thea."

"Neither do I, entirely. But that's where you and I are different. You know my Mama was a bruja. So I learned about a lot of things that don't fit in with the scientific worldview—don't necessarily make rational sense—but they work."

Tom remembered that bruja was the term for a Mayan sorcerer, an aspect of Thea's history that he respected but didn't really understand. He said impatiently, "What has all this to do with Damien ... and you?"

"Because..." she started, and then hesitated. "Please try to understand. There are ways of seeing things..." She stopped and gazed lovingly into his eyes. "Just understand this, Tom: I do not love Damien, I love you. I am married to you. Women are sometimes attracted to other men but that is not love." She reached up and kissed him on the cheek and left.

Tom stood still for a minute or two, thinking. Then he pulled out the small stool hidden under the countertop of the lab, and settled in to read Arnold's notes with deep concentration.

★★★

Peter pushed himself back from the computer desk, stretching and rubbing his eyes. It was possible, he thought, just barely. It was time to call Sam.

"Can you come over, Sam? Believe it or not, I think I have a theory about this bizarre case."

"Sure you don't need to sniff any more leopards? Just give me an hour to get there, Peter."

When Sam arrived in Peter's hotel room, Peter pointed him to an easy chair, and settled on the desk chair nearby. From his window on the seventh floor, there was a view over the bay to the open sea beyond. A few Jacaranda trees in bloom lined the street below.

"So?" Sam enquired.

"I smelled a big cat at your murder site, Sam."

"I'll be damned!" Sam exclaimed. "You did smell something."

"Well it was three days old and extremely faint, so I was very unsure, even after I smelled the leopard at the zoo."

"How the hell would you know that, anyway?"

There was a moment of silence and Sam knew the younger man was trying to figure out how to explain himself.

"You know my Mom was from the Blackfoot nation and I grew up on the reserve," Peter said carefully. "I learned it from an old hunter when I was a boy going after wood caribou in the North. He taught me the faculty was there. You just have to learn to use it, to become open to smell. It's like knowing air pressure, Sam, without looking at an instrument. I learned that too."

"So there's a hell of a lot we whites have unlearnt, is that it?"

"That's it."

"But we checked at the zoo, and there was no leopard missing, not even a privately owned one. Not one had escaped, Peter."

"I know that."

"So?"

"I know that cat smell."

"Oh, for Christ's sake! You mean a pussy cat?" The whole discussion was perfectly absurd.

"Of course not. I mean a large wild cat. I once had to kill a rogue mountain lion on Vancouver Island, Sam, and I'll never forget its smell."

"A cougar is not a leopard."

"Obviously, but they're both large wild cats. They're related."

Okay, Peter, but what good does it do us?"

Peter looked out the window. It had begun to rain. The downpour lasted a few minutes, then gradually stopped.

"None at all, if we think the way we usually do."

"And this would be why I brought you in in the first place, Peter."

"You've heard of clones, right?"

"You mean like Dolly the sheep? So?"

"As you know, human cloning has been banned."

"I see where you're going."

"I did a bunch of research this morning. In fact, there have been a few human clones, though they've been kept under wraps—certain nations wanting to keep it undercover for good reasons." Peter waited.

"You mean in case certain nations produce human clones that are way up there mentally and physically, like a super-soldier. Yeah, I've heard of it. But we're not panicking yet."

"No, but people are getting worried. And I'm sure you've heard of genetically modified genes."

"Well… oh yeah, they're worried about athletes being genetically modified to improve their performance, that's right." Sam thought about this. "But how does that fit in with cloning?"

"If I understand it right, Sam, scientists can genetically modify a clone, and they have experimented with mixing the genes of different species to create animals that combine features of both."

"You mean like genes of a goat can be mixed with genes of a sheep to produce a goeep?"

"Something like that. I've been thinking about the location of the body and the cat smell and last night I saw

DAMIEN

a nature program that featured a leopard stashing its kill in a tree."

Then it came to Sam. "Oh my God. You mean this girl was killed by a human/leopard clone?"

"Exactly, except it couldn't have been half and half, otherwise such a creature would certainly have been noticed. I think it might be a human cloned with selected leopard genes." He paused, "Enough for me to smell it—very faintly though."

Sam sat hunched in upon himself, forced to take this possibility seriously, yet hating the thought. What kind of world were they entering? And how could he propose such a hypothesis to his superiors? They'd probably laugh him out of the room.

Peter smiled. "If I were you, Sam, knowing what the brass can be like, I'd keep this under wraps. I'd just look into it, so to speak, on the side. We already both know how to do that."

Sam nodded. "Yeah, we do." And then he thought of something. "Goddamn it, you got this idea before you started to sniff, didn't you?"

Peter smiled a little. "Not exactly. But the facts don't fit anything else, do they?"

Sam thought about it and grinned. "You bastard. Maybe you've done it again. Maybe. But what a hell of a thing to investigate."

Peter nodded.

"That saliva. We should compare it to leopard DNA," Sam said. "And who had the technology to do this 20 years ago?"

"Yeah. I know where I'd start on that."

"Okay partner, where?"

"With the labs involved in cloning research right here at UCSD," Peter suggested.

"And you're going to assist with that, okay?"

"What about my own case, Sam?"

"You can do that on the side."

Sam's broad visage broke into his most generous smile.

CHAPTER SIX

Peter Gregory was waiting for a call from Helen Murray, who was in San Diego attending a conference. She was a science writer whose last book, entitled, *What We are Making of Ourselves,* about genetic modification and cloning and their implications for the human race, had become an international best seller in the eight months since publication. One of the labs had told Peter about her and confirmed the scientific veracity of her work. She had a degree in bio-chemistry and in her younger days had taught high school science. She'd turned to writing in her early thirties and was now 41.

The phone rang.

"Peter Gregory? It's Helen Murray in the lounge. You can't miss me. I'm the only woman wearing a hat." Fair enough, he thought.

He went to the bathroom and washed his face, looking in the mirror to assure himself he didn't need a shave, though he hadn't shaved for two days. This was one of the benefits of being half aboriginal, he thought. We don't grow as much hair as most white guys. He had a good thatch of fine dark hair on his head, but his arms, legs, and chest were smooth. I'm an anomaly, he thought, remembering sniffing the leopard as he left his room, note-book in jacket pocket—some people might say a little crazy, and only 43.

The lounge was fairly crowded but Peter picked her out even though there were actually two women wearing hats in opposite corners of the room. He was sure it had to be the woman with the broad-brimmed emerald green hat because it was unusual, and he expected an unusual woman.

She was not only unusual, but striking, he noted, with strong features and lots of auburn hair under her hat.

"Peter Gregory, I assume." She smiled, looking up at him. He sat down opposite her. "I've talked to your FBI partner, Sam Schumacker, is it? And he told me you used to be an RCMP officer, one with a remarkable record."

"Not as remarkable as his. I can't think of anyone who's handled as many tough cases, and usually with success."

"You helped him solve two of them, so he said, and now you're helping with the tree murder?"

"Just from the sidelines, you understand."

"So your interviewing me is just a sideline?" Her look was challenging. "I hope that doesn't mean that what I tell you is unimportant."

He had been careless, and kicked himself.

"I don't mean that." He added, "I'm not very good at word games, and you are. It's no wonder you're a successful writer."

"Enough flattery," she said, smiling at him. "By the way, call me Helen." He was about to say something, but she held up her hand. "I don't have very long, so help me. What is your theory about the tree murder?"

"We think it may be the crime of someone who would not see it as a crime."

"You mean a psychopath."

"We think that's unlikely."

"Why?"

"We have reason to think it was a clone with additional genetic modification: a human with leopard genes."

She stared at him for a beat.

"So, assuming for the moment that you have a good reason to think it was a clone, how can I help you?"

"You've written a book claiming that human clones are not just possible but have already been produced by labs in a few parts of the world. You seem to have done a lot of research on this, and claim to know about scientists who have produced human clones, including human clones that were genetically modified. Am I wrong?"

"And you want me to name some of these scientists so you can pursue this unlikely scenario?"

"Well, at least…"

But she interrupted him.

"I'm sorry." She began to pick up her handbag. "I can't help you."

He laid his hand on her arm. "Why not?"

"For the obvious reason that I've sworn to keep information about my sources to myself. It's not public property."

"I understand. But, without divulging the scientists themselves, you do know which labs are engaged in this research. That's all I need right now."

She shook her head slowly but did not move from her chair. His hand was still on her arm.

He continued. "This murderer will probably strike again, Helen. He could even be a serial killer in the making, especially if he's not fully human. So we have to find him. Your whole book is about the dangers implicit in genetic modification and cloning. So why wouldn't you help to stop a killer?"

She sat there, looking at him. "I'll tell you why. It's because I can't believe you. I mean, I don't understand why you would assume that it's a clone and not some deluded human. How could you possibly come to any other conclusion? What's your evidence?"

For a moment Peter was at a total loss. He was not at liberty to share the DNA evidence, especially not with a writer. How could he explain it in a way that would intrigue her and induce her support? Finally he said: "If I tell you that I have a unique ability to use my sense of smell—something that my Indian elder taught me how to develop—and that I smelled a human-leopard mix at the scene of the murder… would you believe me?"

She sat back in astonishment. "You've got to be kidding me!"

Peter looked steadily at her.

Helen studied him carefully.

"If you didn't have such a distinguished career, I wouldn't believe you for a minute. In fact, it goes against my nature, anyway. If you've read my book you know that I research thoroughly, until I'm as sure as I can be. Now you're telling me you've some special shamanic sensitivity which I know little about. I don't believe it.

"This isn't shamanic sensitivity; it's just an unusually good sense of smell."

She paused, staring hard at him.

Helen pointed out, "The creature you're imagining is not a cloned leopard, but a cloned man with some leopard genes. Such a person would not give off the smell of a leopard. That's bloody nonsense, and you know it."

"How would you know? I grant you the smell was faint compared to the leopard at the zoo that I tested it against, but it was there and it initially utterly confused me."

Helen sat there with her arms folded, regarding him skeptically.

"Besides that, we can't find any other theory that fits all the facts," said Peter. "Call it a guess, or an intuition—whatever—it's the best explanation."

"Not better than mine, which is that this was the act of a person under the delusion that he was a leopard." She threw her bag onto her shoulder.

"I grant you the possibility," Peter said, "that it was a deluded human. But find me a person with the super-human strength, agility and skill to carry unaided a 130 pound woman up a tree and deposit her there securely. So whichever way we turn, we're back to having to investigate the possibility of a human-leopard clone."

She removed the handbag from her shoulder.

After Helen left, Peter phoned Sam on his cell.

"Any luck?" Sam asked.

"Maybe. She gave me some names, but only two in or near San Diego, and both in the La Jolla area. One lab belongs to the university, but the other is private."

"Okay. Meantime," said Sam, "I have people checking out labs and scientists in Los Angeles and San Francisco, especially at Stanford and Berkeley. So what about the two she named from this area? Are they high on the probability list?"

"I can't claim that, Sam, except she knew that both these labs had worked or are now working in the cloning field."

"Okay, so will you go see them?"

"Could you put someone onto the university lab? I'd like to try out the other."

"What's so special about that one?" Sam asked curiously.

"I don't know, except the scientist who owns the lab sounds interesting, based on his career. He's a top researcher. Awards and so on."

"What's his name?"

"Dr. Arnold Head."

"I've heard of him, and I think I'll be going with you."
Peter hung up and sighed.

★★★

Thea and Tom were finishing dinner at 6:20 when the
intercom came on. It was Arnold's cultivated English voice.

"Could I see you around six forty-five? Over here?"

"Sure. What's up Arnold?"

"I don't know exactly. I've been contacted by an FBI
agent…" He paused. "I wrote down his name, and I can't
find it now." He sounded exasperated.

"What would the FBI want?"

"I have no idea, but they were quite insistent, so they'll
be here at seven-thirty. I wanted a word with you first."

"Okay, Arnold, I'll be there."

He hung up, frowning, and turned to Thea.

"Sorry, Thea. I can't go to that concert after all. Arnold
wants to see me."

"And you drop a concert just because he wants to see
you? After work hours?" Thea was querulous. She'd been
looking forward to this concert featuring a work by Ravel
which she particularly loved.

"It's not that simple. The FBI want to talk to Arnold."

"Oh? What about?"

"How would I know?"

Tom helped Thea clean up the dishes and then changed
into his cotton trousers and sports shirt.

He stopped in the hallway near the door.

"You're going to the concert alone? Why not see if
Sarah can join you? It'd be a shame to waste my ticket."

"She's on a research trip and it's kind of late to ask
anyone else. I'll be fine," Thea said quietly.

They embraced and Tom headed over to the main house. Tom found Arnold in what he called the library because one wall was covered with books, none of them technical. Tom had already perused the library and found that the titles were nearly all philosophical or biographical or geographical, with few novels. The technical and scientific books and papers were in the lab office.

"What's going on Arnold?"

"I wish I knew," Arnold said. He waved his hand towards a chair.

Arnold looked at Tom with what struck him as a suspicious glance.

"Tom, is there anything about me or my work that you don't know about? Anything bothering you?"

Tom immediately thought of the unlabeled file.

"I wouldn't say anything is bothering me. I suppose I am curious about some things we haven't talked about."

"But nothing in particular? I found an old file of mine on the counter in the lab." Arnold paused, looking challengingly at Tom. "Well?"

He has a noble head, Tom thought. He decided to plunge.

"I was interested in a note you made once. Something about cloning yourself."

Arnold nodded. "I thought maybe that was it." He stared hard at Tom. "Do you think I succeeded? That I cloned myself?"

"You mean you attempted it?"

"I did attempt it." Arnold nodded slowly, watching Tom intently. He smiled faintly.

The silence deepened.

"So did you succeed?" Tom finally asked.

"Where do you think Damien came from?"

DAMIEN

"I wondered about that. He has a look of you. Do you think this is why the police want to see you?"

"I fear that it does look that way." There was a long pause. "I've had a problem with Damien, off and on, Tom, from about the age of 14. He gets into fights. It happens quite rarely, thank God."

Tom wondered if this explained Eden's news that Damien and his father had quarreled.

"The usual thing, Tom. Damien has always been a very good-looking boy, and therefore attractive to girls," Arnold shrugged, "which creates jealousy, of course, and fights between boys. You know all about that, I'm sure. You're pretty good-looking yourself."

Yes, Tom knew about that, and ruefully remembered a couple of encounters, especially one over a girl by the name of Shirley Meehan. He got a bloody nose over that one.

"Anyway," Arnold continued, "a few of these encounters have been..." he hesitated, "somewhat serious." He paused, gazing out the window, "Where the other chap was quite damaged by Damien." His eyes focused on Tom. "I don't mean that Damien started the fights. He swears he never did that. I can understand it happening. I mean, given Damien's looks and his athletic ability, things girls admire, you know." He spoke with the air of offhandedness which the English often use when speaking of something serious. "When I was a boy at school I suffered quite a bit from the other boys, though it had nothing to do with girls, since there weren't any." He managed a thin smile. "I was no good at sports, and therefore had to suffer for it." He sighed. "Now the problem is that Damien is physically superior, I mean not just in muscular strength, though he has a surprising amount of that, but also in speed and dexterity. I can't tell you how pleased I was that he turned out

that way since I didn't. But that's not really the problem."
He paused, as though searching for the right words.
Tom realized he was struggling—unusual for Arnold—
and therefore really troubled, whatever offhand airs he
adopted. "I wish I knew how to say this." He paused again.
"Evidently he never starts a fight, but when it happens,
he's quite violent ... even ... ferocious." Another lengthy
pause. "A few times he has caused some serious damage, in
one case breaking a boy's arm—not his wrist—his arm..."
He said this with an air of incredulity. "In another case,
two years ago ..." He shook his head as though trying to
dispel the memory... "three boys attacked him—three!—
two were found badly injured by a woman passing by, one
having an ear almost torn off. I had to pay for the operation, of course."

"What about the third guy?" Tom asked into the silence.

"That one managed to drag himself off, having been
kicked in the testicles. Luckily no lasting damage."

"So," Tom said finally, "you're thinking this is why
the FBI wants to talk to you. Do they know about
these incidents?"

"I can't think how."

"But Arnold, the FBI are only called in on serious
crime, something usually beyond the scope of the local
police." He thought about it. "It's more likely that this has
nothing to do with Damien. They probably want to talk to
you about something related to your expertise." He paused.
"Maybe they want you to testify on some federal case."

"I hope so," Arnold said, obviously not thinking about
the inconvenience of giving federal testimony. He was
clearly worried, deeply worried.

CHAPTER SEVEN

Danielle was lucky in having very wealthy parents. They had moved from La Jolla to Seattle where she had attended a private girls' high school. After finishing first year at the University of Washington she decided to return to the University of California at San Diego where she had once lived. She'd talked to her cousin, Mabel Fairfield, who'd put in two years at UCSD, and lavishly praised it. Danielle wanted to get out of Seattle and away from the constant attention of her mother, who couldn't understand why Danielle was not that interested in the social life of their Lake Washington friends, old and young. Reluctantly, her parents had seen her fly off, making sure she was completely self-sufficient, which meant quite able to afford apartment rent in a good neighborhood, not far from La Jolla beaches. It was, after all, an area the family had once called home and where Danielle spent her childhood. What finally justified the move in her parent's eyes was that UCSD was noted for its graduate program in organic chemistry, which was Danielle's field of interest.

Danielle was really glad to have gotten back in touch with some old friends, especially Eden, who had been like a much-loved aunt to her. Nearly 20 years older than Danielle, Eden had taken the trouble to teach her the fine points of badminton and tennis, when her own mother was too busy socializing to have much time for her. And it was thanks to Eden that she had become close friends with Damien.

Danielle was troubled about Damien. When they'd swum together he'd seemed as cool and carefree as he'd always been, but he also exuded sexuality with such power that it bothered her, and at the same time fascinated and excited her.

Two days after their swim, she was not really ready for his phone call.

"Hi Danielle," he said in the old familiar way. "Settled yet?"

"Oh sure—well, not quite, I mean…" she laughed to hide her excitement. "I'm still trying to arrange the furniture. And the kitchen's a mess."

"What do you say to a game of tennis and a dip in the ocean?" There was a pause, while she thought about how to answer. And then his voice altered a little, sounding deeper, yet still offhand. "Then maybe you'll let me have a look at your new digs."

"Why not?" she answered quickly, before she'd meant to.

"Saturday afternoon then? About three? At the court."

"Okay." Of course there was only one tennis court for them, the one where they always used to play. "Sure… see you there." And she hung up.

She sat down, putting her cell phone on the table, and found she was trembling. What was going on with her? She'd had other boyfriends, especially Curley Moran, her Seattle flame, who'd become her first lover. It was a relationship she controlled, played by her rules. When she'd left he told her he'd like to come down and visit her sometime, and she had been looking forward to it. She liked Curley a lot. He was so sweet and gentle that it was hard to believe he was such a good football player. Besides being lovers they were good friends.

While in Seattle, she'd remembered her childhood friendship with Damien and the fun they'd had together being adventurous and daring. Then, in the last year before she left, when they were 14, things had begun to change. His voice had deepened and she'd found him looking at her in a way which made her vaguely uneasy. And now, as a mature woman, she found herself positively overcome by his physical presence. So why did that frighten as well as excite and disturb her?

She recalled her experience with him at the pool. It was something he seemed to exude from his very being. Whatever it was, it was primitive, and sent a shiver up her spine. She could not relate it to anything she knew or had ever known.

★★★

Their afternoon together began much the way so many of their childhood afternoons had. They played an intense game of tennis, and though he won the set she proved herself a worthy opponent, a few times shorting him at the net. He laughed, enjoying her tricks.

After cool drinks in the beach-house, they went for a swim, both of them having worn their suits under their tennis garments. The water was bracing but not cold and they splashed one another, then swam far out to float on their backs, gently lifted up and down on the great swells.

"Are you glad you came back to La Jolla?" Damien asked.

"How could I not be? Seattle has nothing like this to offer."

"They tell me there's only one place better than this for swimming and that's Cancun. So one day I'll go there."

DAMIEN

That was typical Damien, not: "I may go there," but, "I will go there."

"I'm still curious, Damien, about what you were telling me at your Dad's place—that Thea said your mother was Guatemalan. You didn't say how she knew this."

"I didn't because I can't. Thea wouldn't tell me."

"I wonder why she said that. You don't look Guatemalan, in spite of your tan and dark hair. I actually think you look a bit like Arnold even though you're so much taller."

"I don't know." He thought about it. "I think she knows more than she's willing to admit. She's a deep one."

He rose upon a wave and she lost him for a moment.

When he was beside her again he said, "Did you know that Thea's mother is a shaman? Actually, the term there is bruja."

"You don't mean she casts spells and predicts the future?" Danielle asked incredulously.

"The Maya are supposed to be good at that."

"I don't understand why Thea wouldn't tell you what she knows." He was hidden behind a wave again, then rose, "Or guesses—I mean about your mother."

"Neither do I. She said she might take me to Guatemala and get her mother to tell me. I want to do that. Let's race for shore."

So they raced, and Danielle won because Damien let her, she well knew.

Wrapping their towels around their bodies while they removed their bathing suits, for it was a public beach, they slipped on their tennis shorts and shirts and drove to her apartment.

Standing on her little balcony, he was suitably impressed by the view. Though her apartment was set back a couple of blocks from the sea, it was high enough to offer a view over the distant ocean.

"Would you like a beer?" she asked as he came in.

"No thanks. I'm fine." He was now looking at her paintings. She had developed a liking for primitive art and he seemed completely engrossed in it. Looking at him, his lean compact body, his buttocks so clearly outlined by his shorts, she felt a surge of desire. He turned to her, his face slightly flushed.

"I like your place," he said quietly. He stepped toward her. She was aware that her nipples had become taut with excitement. She flushed and turned to switch on some music which filled the room.

"I want you," he said huskily, and she turned back to find his lips on hers, her mouth opening slightly to welcome him, her body pressing against him so that she felt his hardness against her, and she moaned in her desire, giving way completely, surrendering herself to him, and, forgetting her fear, stripping for him.

He stepped back then, dropped his shorts. She watched his muscles flexing as he pulled his shirt off. She had never felt such lust. He was a primitive god, with his giant hooded phallus and glazed wild eyes of brilliant sunlight pouring into her and flowing over and through her.

DAMIEN

CHAPTER EIGHT

Tom opened the door to admit the two officers. The older one, Sam Schumacker, showed his FBI card and nodded at his companion.

"Detective Peter Gregory… working with me."

Tom introduced himself as Arnold Head's Assistant, and led them into Arnold's study.

"I'm very pleased to meet you, Dr. Head." Sam began." My associate and I have a few questions about your area of expertise in relation to a case we're working on. I'm sure you've heard of the body of the young woman found in a tree on the university grounds."

Arnold looked vaguely bewildered.

"Yes, I did hear of it, though I can't imagine how I can help you."

"Then let me explain, sir. The young woman was found stashed about twenty feet up a tree. As you probably know from the papers, the cause of death was loss of blood from her severed throat."

Arnold waited without even a nod.

"Now, sir," Sam said carefully, "we have reason to think that the attack on the young woman might have been made by a completely new kind of creature: a human cloned with selected leopard or other wildcat genes." He paused. "I'm only an FBI agent and so find this pretty unbelievable, but I am told that such composite creatures are now scientifically possible. Is that true, sir?"

"Yes, it is," Arnold answered, "but only in recent years."

Tom looked quickly at Arnold, surprised at his bold-faced lie.

Arnold continued, "So if you are talking about a human clone committing this act of murder I strongly doubt it. If you recall, the first scientifically recognized clone of any consequence was Dolly the sheep in 1996. Since then, there have been many other animals cloned, and most have not lived long. By now, it's hard to imagine that a human clone has not been produced somewhere, but it wouldn't be old enough to commit a crime like this."

"Yet you've been quoted as saying that, in 1990, there was a two to three per cent chance of such a clone being brought into the world," Sam said.

There was a pause. "I did say that, but I was being optimistic. Other scientists would have said the chance was negligible."

"Why?"

"Because back then there were fewer than a half dozen very gifted bio-scientists who might have had the knowl-edge and institutional support to approach that capability."

"Would you put yourself among that number?"

Arnold shifted uneasily."Why do you ask?"

"Because you have been identified by experts as one of the few who might have been capable of such a cloning."

Arnold was obviously becoming just a little perturbed.

"Ask my young partner, Tom, if he thinks I deal in 'might-haves.'"There was a moment of silence. "Go on—ask him."

Sam turned to Tom. "Well, sir, what is your opinion? Could Dr. Head have cloned such a composite creature?"

"I was not around in 1990, so I could not possibly know. But there's something I'd like to ask you. Why do you suspect such a clone? Why specifically a human with a leopard?" Tom asked.

"Because a leopard is about the only predator that often carries its kills into trees to store them more safely," Peter interceded. "And of course, the jugular being ripped out by teeth was certainly animal-like, though not specific to leopards."

"But why not some big cat, like a cougar which is at home here in California?"

Peter responded, "They don't carry their kills up trees. Only the leopard, and sometimes the jaguar, does that."

Tom nodded, remembering that Arnold's father's zoological specialty was leopards and that Arnold's childhood and part of his youth had been spent at Kruger National Park where leopards abounded. Tom didn't think it was a coincidence, either, that he and Arnold had spent so much time in Guatemala looking for jaguars in that first year of Tom's employment with Arnold.

After a moment, Sam climbed to his feet. "Thank you, Dr. Head, for giving us your time and answering our questions. If you do think of anything related to this case, I'd appreciate a call from you." He nodded to Peter, and Tom got up to escort them to the door.

Just as he was about to leave, Peter turned back.

"By the way, sir, do you have a son?"

Arnold looked baffled, "Yes, I do."

"And he's what age?"

Arnold hesitated before answering. "Twenty." He was clearly perturbed. "Why do you ask?"

"Just wondering," Peter said. The two officers left.

"Incredible," said Arnold when they'd left.

DAMIEN

"I didn't like that question about Damien," Tom said. "I really don't think he could have done something like this."

Arnold took a deep breath. "I can see why they've developed their theory and even why they've come to me. But why would they think I would help?"

"Maybe they're after scientific plausibility."

"I hope that's all..." There was a difficult pause.

"I guess you're relieved that they didn't bring up Damien's violent disputes," Tom said.

"The police were never called in, so they've no record of them." Arnold paused, and then went on, "Damien was with a girl when the three young fellows I'd told you about attacked him. She witnessed the whole thing and came to tell me about it. I think she came to me because she couldn't quite believe what she'd seen. She said the three young men never had a chance because, aside from his strength, Damien moved with such speed they were put out of action before they knew what happened. And—this is what really shocked her to the core—she said he moved not only swiftly but with incredible precision, without a miss."

"Even when breaking the guy's arm?"

"That was the first thing he did, she said—broke the young man's arm by smashing it against a lamp post. No doubt the fellow's scream somewhat paralyzed the other two, shocked them into a moment's hesitation. The second fellow was down the next instant with a kick to the balls, and then evidently Damien grabbed the third by the head and bit his ear, tearing it half off, leaving the lad screaming on the ground." He stared at Tom. "Guess what Damien did then."

"I can't."

"Nor could I at first."

"What?"

"Completely calm, Damien phoned for an ambulance, then took the girl's hand and said that he had better take her home, and not to worry because everything would be just fine. She said she was terrified, not because she felt threatened herself in anyway. But what he had done and the way he behaved weren't quite human, she said."

There was silence between them.

Tom wished Arnold hadn't told him all this. He had a strong desire not to be involved. "Did you speak to Damien about it?"

"Of course. You see, I felt desperate and I'm afraid I shouted at him. I was beside myself with fear for him."

"And his response was...?"

"He said that the girl was telling a story, and he didn't know why."

"Oh come on."

"And that no incident occurred, at least any that involved him."

The silence deepened.

Finally: "Did you believe Damien?"

"Yes, I did. I've thought about it a lot, and phoned a psychiatrist friend. I didn't tell him about Damien. I just asked if he'd ever heard of people blanking out... I mean if it's possible for a person to be unable to recall an incident they've been involved in, even a recent incident. He said that, in certain cases, especially those of extreme violence, people have been known to dissociate so completely that they lose all memory of the incident."

"What do you think this means, Arnold?"

Arnold shook his head slowly.

DAMIEN

★★★

Sam drove Peter to his hotel. They said nothing on the way. Stopping in front of the hotel, Sam turned to Peter.

"That question of yours was exactly the right one. Strange I didn't think of it. Arnold has a son and your question could have been: was he a clone?"

"Yes."

"I could see it bothered the hell out of the old man."

"Yes."

"I'd like you to get to know more about this son."

"You mean whether he has leopard spots?"

Sam laughed loudly. "You're a wonder, kid."

Peter opened the car door and got out.

"I've only got three more days on your case, Sam. And then I've got to get onto my own. The easy days of police work are over for me."

Sam smiled. "Okay. For you, three days should be more than enough. Good luck, kid." And he drove off.

CHAPTER NINE

Danielle did not know that there could be such violence in love-making. Far from dampening her passion, Damien's huge convulsions had wildly inflamed her. He had literally attacked her, never bothering with a condom. It could be said he raped her but, if so, she gloried in it, crying out for him, writhing as he thrust deeper and deeper into her, opening a gulf of ecstasy which she would not have believed possible.

Now he had left and she was lying in her bath, wallowing in the warmth, though her back stung from deep scratches there and the back of her neck was sore where he had bitten her, but she remembered that her teeth had pierced his flesh too. When he'd growled fiercely and bestially, she had felt a surge of fear but her lust had consumed it and intensified her need. They had been wild animals.

Did she love him? She did not know. They had a deep connection, certainly. Did she desire him? Yes… yes, desperately. But a long term relationship? It was far too soon to begin thinking of that. But she had learned something about herself—oh yes—more than she quite knew how to handle.

★★★

That evening the phone rang insistently at Tom's place. It was nearly 10:00 PM. "Hello?"

"Hello, we met earlier today. I'm Peter Gregory, assisting Sam Schumacker of the FBI."

"Oh yes." Tom was not happy about the call.

"I was wondering if I could see you sometime in the morning?"

"What about?" Tom gathered himself. "I'm sorry, but I can't imagine how I can help you."

"I think maybe you can help me." Peter answered. "If you can't help I'll find that out." There was a pause. "It's important."

Tom felt helpless. Thea had come into the room and was looking at him.

"I start work in the lab at 9:00 AM. We'd have to meet at 8:00 AM." Tom told Peter.

"Fine. How do I get to your place?"

"Dr. Head gave you his card. Why don't you just talk to him?"

"Because you're first on my list. Do you have a separate address?"

"If you must meet me, drive to Dr. Head's address which is on the entrance wall to the property. You drive in and park in front of the big house which is Arnold's, then take the path around the right and stay on it until you come to my bungalow." Then he added with acidity. "You ring the bell."

"Thank you. I'll be there." And Peter closed off.

"Who was that?" Thea asked.

Tom couldn't help admiring her lovely form in that cream negligée, with black lace lining that accentuated her eyes. She came and sat beside him, taking his hand into her lap.

"It's the damned detective working for the FBI."

"And?"

"He wants to talk to me, that's all."

"You're worried."

"I know what he wants to talk about, Thea."

"Damien," she said.

"Yes, Damien. At least that's what I think. It sounds completely wild, but they're asking about the possibility of a human clone augmented with leopard attributes."

"Why?"

"Well, apparently leopards stash their kills in trees."

"What's that got to do with Damien?"

"Well…" Tom was miserable.

Thea looked closely at him. Suddenly all she knew about her mother's interest in Damien, his extraordinary physical prowess and sexual magnetism, and Arnold's fascination with jaguars came together in her mind.

"Oh my God!" She exclaimed. "They don't think it's him, do they?"

"I think they're curious."

"No!" Thea exploded. "He wouldn't hurt a girl like that."

Miserably, Tom shook his head in agreement.

After a pause, Thea said slowly, "His being a clone does make an awful kind of sense, though."

"What do you mean?"

"Well, we knew Damien was different, not just gifted, didn't we? And I always wondered how he could look so much like Arnold—a bigger, stronger, faster Arnold—when he was supposedly adopted. But even if he's a clone it doesn't mean he killed that girl. But how could Arnold have made a clone so far ahead of everyone else? Is that even possible? What did Arnold say?"

"Arnold told the detectives that he thought it was possible—though barely— that someone could have created a viable clone in the early 90s. That would have been years before Dolly the sheep, though, and everybody thought that was the first cloned mammal."

"So why did he say it was possible?"

"Because it was, barely. He didn't tell the police what he'd told me just before they came: that Damien was his clone."

"It's true, then." Thea said heavily.

Tom nodded mutely.

Thea searched Tom's eyes in that way that made him uneasy, as if she were reading his soul.

"So why are you so sure this detective wants to talk about Damien?"

"This guy—his name is Peter Gregory—just when they were leaving, he asked Arnold if he had a son, and of course Arnold said yes. Then when they left, Arnold told me something else that clearly worried him a lot."

"Which was?"

"First, that Damien seems to have a violent streak, at least when he's threatened by someone. And he always wins because of his amazing strength and agility." He thought for a moment. "And, secondly, apparently he completely blanks out the most violent episodes. He can't remember them."

"Oh. That's not good at all. Has this happened often?"

"Not for years. And it only happened when boys tried to bully him or his friends."

"Does your FBI man know this?"

"None of it. And that's what bothers me. Should I tell him about all this? I mean if I do, it will lead to his thinking that Damien..." He broke off, unable to say it.

"That Damien killed that poor woman?"

At first, Tom could only shake his head.

"I know the kid... I can't believe that."

"Neither can I." Thea moved swiftly to embrace Tom. "Neither can I."

★★★

At 8:10 AM the doorbell rang.

"Sorry I'm late," Peter said, stepping through the door.

"I'm glad you are," Tom said. "At 8: 00 a.m. I was brushing my teeth." He led Peter into the small sitting room which doubled as a study. Peter immediately noticed a few small stone figurines on the wooden shelf that ran along the side of the room. "Interesting," he said.

"They're Mayan," Tom answered. "My wife likes them."

They were more than interesting, Peter thought. They were from the world of sacred objects like the medicine bags he had known as a child in the Blackfoot village... very different, but having a familiar resonance.

"So what do you want to know?" Tom asked after they were seated and Peter had taken out a notebook.

It seemed that Peter Gregory wanted to know everything: first the nature and scope of Tom's work, his background and how he had got to know Arnold; about his wife Thea, and how long they'd been married; about Arnold in even greater detail, and his secretary-nurse Eden; about Damien, his age, schooling, university course subjects and marks, boy and girl friends, special talents. Tom was in the middle of this when Thea entered.

DAMIEN

"I have some coffee ready if you'd like some," she said. Tom looked at Peter who nodded. "Thank you." And Thea left, Peter noticing the grace of her movements, her bearing, her self-possession, and something more. She was clearly Indian or part Indian like himself.

Thea returned with three cups of coffee. Handing one to Peter, for a moment she looked intently at him and he returned the look. He felt her searching him...inside. His own mother, who had shamanic abilities, would do the same thing. After handing Tom his coffee, Thea sat down with hers.

"I don't know why you're asking me all this about us," said Tom.

"I don't know yet," Peter responded, "so you may say I'm wasting your time. Right now we're like sailors trying to capture every puff of wind. Our only lead, to be frank, is that Dr. Arnold Head has been identified as one of the few scientists who could have produced a clone in the early nineties. Given that fact, we have to be curious about his son Damien."

"You think Damien might be a clone?" Tom asked.

"I know the chance is remote, but it's all we've got."

"Damien wouldn't do a thing like that," Tom said flatly.

"Damien is a sensitive soul," Thea said.

★★★

After Peter had left and Tom had gone over to his desk to gather a few papers, Thea came up to him.

"What did he want to know at the beginning, Tom?"

"Everything."

"I'm afraid of him."

Tom turned to her. "He's just doing his job."

"He's no ordinary policeman, Tom."

"What do you mean, Thea?" Tom asked, turning away. "Sorry, Thea. I'm just not myself, and I need to get to work." Tom fled to the lab.

Thea stood still. In some important ways, Tom remained a stranger to her, or was it the other way around? She wasn't sure. She didn't regret marrying him, though. Thea loved Tom dearly for his open personality, his blonde American good looks and most of all for his depth of intellect and spirit. He was not shallow or cold as so many people were.

As a child, Thea had learned that there had never been and never could be any real communication between the Maya and the white landowners, who might have come from a different planet. Those people, it seemed, simply did not appreciate the ancient world of huge and beautifully carved buildings in cities like Tenochtilan and Uxmal, built by worshippers of jaguars and feathered serpents. This alienation was not helped by the systematic slaughter of Mayans which began with the Spaniards, and continued intermittently into the 1980s, when Guatemalan special forces representing the landowners and reportedly supported by the CIA "disappeared" tens of thousands of Mayans.

But Thea had always had difficulty believing there could be so little common ground. Certainly, she and Tom had a deep unspoken connection, even though, at 31, Tom was seven years older than her and from such a different culture.

Thea's bruja mother had taught her never to try to explain the Way to white people, and she had found that even Tom had difficulty fully understanding this side of her.

The phone rang, startling Thea out of reverie. Somehow, she was unsurprised to hear her mother on the other end of the line, though she hadn't heard from her in six months. Thea told her mother about the killing and the police's interest in Damien, and asked about Arnold's first

DAMIEN

visit to Guatemala, when she had been conceived. When Thea hung up, she stood very still and breathed deep into the soles of her feet and out into ground below, then back in, rooting her body, drawing energy up from the earth and exhaling to the sky, opening a channel, holding it open, waiting. At last, she felt the spirit of the serpent God, K'uk'ulkan, expand within her, giving her the power she needed.

She would begin with Arnold Head.

CHAPTER TEN

The opportunity came the next day when Thea knew Eden would be away most of the morning in San Diego visiting the accountant. Thea buzzed at Arnold's door and after a moment he answered, "Yes?"

"It's Thea," she said. "Can I talk to you?"

"Of course, I'm in the study." The door opened automatically.

Her father was seated in his wheelchair sorting papers at the desk, but turned to receive her light hug. Even after six years, they were still a bit awkward with each other; sometimes she wondered if he would ever fully relax with her. There was a great deal she didn't know about him and on occasion she felt alienated by his English propriety. He was so different from Tom, in whom nothing was hidden.

"What can I do for you, my dear?"

"Well, Father, I need to ask you about something."

"And what could that be?"

"Damien."

His brow furrowed.

"What about him?" he asked, dropping his voice.

"You know he killed that girl in the tree."

There was silence. Then Arnold quietly shook his head, "No, I don't know."

"Yes, you do. He's your jaguar clone. Who else could tear out a girl's throat, then stash her up a tree? And you know Damien blacks out his violent episodes."

Arnold lowered his head and closed his eyes. At last, wearily, he said, "There's no proof. He's never hurt a girl before. Did Tom tell you Damien's my clone?"

Thea sat down and leaned close to him.

"He did, but I already suspected something like this. When you first met Mama in the jungle, you said you were looking for jaguar blood for experiments back in San Diego. But that was not your only purpose. You were searching for an extremely rare variant of the ayahuasca plant—one with special powers."

She watched him carefully as she spoke, looking for some hint of denial.

"You knew that use of the hallucinogenic ayahuasca-based drug was suspected of enabling Mayan shamans to develop a superior calendar and recognize the importance of the number zero in mathematics, among other things, long before the Europeans had even thought of such things. You thought you could use it yourself to achieve a personal goal, didn't you?"

"Your mother told you this," Arnold murmured.

He seemed suddenly very old.

"Mama may have been only 22 and living in a commune in the jungle, but she was a bruja who knew what you were after and also knew she was meant to help you. The jaguar is sacred to Mayan people and brujas are interme-diaries between the sacred and the secular. Some are even shape-shifters, but you know that."

In spite of himself, Arnold nodded slightly.

"Though you believed you were following your own path, Mama knew it was pre-ordained. So she not only loved you but was prepared to go to the risk of getting you what you wanted."

Arnold turned his palms up and looked at them.

"If it really is Damien who did this terrible thing…" he faltered. "Did… did Ahmal have any foreknowledge of Damien's future?"

"She didn't understand your science, but she knew that a human-jaguar combination would be incredibly powerful and a gift to the Maya. But I can't understand why you would do such a thing. Why did you do it?"

There was a long silence. His head had fallen further as he stared at the floor, breathing heavily. At last he spoke hollowly.

"I wanted a son who was at least equal to me mentally, but also much superior to me physically. I was always so frail. I always admired leopards and jaguars for their extraordinary strength and agility. Ayahuasca enabled me to think differently about how to engineer the first human-animal clone… and it worked. Damien really is superior not only mentally but physically too."

"Except…" she said.

"Thea…" He grasped her hand. "I could not believe it… when I heard about the girl who had… been killed… and found in a tree…" His voice wavered tremulously on the last few words. "I still can't… I just…I can't."

He gasped, weeping now, head down.

Thea felt his suffering… but she had a purpose.

"Father—the police will find Damien. Either you or I must tell them." There was silence between them. "You know that. Otherwise…"

"Leave me," he gasped. "I will do it. I promise you."

"Soon, Father."

"Yes, soon, yes …"

"No one else must die."

DAMIEN

He was silent, but nodded slowly. She stroked his hand, thinking how much he meant to her. He had been so good to her, the byproduct of his ambition, accepting her as his unseen daughter, supporting her financially throughout her childhood, and then welcoming her into his home as a young adult. But, Damien…

★★★

That night Thea got into bed in a turmoil. She turned on her side and then again on her back, and then back again. She hadn't had a chance to talk to Tom about her conversation with Arnold before Tom had to leave for an overnight visit to a specialist lab in L.A. He was working on something terribly important—trying to identify a genetic link to asthma in the hope of eventually reducing or eliminating its symptoms. She loved this about Tom: his deep commitment to lessening suffering, his desire to help the unfortunate of the world. She knew something about suffering, though so far she had escaped most of it herself. Her mother's people, the Maya, they knew all about it. Oh yes. And now, her brother… she sat up, tense, facing the nightmare truth about Damien. How could such a gentle soul be so violent? But Damien was the victim of Arnold's obsession with perfection. Instead… what had he produced? A monster. Yes. She did not wipe her tears. And a beautiful young man—beautiful beyond imagination. A soul who loved hummingbirds. Yet also a monster. Throw this incredible being into a jail cell? Destroy him? That couldn't be right.

She began to call on her resource—the only one she knew—K'uk'ulkan. She threw herself on him, emptied herself… desperate, bereft. Breathing, offering herself, she waited for awareness of that other dimension. Slowly, so slowly, the God responded and the power rose through her loins, gathering strength and force as it moved upward, until her eyesight dimmed and her mind grew clear… and she knew what she had to do.

★★★

By 11 the next morning, Eden had not heard the buzzer from Arnold's room which meant she could bring him some breakfast. She'd made Damien his favorite breakfast of eggs benedict—an odd choice, she had always thought, for a boy. She thought fondly of when he was a youngster with dancing golden eyes. Those eyes were more serious now, most of the time. After breakfast he'd left for his first lecture at 8:30. She was worried about Arnold. He hadn't been an easy man to get along with, but he had never allowed himself to become depressed. And now she had to wonder. If he was not actually medically depressed, he was depleted, ennervated. Could it have something to do with his worries over Damien? She was sure she knew what the problem was—that little bitch Thea. Ever since the girl had come six years ago, things had not been the same. Arnold had become preoccupied with Thea's education and then her developing relationship with Tom. Eden was glad of Tom and Thea's marriage, but knew that it had upset Arnold. After all, the girl was his only daughter—allegedly. Obviously, Thea didn't give a damn for him. And then to make matters worse, the hussy had begun to flirt with Damien. It was too much. Eden was supposed to stand by and witness the whole sordid business. She was sure that the relationship had gone beyond flirting—the slut had surely lured young Damien into her bed. It made Eden want to scream. And then, when she and Thea had argued, the little tart had had the nerve to throw her, Eden, out of

Arnold's bungalow. Well, enough was enough. It was her duty to tell Arnold what was going on, especially because she was certain Arnold suspected something, and that was why he was depressed. If he knew that she supported him, he would surely throw Thea out. She was sorry about Tom. But he had to find out sooner or later who he had married.

There was no question. Eden would take some coffee up to Arnold and then tell him the dismal truth and assure him of her full support.

★★★

Danielle phoned Damien at 11:30 that morning when she knew he would be between classes.

"Hi Damien."

"Hi Danielle. How goes it? Recovered from our get-together?"

"Well, not entirely, Damien. I'm still nursing some wounds."

He laughed. "So am I."

"Want to give some more?"

"Anytime, just name it."

"Okay. How about dinner tonight? I mean here at my place. I'll promise to feed you something first this time."

"Call it done."

"Make it seven?"

"Seven it is."

"I'll have it ready," Danielle promised.

"I want it more than ready."

"You'll have it, big boy."

They both giggled, and cut off.

CHAPTER ELEVEN

Peter Gregory woke up feeling hemmed in as he had when as a small boy he dreamt of being in a room which was slowly contracting around him. At breakfast he pored over all the notes on the tree murder case, especially those dealing with labs that might have had cloning capability. The saliva test had come back showing similarities, though not an exact match between the unusual DNA and leopard DNA. Tests were now being made on the DNA of close relatives to the leopard, so it seemed fairly certain that they were looking for a genetically enhanced human rather than a Halloween vampire.

Peter couldn't say why, but his attention kept returning to the interviews with Dr. Arnold Head and Dr. Tom Delaney. Maybe it was their discomfort when he asked about Dr. Head's son. They were protecting him, Peter was certain, but why?

His sense of urgency was growing; the killer could strike again at any time. Humming in his head was the question: of all the avenues of investigation, which was the most promising?

Peter rang Damien.

"Hi," the young deep-throated voice said.

"You're Damien Head?"

"As far as I know," came the easy answer.

"I'm Peter Gregory, Damien, and I've been speaking with your father and Dr. Delaney about a case we're involved in. I would like to talk to you too. As soon as possible. In fact, today."

"Oh God," Damien said. "Today is really packed. Lectures all day."

"Tonight then."

"Impossible—I've got a previous engagement. What's this all about anyway?"

Peter ignored the question.

"Are your classes over by 5:30?"

"Yeah, but…"

"Fine. I want to see you at 5.30. I'm afraid there are no ifs or buts."

"I guess it'll have to be out here at the university, then. But I still think you should tell me what you want." There was a pause. "Have I done something I shouldn't have?"

"Let's say I just need some information from you. How about we meet at the coffee shop by the main bus stop."

"I guess so," Damien agreed grudgingly and hung up.

Peter was thinking of the saliva sample he intended to obtain from Damien's used cup when his phone rang.

"Hello," a female voice said. "Peter Gregory isn't it?

"Yes—"

"Once RCMP, now doing a job for the FBI. Can I see you again? It's Helen Murray. I have some information you'd be interested in—or should be."

"Okay, but not tonight. It would have to be sooner—say early this afternoon—or tomorrow?"

"This afternoon's fine. Your room number?"

"Seven twenty one. See you at 1:30?"

"I'll be there." She rang off.

★★★

Eden opened the door to Arnold's room with one hand while balancing the tray with the other. Arnold was sitting up in his bed writing on a pad. She thought he looked terribly pale, and for a moment wondered if she should talk to him as she meant to, then decided she really had no alternative.

"Here's a little brunch for you Arnold. I know you didn't ring but it's after 12:30, and you've had nothing."

He nodded in her direction but continued writing.

She settled the tray in front of him, and sat down on the chair beside the bed, something she seldom did these days, since they hadn't been intimate for several years now. She knew she was good in her multiple roles of mistress of the house, secretary and housemaid for a very important man, and worked hard to keep Arnold dependent on her. It was a kind of marriage in which Arnold definitely played the boss, in name if not in fact. She never asked herself if he really cared about her. His dependency was enough.

"Arnold, I need to talk to you about something that has been troubling me a lot."

He looked vaguely at her, so that she wondered for a moment if he had heard her. Then he nodded slowly, though still with an air of absence.

Eden smoothed her skirt over her generous thighs. "It concerns, I'm afraid, your daughter Thea, Arnold. Actually Thea and Damien."

His old-looking eyes began to focus on her.

"I truly hate to tell you this, but I'm afraid I must. I really have no alternative." She paused and smoothed her skirt again.

"Go on," he said, sounding frail.

DAMIEN

"Arnold…" She paused again, wanting him to register the import of what she was going to say. "I'm sorry to say that Thea has seduced your son."

He looked bewildered.

"They are having an affair!" She almost shouted it, as though his hearing had gone. "This is very bad for Damien." She found herself increasingly carried away. "To be seduced by the woman married to your own assistant—though Tom knows nothing about this, I'm sure," she hastily added.

Arnold stared at her so blankly that she was not sure he fully understood the import of what she was saying.

"I know it's terribly hard for you to hear this," she said fretfully. "And I wish I didn't have to be the one to tell you. But there it is. And I must emphasize that this is not good for your son!" Did he really hear her or not? "Under your own roof, Damien is sleeping with your employee's wife, who is—allegedly—your own daughter!"

He slowly raised his arm and pointed a shaking finger at the door.

"Get out!"

She could not believe it.

"But—"

"Get out!" he shouted hoarsely.

In shock, she stumbled toward the door.

★★★

Peter Gregory was feeling pressure on the missing girl case he'd come to California to solve. His Vancouver client had phoned demanding to know how the search was going and Peter had assured him that he was making progress. This was true because Sam had pulled strings at the FBI to get them to provide some invaluable leads about the most likely suspects—leads that it would have taken Peter days to track down on his own. He was anxious to see the poor girl returned to safety as soon possible.

But Peter had promised Sam two more days on the tree murder. Only two days to solve one of the weirdest cases he'd ever known.

He wished that he had told Helen Murray he couldn't see her, at least not right now. That made him wonder about himself. He still missed his wife. When she'd died three long years ago, he was bereft. They'd had six years that felt like an endless honeymoon. But now. Now he was attracted to Helen and knew he needed a woman.

When he opened the door to Helen, she stood there in one of her marvelous hats, wide-brimmed and a dark green which seemed to match her eyes. Only Peter knew they were not green, but grey, and it must be the large hat brim reflected in them. He liked the droll look she gave him as she lounged into the room, her ever observant eyes taking in everything.

"You have a limp," she noted as she sat down on the sofa. "Is it permanent?"

"Afraid so. Some toes froze off in a snowstorm." He said, as he settled next to her, but not too close.

She waited.

"The high Arctic," he explained. "I was on patrol. Snowmobile broke down. Blizzard lasted four days."

"Ouch."

"Ouch," he responded. "So, you have something for me?"

"You're in a hurry."

"I have to be."

She took off her hat and laid it on the small glass table in front of them. Her hair was loosely gathered in a bun, wisps escaping round her square face. She wore a grey suit and now her eyes were grey and her mouth generous.

"Then I won't waste much of your time," she said in an ironic tone, opening a small zippered briefcase and taking out a sheaf of papers. "I talked to a psychiatrist friend of mine." She glanced at the typed pages before handing them to Peter. "She thinks, as I do, that this killer of the young girl was not a clone but a split personality—actually, a double personality."

"Why not a clone?"

"Because a human clone who has been genetically modified to include some leopard DNA probably would not exhibit leopard behavior. Not without having some of the physical characteristics of a leopard. And such a creature would hardly be taking a young university girl for a date."

"True. But why would he need to look like a leopard?"

"Because it actually performed like a leopard in climbing a tree like that—not alone, but dragging along a human body. In her view that would require a body having leopard-like capabilities."

"I know it's unusual, but he could still *look* entirely human."

"If so, that leads to her main point that this is probably a double personality—a real Jekyll and Hyde type—Jekyll not knowing anything about Hyde and vice versa. She says that, though rare, there are documented cases of such double creatures, in fact multiple creatures. You don't need a clone. So this should help to focus your search."

Peter wondered why Helen was ignoring the fact that a double personality would not have the strength to take that girl up the tree. She was an intelligent woman. Then he suddenly realized that Helen hadn't come merely to bring him that information, for there was nothing completely new in what she was saying. Just as suddenly he realized that he wanted her. Now.

He slid his arm around her and, feeling her melt into him, kissed her warm firm lips.

"Don't you want to hear more about your supposed clone?" she said softly, as she broke away from him and stood up to remove her jacket and slip off her dress.

"No," he said.

★★★

On her way to the university shortly after three in the afternoon, Thea phoned Damien, who answered in a low voice, explaining that he was in the chemistry lecture theatre and wouldn't have answered the phone if he hadn't been in a row by himself near the back of the room and bored out of his mind by a large-screen lesson on an intricate lab procedure.

"Damien, I can't talk about it on the phone, but we've got an emergency. I'm half way to the university and I want you to leave your class right now. Where can I pick you up in less than fifteen minutes?"

Compelled by the urgency in her voice, Damien told her, gathered his books and left the lecture room.

When he opened the car door, he immediately noticed shadows under Thea's eyes and a strained look about her face. He was hardly in the car when she told him.

"I think the police are about to arrest you for murder."

"What?!"

"That girl who was found in the tree. You're a prime suspect."

"But I didn't do it."

"That doesn't matter. The police believe you did. So you can't go home unless you want to be arrested."

DAMIEN

"It's true I knew Catherine, but I would never have seriously harmed her. How can they believe I'd do a thing like that?

There was a long pause.

"We're going to Mexico. A little earlier than planned." Thea said.

★★★

Sam Schumacker was not in a good mood when the call from Eden Hearn came in at 3:10. His division chief Hal Tornbrook had demanded a progress report on the tree murder case that was attracting so much media attention. Making such a report would be wasting precious time. The call from the Hearn woman confirmed this. She was close to hysterical.

"Please come… come now. He… he's dead. I think. He shot himself…I heard…" she broke into sobs.

"Who?" he demanded.

"Arnold… Arnold Head… Oh God… please come… Arnold… he… he shot himself" Again she broke down.

He called the homicide unit, then Peter Gregory.

"Hello," Peter answered. "Sam?"

"Eden Hearn phoned. Dr. Head just shot himself. I'll meet you there."

Peter dressed rapidly.

"A call from Sam Schumacker, my FBI friend," he said to Helen, naked beside him on the bed, her hair flaming luxuriantly over her shoulders. "Got to go."

"An emergency?" Helen asked, lazily stretching.

"You might say so. You can stay here if you like." He zipped his pants and grabbed his keys. "I'd like." He smiled at her.

"No," she said, sitting up. "I've got work, too. But I'd like a shower first." Her eyes had that ironic look, "with your permission."

"Of course," he said, heading for the door. "Glad you dropped by." He grinned at her again.

"I'm glad, too," she said.

★★★

"I figure it happened about an hour and a half ago," Sam said to Peter staring at the body of Dr. Arnold Head.

"Did he leave a note or anything?' Peter asked.

"Not that we've found so far," Sam said. "Kind of surprised that he didn't, but maybe the Ident Team will find something. They should be here by now." He looked at his watch, frowning. It was 4:12 PM.

Arnold was staring straight upward, his face expressionless. Blood was splattered on the head of the bed behind him and on the wall above. His right hand lay sprawled open on his chest and the gun, a .38 revolver, lay partially under it.

"It looks like suicide," Sam said meaningfully.

"Yes," Peter said. "She could have done it easily."

"And the fact he didn't leave a note adds to the possibility," Sam said.

"Of course being on the bed at this time of day, he might have been having a nap, or sick, maybe very sick. Aside from your med team it might be a good idea to check with Arnold's physician, Sam."

Sam glowered at Peter. "God damn it, Peter, I've already done that. He'll be right over."

Peter shrugged.

"Sorry, Sam. In some ways I'm still a police inspector, always crossing my T's."

DAMIEN

"Oh shit—you too?" And Sam grinned back.

They went into the adjoining room, Arnold's study, where Tom sat with his arm around Eden's bent shoulders, comforting her.

Sam stood by them, looking down.

"I'm sorry about this, Ms. Hearn, but I have to ask you a few questions."

Tom looked up. "She's very upset. Couldn't you wait a bit?"

Her head was still bowed.

"I'll only ask one question right now. You're sure that Dr. Arnold Head left no note?"

Her head remained bowed, but she slowly shook it "None," she muttered.

"Thank you Ms. Hearn. I'll need to ask you more questions very soon. Meanwhile, Dr. Delaney, have you anything to say that could throw any light on this?"

"Nothing," Tom said, but there was an edge of uncertainty in his voice.

CHAPTER TWELVE

The events of the afternoon struck Peter as bizarre, but then life was sometimes like that. What was hardest to live with was the sense of impending disaster. Shakespeare caught this feeling when he wrote: "Light thickens, and the crow makes wing to the rooky wood." That was just before Banquo was murdered. Had they come to a point like that in this case, Peter wondered as he looked out Arnold's study window. He felt increasing unease, remembering a king murdered by his trusted host, Macbeth. Even more so, Hamlet, where the king is murdered by his brother who then marries the king's wife. So many of Shakespeare's plays were like that, when Peter thought about it, cases of murder as though life itself was intrinsically not only dangerous but also entirely unpredictable. Like this afternoon—Peter having a tumble in bed with someone he hardly knew while the brilliant scientist he had interviewed the day before was blowing his brains out. *If* he was the one who actually pulled the trigger.

Peter looked at his watch. It was just after nine.

"Oh damn!"

"What?" Sam was startled.

"I was supposed to meet Damien at the university bus stop at 5:15. And he said he had a date tonight."

Peter phoned Damien's number, but there was no answer. He waited, hearing the hollow ringtone. His sense of unease grew, remembering as a boy in the snowy moonlit foothills of Alberta hearing the wolves calling from far away. They carried a message of warning. The old ones of the tribe heard it and understood.

"We'd better see if Eden or Tom has talked to Damien." said Sam.

The Med team had given Eden Hearn a little sedative, so her convulsive sobs were fading away. A paramedic put her on the sofa and placed a blanket over her. Her eyelids were fluttering closed.

Sam turned to Tom. "She'll rest for a while now. We need to talk to you."

But Tom's cell phone rang.

★★★

That evening, Danielle got no answer when she phoned Damien to ask him why he hadn't turned up. It was unlike Damien to just not show—especially when they had such an evening planned—so she tried Thea's cell phone before it got too late, but again there was no reply. Something felt wrong, so Danielle finally looked up Tom's number and phoned him.

"Thea?" came Tom's worried voice. And then. "Who is this, please?"

"It's Danielle, Tom. Damien didn't come and I can't reach him. Is everything okay? "

"No," Tom said. "Something terrible happened today, Danielle. Arnold's dead... he shot himself."

"What?!"

"The FBI is here. They want to talk to you." Tom explained that Damien hadn't shown up at Danielle's as he handed the phone to Sam.

"Hello. Detective Sam Schumacker here. You're Danielle Deneuve?"

"Yes." She felt caught in a whirlpool.

"Has Damien ever done that before, made a date and not shown up?"

"No. But is this true—about Dr. Head? Did he really kill himself?"

"So it would appear. Did you know Dr. Head well?"

"Yes. I mean, he was like an uncle to me. But… where's Damien? I mean his own father! …What's going on?"

"It's a good question, Ms. Deneuve."

"I'm coming right over…"

"We'll wait for you."

★★★

Sam and Peter and Tom went into the sitting room opposite the study.

"Have you told your wife or Damien about their father's death, Dr. Delaney?"

Tom looked worried. "I haven't been able to reach either of them."

"Does your wife usually respond promptly to calls or texts?" asked Sam.

"She's pretty good about that most of the time."

"When did you last see her?"

"Yesterday. I was away overnight visiting a lab in L.A. But we talked this morning. It's not like her to be out of reach like this."

"When did you get back?"

"This afternoon."

DAMIEN

"So what did you find when you got here?"

"Eden called in hysterics. I found her in Arnold's bedroom holding Arnold's body," he hesitated, then took a deep breath. "There was blood everywhere... I managed to help her into the study and tried to find out what happened, but the most I got was she heard a shot and ran into his room to find he'd killed himself."

"Do you have any idea why he'd do that?"

Tom looked uneasy. "No. Not really."

"What do you mean 'not really'?"

"I mean... I knew he was worried about Damien...but I can't believe that would cause him to shoot himself. No. I don't... I can't believe that."

"Do you know what was worrying Dr. Head about his son?"

"Only that the boy had... a wildness... and sometimes... got into a little trouble." Tom said, frowning.

"What kind of trouble?"

Tom had to say it. "He had a violent streak. I mean if he thought he was being unjustly crossed or interfered with..."

"But was it assault?"

"Well, you know, boys fight."

"You know, don't you, that Damien is a suspect in the recent murder at the university."

"Yes, but I'm not clear why. Is there evidence to suggest his involvement? I certainly can't believe that Damien would do such a... totally horrible thing."

"The point is, did Dr. Head think Damien was guilty? Could that be why he committed suicide?" Sam paused, staring hard at Tom. "I mean if Damien was a clone of Arnold himself—a clone which went wrong?"

Tom was speechless.

After a moment, Sam said. "There's something you're not telling me... and I want to know what it is."

"Before someone else is killed," Peter added.

Tom hesitated. "Let me be clear. I have known Damien for six years. He is a remarkable individual, brilliant and charismatic and kind, and I think he will do amazing things in his life. Whatever his origins, I don't believe that he would in his right mind do something like this."

"Whatever his origins? Do you think he's a clone?"

Tom sighed heavily. "Yes, I'm afraid so."

Sam and Peter looked at each other.

"Do you have any proof?"

"Not exactly. I did come across some lab notes from 1989 which I asked Arnold about."

"What did he say?"

"He didn't deny it."

"Can you show us the lab notes?"

"We have to go to the lab."

But when Tom opened the drawer in the lab, he found the notes were gone.

"Do you remember what the notes said?"

Tom looked away. "I remember one thing: 'And what animal will I clone? Myself.'"

"That's what it said word for word?"

Tom nodded.

"And the date?" Sam asked.

"May 21, 1989."

Sam and Peter looked at one another.

"Did the surrounding notes relate to cloning?" Peter asked.

"Yes, but they were very hard to read. I don't know if I could interpret them. He had his own kind of shorthand."

"Just the same, we'll search for them."

DAMIEN

"How did your wife get along with Eden Hearne?" Sam asked.

Tom studied him for a moment. "Not very well."

"Do you know why?"

"She thought Eden had too much influence over Arnold. But it was mainly coming from Eden. I think Eden resented this new daughter coming onto the scene and stealing her father's affection."

"Anything more than that?"

Tom looked carefully at Sam. "Why do you ask? Is it important?"

"It could be. I don't know." Sam paused. "I'm trying to understand why Dr. Arnold Head killed himself—or was killed."

"You think he was murdered?!"

"That's unlikely. Suicide seems most probable, but we have to be open to all possibilities."

"I'm going to go look for my wife," Tom said agitatedly.

★★★

Sam turned to Peter Gregory.

"I'm assuming that Damien and Tom's wife are together, Peter. Otherwise nothing makes sense. I'm assuming they're on the run; that somehow Thea knows Damien is our main suspect. I'm assuming she talked to her father about Damien and it was something the old man already feared."

"The idea that his most brilliant creation could be so flawed… he couldn't live with that," Peter added.

"I'm afraid so. Do you think Tom understands?"

"I think he suspects, as hard as it is for him to accept it," Peter acknowledged.

"I've put out an all-points bulletin," said Sam. "What with having a complete description of them and the car license number, we should be able to round them up."

"That depends on when they took off," Peter said. "It could have been early this afternoon. By now they'd be some way into Mexico."

"I've alerted the Mexicans, too."

"Good."

Sam changed tack, "Danielle's experience of Damien doesn't support the idea he's a killer, though. What do you think, Peter?"

"I think Danielle's desperately in love with him and would do anything to protect him."

"Do you think telling her that we think Damien's a clone would have changed her response?"

"We may have to test that," Peter replied.

"Well, for now it's a simple chase, Peter. So I guess you're free to work on your own case. I owe a lot to you, pal, but one thing I've been wondering about. You put on that act of smelling leopard, didn't you? I don't believe you smelled a god-damn thing."

Peter smiled.

"Yet I did believe you were sure a leopard was involved. How'd you figure that?" Sam continued.

Peter's smile widened. "Lucky guess?"

"Some guess. Okay, just go on doing whatever you do. But keep in contact, okay? I'll probably need you before this bloody mess is over."

"You may want me around tomorrow, Sam, if Eden starts to talk. I mean, depending on what she tells us."

Sam blinked. "It could be so."

★★★

Thea drove through side streets looking for somewhere to leave the car. They were on the U.S. side of the Tijuana border crossing. She had brought their passports, cash, toiletries, and a change of clothes for each of them. Damien, who had sat by her in utter silence ever since they had left San Diego, had nothing but the T-shirt and jeans he was wearing, his textbooks and what little cash was in his wallet. Thea had used her credit card for the last time to buy lunch for the road just before they left La Jolla.

"Does Tom know?" Damien stared expressionlessly out the front window.

"No. not yet."

Long silence.

"Let me off. Then go back to Tom."

"I thought about that," she said.

"And?"

"I can't. I know they'll find you if you're on your own. But with me you have a chance because we can go to my mother's people."

Again there was silence.

"I want you to know," he said in a low voice, "that if I killed Catherine I have no memory of it. None. I really liked her. I remember walking with her through the park. We came to a mossy place near a pond and got naked. She wanted to do it. We were playing, and I chased her..." Another silence. "She wanted a condom... but I didn't have one..." he trailed off. "She got mad... and... I don't remember." Thea looked over at Damien. He had scrunched himself down in his seat. "I don't remember anything after that... nothing... I wondered why my clothes were damp when I got home."

Thea pulled over. "Oh Damien," she said softly, wiping a tear from his cheek. He looked so like a lost little boy in that moment.

She looked down the road at the steel wall and no-man's land on the U.S. side of the border, and hovels crowding close to the Mexican side.

"We've simply got to get across this border now."

There was the usual lineup at the border, downtown Tijuana holding many attractions on a Friday, but the line moved rapidly. Thea went first, presented her Mexican passport, and, speaking her native Spanish, told the officials that she was taking Damien over the border for the first time to enjoy the delights of Tijuana. She winked at the Mexican guard, and of course he understood perfectly, smiling broadly when she folded a twenty into his hand.

"You'll enjoy Tijuana, my friend," the guard said to Damien, grinning lecherously at Thea and stamping Damien's American passport.

Thea took Damien's hand as they stepped into Mexico.

CHAPTER THIRTEEN

Sam woke up the next morning swearing at himself for sleeping in. It was nearing 8:45. Then he remembered hearing from his wife, Ruthie, the night before. She would be coming home in two days, on Wednesday—bless her! No more meals bought on the run. At least he could make his own breakfast: a glass of orange juice, a boiled egg and toast, a cup of coffee. And after breakfast he would think about the day ahead while smoking a cigarette, one of only five he was allowing himself, in hopes that the need would slowly fade. But it was a bugger how the craving hung on. Two years ago he had cut down to twenty a day; next month his schedule would put him onto four a day. He figured by his forty-sixth birthday, the year of his twentieth wedding anniversary, he'd be quit of the habit forever. He must have a streak of masochism to go through this slow, agonizing self-denial.

★★★

Peter Gregory woke up a little later, at about 9:15, feeling a hand caressing his skin from his chest to the hair curling below. Helen Murray lay close, kissing him, and he felt life surge. For more than two years after Cathy died, he had been without this pleasure, curled within himself like a snail. Then he had begun to live again. Cathy had wanted him to find another woman, for she knew him. He remembered her once calling him Crazy Horse in the middle of love-making, referring to the nineteenth century Sioux warrior. And then the cancer came down on her. He could not believe how rapidly she sank—the woman who loved life. She just… sank away. After that, a blankness. Then, he'd met Molly who lived for fun; who had no depth at all. He could forget himself when he was with her. Their affair lasted for nearly a year, and she told him he was her first lover who had lasted long enough that she would not forget his name.

Now Helen. She was special in her way—a woman of discernment and inner strength, as well as unself-consciously attractive, though he would not describe her as beautiful. Her mouth was too wide and her hands and feet were large, but somehow that made her more attractive to him. Her love-making was like a challenge which she threw at him. He liked that. But he did not like the phone ringing before they'd quite finished. She shook her head, but he answered anyway.

"It's me. Can you come right over?"

Peter cursed under his breath.

"What's up, Sam?"

"Eden Hearn wants to talk to us."

"Be right over."

★★★

Eden managed to dress herself in a dark grey suit and brush a little color onto her face, while her faded eyes looked vacantly back at her.

When she entered the studio she saw that the nice young detective, Peter Gregory, was looking intently at her, and of course that big hulk of a man, Sam Schumacker, whom she trusted though she was not sure why. She handed him a sheet of paper.

"I wasn't ready to show you this before," she said.

After scanning the note, Sam handed it to Peter and focused his attention on Eden.

"It's all there," she said. "He was sitting in bed writing it when I brought breakfast to him. I had to tell him about Thea and Damien's love affair. It's my job to keep him informed. But he only yelled at me to get out."

Eden tried to ignore the prickly sensation in her eyes as she smoothed her skirt.

"I was shaking all over I was so upset."

"What happened then?" Sam asked gently.

"Then I heard the bang. The whole house seemed to shake—and I ran in… found him…" Now she wept helplessly. "Blood all over—it was awful. My dear man. And his eyes open, looking at me, like he was accusing me. Me!" Her chest shuddered as she sobbed.

The two men glanced at one another and waited until her sobbing softened.

"And you found Arnold's note," Sam prodded.

"I thought I'd killed him," she said peering tearfully at the men, "because of what I'd said about Thea and Damien. I don't think I said they'd actually slept together… surely not… I think I only said Thea was leading him on." And she wept again, feeling that she must pull the fragments of her life together. They *must* be told the truth.

"But I was wrong, you see. Late last night I read Arnold's …"

There was a long pause. She was struggling, feeling that she'd reached a summit and must now plunge down the other side. The tears were over.

DAMIEN

"All these years I've worked for Arnold, I knew there was something very special about the boy—only I didn't know what." Eden went on. "I was responsible for Damien's upbringing, so I thought I should know. I asked Arnold, but he just said Damien was gifted."

"Did you think that was it?" Sam asked.

"Well, for a time. Then one day I was tidying up and noticed some receipts in Arnold's drawer there," She pointed to the large desk in the study corner. "They were for a lot of money and they were made out to a woman."

"Was Arnold having an affair?"

"That's what I wondered. The woman had an unusual name, Adella Cronenburg—I still remember it—and her phone number was on the receipt. So I called her and told her I was Dr. Arnold Head's secretary and he was wondering if she was still in business."

"That was clever," Peter observed.

Eden smiled dimly at Peter, "Right away the woman said, 'Oh my no, that was twenty years ago. Being a surrogate mother was a good business while it lasted. Dr. Head's baby was a rough delivery, though.'"

"What did you think?" asked Sam.

"I was stunned. I'd always thought the boy was adopted. And I wondered why Arnold hadn't told me that he was Damien's natural father."

"Did you ask him?"

"No, I didn't feel I could when he'd told me something different. And I didn't think it mattered that much. It did explain why Damien was so very smart. Such a handful," Eden smiled to herself, thinking of the boy.

"But not why he was so athletic. Did you think about that?" Sam enquired.

"Maybe that came from the mother. I did wonder who she might have been and what happened to her, but Arnold was very private."

"So you never had any notion that Damien might be a clone of Dr. Arnold's?"

"Oh my no! I never dreamt of such a thing. Then I read what Arnold wrote in that note." She glanced over at Peter who had been reading Dr. Head's suicide letter while she spoke.

"And I've never been so shocked in my life. I mean to think that Arnold thought Damien might have killed that poor girl… I don't believe it for a minute. My boy!" She gave way to tears again. She was in a morass.

"Ms. Hearn," Sam said, "you can be glad of one thing. In this note you've given us, Dr. Head said he couldn't live with the idea that his clone had killed that girl. So it wasn't what you told him that caused him to commit suicide."

She looked at him with brimful eyes, and nodded. This detective: he was a kind man.

***

Sam and Peter went to a nearby restaurant for lunch, and Sam read Arnold's note again while they waited to be served. Each ordered a hamburger and coffee and ate without speaking until they'd finished.

"What do you think of this note?" asked Sam.

"It's a clear and complete confession, Sam, that Arnold cloned Damien and believed him to be the killer. You've just got to find Damien."

"But bloody hell, why do these other complications continue?"

"You mean about Thea and Damien."

"You bet."

DAMIEN

"That's a tough one."

After lunch they found Tom in his lab hunched over some notes.

"Interesting reading?" Sam asked as they entered.

"I'm still looking for those old notes of Arnold's."

"Maybe you won't need them," Sam said, holding out Arnold's deathbed confession.

Tom read it, frowning and shaking his head. "So that's it then."

"Of course, there's nothing about how he did it," Sam said, "just that he cloned the boy."

"With the help of ayahuasca," Peter added.

"Yeah," Sam said, "what's that all about?"

"Ask the Maya," Peter said.

Sam obviously wanted to move on, "Did your wife know the truth about Damien?"

Tom sat back, his hands tight on his knees. "I think so," he said. "But none of this actually proves that Damien did it. It's all circumstantial isn't it?"

Ignoring Tom's question, Sam asked, "Ms. Hearn said she told Dr. Head that your wife was after Damien. Did you know about this?"

Tom waved his hand dismissively. "I knew she was attracted to him. She told me so. But I never thought it was more than that. Just an attraction. He is her brother, after all."

"Well, Ms. Hearn's statement seems to fit with the fact that both your wife and Damien have gone missing."

Tom only shook his head. "That doesn't mean an affair, necessarily. Thea always looked out for Damien."

"Whatever her motives, if Thea's with Damien, she's now a fugitive from the law." Sam observed Tom closely.

Tom said nothing.

"Have you heard from her?" Peter asked.

"No."

"Thea's car has been found parked near the Tijuana border crossing," Sam said. "So we think they've fled to Mexico."

"They're both officially wanted persons," Peter said.

"We need good photographs of Thea and Damien," Sam added. "And we'll need your help. Which of her clothes are missing? Describe her handbag or anything she might have carried with her. How much money did she take? Does she have access to Mexican accounts that her mother might have set up for her? Do you know where her mother is now, or how she can be traced? Anything that could help us find her?"

Tom nodded.

Tom provided the information they requested, then sat immobilized after Sam and Peter left. His life had fallen apart and he could not even weep. She had gone—and Arnold Head was no more. Should he follow them into Mexico? He'd never find them even if he knew Mexico well, which he didn't. Or spoke Spanish, which he didn't, at least not well. She'd left nothing—not even a note. What was she thinking? If the police found them, she'd go to jail for a long time. And if the police didn't find them, what kind of life would she have? Wherever he reached out, there was nothing—nothing at all. His life had discarded him.

DAMIEN

CHAPTER FOURTEEN

At three in the afternoon on the day after Dr. Arnold Head's death, Sam Schumacker visited Dr. Head's lawyer.

Henry Franks had dark-rimmed spectacles and brown hair touched here and there with grey. With a distracted air, he kept straightening papers on his desk.

"Well, Mr. Franks, you know I need to see Dr. Arnold Head's Last Will. Can you tell me the gist of it?" He paused because Franks seemed vaguely disturbed by the request.

Franks looked grave. "My only concern is the possibility of a civil suit by one of the parties named in the Will. It's not that I am anticipating one, but you never know. Actually the Will is quite straightforward."

Franks picked up a type-written page. "His daughter, Thea Maria Arenden Delaney will inherit all real estate and intellectual property, including Dr. Head's patents, and therefore the ongoing income from same, a substantial cash flow. Next is his son, Damien Head, who appears to have no middle name…." The lawyer frowned as though this were an egregious oversight. "He will inherit 80 % of Dr. Head's investments, only excluding royalties on the patents already mentioned. Then there's Eden Hearn, named as Dr. Arnold Head's secretary. She will receive a substantial cash amount. It appears to be valued at more than six million dollars liquidated from assets in Dr. Arnold Head's investment portfolio. Her amount adds up to about 10% of the total. The final recipient is one Ahmal Arenden, named as Thea's mother. She will receive three million dollars in cash; the remaining three million dollars are allocated to various organizations and institutes Dr. Arnold Head wanted to support."

"I hope that Dr. Arnold Head included Thea Delaney's mother's address."

"Oh yes. Although it's a bank in Mexico City."

"Good. So that's it?"

"That's it. Oh. Not quite. Dr. Head names Thomas Henry Delaney as recipient of all his files and lab equipment and as one who should take charge of ongoing projects, though of course his wife Thea will actually own the lab."

Sam nodded, placing the Will in his brief case.

"I believe you have been Dr. Head's attorney for a number of years."

"Seventeen to be exact."

"As you know, Dr. Arnold Head's death is under FBI investigation. I need to ask you a few questions."

"Naturally."

"Are you aware of anything that could throw light on Dr. Head's apparent suicide? I'm asking not only for something specific, but also more general concerns or problems that may not appear in your file."

The lawyer fidgeted with his papers. "Only one thing sticks in my mind because I found it pretty odd, and couldn't see how it related to my client. About a year ago I received a call from a man who claimed to be a member of Mexican military intelligence. I've forgotten the official title, but I've got it all on file. Anyway, he asked me if I was Arnold Head's attorney and if I had any information, preferably an address, for Thea Delaney's mother's place of residence."

"What did you say?"

"I said no, naturally. Then I called Dr. Head about it."

"What did Dr. Head think?"

"Dr. Head was quite annoyed, saying that if he had her home address he would not pass it on to anyone, and hung up." The lawyer paused, fidgeting again. "I always remembered that incident."

★★★

It was nearly noon the next day when Danielle rang at Tom Delaney's door, but there was no answer, so she walked up to Dr. Head's place, and with a feeling of dread buzzed the intercom.

"Oh hello," Eden said. "Yes, Danielle, it's a sad time." She opened the door wide. "Do come in."

Noticing Eden's faded eyes as they sat down in the study, Danielle was struck by the age gap between them.

"Back when I almost came to live here—it was like my second home here—you were wonderful to me, and I'll never forget it. Never forget you."

Eden was looking out the window. "They were good days for me too." She spoke softly. There was a silence.

"How could this happen, Eden?" Danielle asked in anguish. "I'm sorry—but I just can't… understand it. And where is Damien? The police wouldn't tell me anything about him last night."

She waited. "Please tell me."

Eden spoke slowly as though to herself, "We don't know." She was silent again. "He left… with Thea."

"What about Tom? Has he heard from her?"

DAMIEN

Eden shook her head. "The FBI found her car parked near the Tijuana border crossing."

"Is this because of what happened to Dr. Head?"

"No. They don't know."

"They don't know their father's dead? The whole thing is..." Danielle could find no adequate word... "unbelievable."

"Did the police ask you about Damien?"

"Yes, but what could I tell them, Eden? I haven't a clue why Dr. Head killed himself." There was a pause. "Did he leave a note?"

"Yes. But it's up to the police to tell you about that."

"I may be young, Eden, but I am a woman now. You know that Dr. Head was like an Uncle to me. He liked me... I need to know... I have the right to know!"

"Oh my God..." Eden's eyes were cast down... "Don't ask me."

But Danielle had to know. "Tell me, Eden."

"Arnold shot himself... because... because of Damien." She broke down and wept, and Danielle waited.

"What about Damien?"

"That Damien... killed that young woman in the tree ..."

Danielle could not believe what she was hearing. "What?!"

Eden struggled on, almost in a whisper. "...And it was Arnold's fault ... because he... he..."

"He what?" Danielle leaned forward, wanting to shake the information out of Eden.

But Eden rose to her feet and ran out through the study and hall, hurled herself into her own room and slammed the door shut.

Danielle stood up, and then sat down again. She looked around at the room, seeing bits and pieces that did not fit together. Slowly she rose, walked carefully to the front door and out into the sunlight. For a moment she stood there blinded by it, and then gradually felt its warmth spreading. She walked down the path to stand outside the laboratory, and then knocked on the door, hoping Tom was back. After a moment Tom opened it and she went inside. A pile of notes lay scattered on the desk to the right.

"I need to talk to you."

He invited her to a chair near the desk. "I guessed you would," he said.

"I've just come from Eden. She told me about Damien and Thea." Danielle could not help the catch in her throat, but continued: "I do not believe it, Tom. I know Damien." She saw him frown and shake his head and was suddenly angry. "We grew up together, Damien and I."

"Danielle," he said, "Please... I'm sure in a way you do know him better than any of us. But you don't know..." He shifted in his chair. "...Damien is Arnold's clone."

"What?! No! How is that possible?"

Danielle thought about Damien and went on, "No!" "He can't be. He's so different. Different eyes. Physically powerful where Dr. Head was weak."

"Arnold added other genetic material to achieve Damien's strength and power. Selected jaguar genes."

"What?"

"Jaguar genes."

"Oh my God!" Remembering glowing yellow eyes, growling power, savage sex—Danielle suddenly knew it to be true. She remembered quite suddenly how well he could see in the dark. He would forget to turn on lights at night, and yet never seemed to bump into anything.

"It's all in his last notes Danielle. Arnold wanted his creation to have his high I.Q. and the physical prowess he never had."

DAMIEN

There was a moment of silence. Then: "But this doesn't make Damien the murderer."

"The probability is pretty overwhelming, Danielle. I'm having trouble believing it too, though. He is so gentle."

"Oh my God…" Danielle groped for balance. "But is there any physical evidence?"

Tom considered this: "Well, no…"

A sudden thought struck her. "But doesn't this mean Thea is in great danger? Are you just going to sit here shuffling notes?" She felt an unaccountable directionless anger.

Tom sat back. "What do you expect me to do?"

"Go after her, Tom—bring her back!"

"Go where, Danielle? If you could tell me where on earth she is I would go. I'm hoping to hear from her." He paused.

Danielle saw Tom's dilemma, but it didn't mitigate her anger.

"I'm truly sorry, Tom. But I can't do the same."

After a moment he said, "You know, Thea often had real insights. She had a reason for doing this. I know she'll contact me when she can. And I need to be ready for her when she needs me."

"I'll go after them."

"That's crazy."

"No," Danielle responded slowly. "It makes a weird kind of sense. I've got the money and I speak Spanish and I can get leave from the university."

"You'll need help. You might want to talk to Peter Gregory."

"Who's he?"

"The private detective that has been assisting the FBI. Thea was impressed by him. In fact when I think of it, she was afraid of him in some way, maybe because she figured he was on to Damien. Anyway, maybe he could help you. He'd be expensive, though."

"Isn't he still working for the FBI?"

"I think he's independent. You can probably get his number from that FBI guy, Detective Schumacher." Tom suddenly lowered his head and put his hands over his face. "It'll be terrible if the FBI find them first. God! I hope they don't!"

Danielle was thinking desperately. "Tom," she grasped the wrist of the hand covering part of his face. "Let's start looking right here."

"Where?"

"Why would they go south? What's down there?"

"Oh! Thea grew up in Guatemala and Mexico. She must be going to her mother. Ahmal is powerful among the Maya."

"So can I have Ahmal's address?"

"We don't have it. She was always moving around."

"But Thea and Dr. Head must have had some way of contacting her. Maybe there's something in Dr. Head's papers. She's the key, Tom, the one who can help us—Thea's mother!"

"Oh God," groaned Tom. "I want them to get away. But if Damien's a killer…"

★★★

The next morning Tom found a letter from Thea in the mail.

Dearest Tom,

I have to pick Damien up from the University. He's going to be arrested for murder. Arnold believes it was Damien and

DAMIEN

admits to cloning him from his own genes and a jaguar's.

But Damien hasn't the heart of a killer. He's a new being who needs a chance to sort himself out. Being tried for murder would destroy him.

I love you, Tom, and only you. Damien's my brother. I'll see him safe and then come home to you.

Love,

Thea

P.S. Destroy this when you've read it. Sorry it's so rushed.

PART TWO

CHAPTER FIFTEEN

They had not gone many blocks into Tijuana before they found a nondescript little restaurant where they chose a window table and ordered coffee. Thea searched her notebook for the phone number she needed and asked to use the phone.

"Ramón?" she said, speaking Spanish. "Good, it's Thea, Ahmal's daughter ....Yes. I'm here with a friend. Could you pick us up, please, Ramón. ....Thank you—yes." She gave him their location and returned the phone.

"He's coming right away."

"Who is he?"

"A fellow who's involved with my mother's political network, the Savonards. The Mexican government treats them as criminals although their organization would be legal in the US. Without their help we don't stand a chance, but we can't ask questions. I'll explain what I can when I can."

"Okay, Thea."

"So far so good..." Thea sighed. "When I see Ramón's car, we'll walk to the corner to meet him." Thea paid for the coffee.

"Do you think the police will follow us down here?"

"I think they might try. I'm banking on the fact that the Mexican police—at least the street cops—are not that interested in cooperating with U.S. law enforcement. That's assuming word has gotten down to them, which I doubt... at least not yet. Still, we should be careful."

Damien was silent, staring at the circles his spoon made in the coffee.

"There's Ramón. Let's go," Thea said.

They walked to the corner, and slipped quickly into the battered-looking Chevy station wagon that drew up beside them.

"Good to see you, Ramón. You don't look a day older," Thea said in Spanish.

"Good to see you too, Thea... You do look a little older." Ramón, who appeared to be in his mid-thirties, grinned at them, "Then you were a teen-aged girl, now you're a beautiful woman."

Beside him sat Genera, a younger man who nodded to them.

"And who is your boyfriend?" Ramón asked.

"He's my American brother Damien."

"Hello, Damien," Ramón said in English and then in Spanish to Thea. "Are the police after him?"

"Yes, for a crime he did not really commit. But, that's not the point. Ahmal wants to see him."

Ramón nodded. "Anyone who interests Ahmal interests all of us. We will help, but we have little to give."

Ramón drove carefully through the darkening streets, avoiding the downtown area.

"We don't need money, Ramón... We need shelter and then to get over to San Felipe, where I have another contact."

"Yes, I know him... Montago... the old man."

"Yes... him."

"Good, and how soon?"

"Something to eat and some sleep would be good… Could someone take us to San Felipe in about six hours?"

"Leaving about 2 AM?"

"No later."

"It is done, Thea. While you are sleeping we will prepare tourist visas for both of you for the Puesta checkpoint on the way to San Felipe."

"I forgot about that. Is it a police checkpoint?"

"No… only army, who won't know anything about your friend. They're there to stop drug traffickers and they're not even good at that."

Thea smiled. "Dear old Mexico."

"Only God loves her. Anyway, my wife is looking forward to meeting you. And of course will welcome the good-looking American. Oh yes."

As they drove along, Thea asked Damien how much he'd understood.

"I got the gist of it. Where's San Felipe?" Damien asked.

"It's on the Sea of Cortez, where the whales are."

"I like whales," he said.

★★★

After they'd slept, the young man Genera drove them past Enseñada and through the San Pedro Martira Mountains toward San Felipe. They left at 3 AM, seeing little traffic.

Damien was scrunched down in the back seat in darkness.

"Are you asleep, Damien?" Thea said softly.

"No." His voice was muffled.

"Do you want to know more about where we're going?"

"No… whatever." Damien was thinking about his dream. He'd dreamt again about the hummingbird,

DAMIEN

Zynta—the vibrant colours, minute body—only this time it had transformed into Catherine, her long dark hair and delicate bones and… He couldn't, wouldn't go there where the blackness lay. What had he done? He balled himself tightly into the corner.

Thea waited, thinking hard, and the dark miles passed. Finally, she turned to the young Mexican.

"We are not in a race, Genera. You have hit several bad potholes which have kept me wide awake, and about to use bad language. You don't want to hear such words, do you, Genera, you being so young and innocent."

The young man grinned. "Why, no, I might learn words I never heard before, being so young and innocent… almost a virgin."

"Well, I would not want to be the cause of you losing your virginity would I, Genera? But if you don't slow down this fucking vehicle I may change my mind."

"Oh, good God in heaven," Genera intoned, "and the Blessed Virgin. That tempts me to step on the gas. But you are married and I would not want to be the cause of your damnation, so I will slow down, and may the Saints bless me." And he did actually slow down.

"Tell me, Genera," Thea said, "do you understand English?"

"About five words, which I would not want to repeat to you."

"We'll stick to Spanish then," she said.

Thea turned to look at Damien, who was still lower in his seat. "Damien, how are you feeling?"

After a long silence, his voice was fragile. "Why are you helping me, Thea? What if I really am … what they say…. a killer……….. what if I killed Catherine?"

She had to strain to hear him. She turned to Genera. "Stop the car, please. I need to get into the back."

With a screech of brakes, they came to a halt, and Thea quickly climbed in beside Damien and wrapped him in her arms as Genera drove on. For just a moment Damien yielded, but then he stiffened and Thea released him.

"If I did and I don't remember it, I could be a danger to you. Maybe you're not safe with me. Maybe no one is." Damien shrank further back into his corner.

"I don't think that's true."

"You don't understand, Thea. I get angry sometimes, and then I can't remember afterward. People have been hurt before. I don't know where it comes from or how to control it or even why it happens. It scares me. I don't want to hurt anyone."

"I know," Thea said soothingly. She laid a comforting hand on his lean thigh. "You need to know something about yourself, Damien."

He said nothing.

"This is hard, and I don't know how to make it easier for you."

Damien looked steadily out the black window.

"You're not actually adopted, at least not in the traditional way."

"Why am I not surprised." Damien grunted.

"Arnold cloned you from himself, so he is your natural father."

"No!" Damien bolted upright, hitting his head on the ceiling. "Ow!" He grabbed his head, groaned. "But I'm not the same as him. Wouldn't I be identical?"

"Yes. But he wanted you to be better than him, more physically adept, so he gave you genes from a jaguar, too."

"Fuck!"

Damien rubbed his head.

DAMIEN

"Fuck! Why the fuck would he do *that*?" Damien reached for the door handle. "Stop the car. Now!" He shouted at Genara.

Genara slammed on the brakes and Damien leapt from the car before it had even fully stopped, hitting the ground running. Thea jumped out after him, only to see him vanish, navigating unerringly over the rocky ground and around the stiff cacti whose forms were barely darker than the night.

"What was that?" Genara called in astonishment.

"He'll be back." Thea replied over her shoulder. At least I hope so, she thought.

And so they waited. And waited. Genara looked at his watch.

"It's been an hour. How long are we supposed to wait?"

"Until he returns." Thea laid her head back against the seat and closed her eyes.

Thea didn't think she was sleeping, but she was jolted awake when Damien finally opened the door and slid in, sweat drying in his hair.

"I'm so glad you're back." Thea said gratefully.

"You shouldn't be. I could kill you too. I really liked Catherine, you know? I really like you too. Part jaguar. Holy fuck. No wonder I'm dangerous and can't control it. I killed Zynta too, you know."

"Who?"

"Zynta. Oh forget it. Maybe it'd be better if I'm dead. I'm out of control." He reached for the door handle again, but Genara suddenly accelerated away from their parking spot and Thea grabbed Damien's arm.

"You can't do that."

"Why?"

"You just can't. You're too important. You're the only one of your kind and you're amazing and you're gentle and now you know about it you'll be able to learn to control your jaguar side."

"Yeah, sure." Damien looked out the black window. "How was that even possible, to clone me like that?"

"You know Arnold was way ahead of his time."

Damien drew himself even further away and sat rigidly, staring into the night.

"So why'd you tell me I had a Guatemalan mother?" He asked angrily.

"At the time, that's what I thought, and I was pretty sure Mama knew the whole story. Turns out I was right about that—Mama knowing—but so wrong about you."

Damien grunted.

"You see, when the detectives came to see Father and then Tom—"

"When was that?" Damien asked sharply.

"Tom the day before we left, and Father the day before that. Anyway, there were too many questions, so I talked to Mama and then confronted Father about it."

"That must have been something to see,"

"Father was pretty upset." Thea admitted.

"So I'm basically a clone of Father, with a few jaguar genes thrown in for physical prowess." Damien shook his head, as if to clear it. "So that'd be why I don't look exactly like him, I suppose…. and…oh my God—jaguars stash their kills in trees." Damien looked at Thea in horror. "I'm a freak!"

"You're different, but that doesn't make you a freak, more like a kind of superman," Thea said, then struggled with her words.

"Damien, somehow you have to learn to live with your animal side. The fact is you're a new kind of…composite being. And only you can find the way to make that work. What happened to that girl…that was not the human part of you, it was the jaguar-you. That's why you've no memory of it."

"So I'm a monster."

Thea tried to reach though the darkness that was settling over him.

"I'm saying it's the jaguar-you that did it; not the human-you."

"Like temporary insanity."

"A bit. But you are mostly human. You can learn to control your jaguar side."

Damien voiced his despair, "The real me... man and animal... freak. Jekyll and Hyde."

Thea searched to free her meaning. "You know something?" She blurted out. "All of us are composites. Important parts of our brains belong to our lizard selves— there when we slithered out of the water, and still there now, and... and those animal parts still struggle with our reasoning selves, those so-called higher functions that were the last to develop."

She tried to read his face, but there was no light.

"I'll go further, Damien. Sometimes our lizard brains take over and we do terrible things. All of us. We kill in the heat of the moment, not fully realizing what we've done until our higher brain regains dominance. But we can and do learn to manage our lizard selves."

"So... I can learn to manage the jaguar-me?" He said in a low tone. "Is that it?"

She hesitated. "Yes...I think so."

"Bullshit."

"No, really. I think maybe Mama can help you with that."

"You talk like a professor, Thea." Damien subsided again. Then, "Actual jaguar genes are a wee bit different from ancient lizard-brain, though."

"True, but I think you can figure it out—with Mama's help," Thea said.

"If it happens again…? And…" He struggled, thinking again of Zynta… and Catherine… "I don't know when… it might…" He could not finish, and the car rumbled on through the dark night.

★★★

On the east coast of the Baja, near where they turned from the interior to the coast road, they passed through the army checkpoint. It was a bleak landscape, with no touch of green and few dwellings. Since Enseñada, they'd only seen one ponderous truck heading the opposite way. The soldier yawned as he compared their tourist visas to their faces.

They arrived in San Felipe at nearly 9:30 AM. Genera drove straight down to the fisherman's harbor and found Montago's fishboat. It was old, like the man himself, who sat in the stern chewing on chilli peppers. Genera got out of the car.

"Hullo, Montago," Genera said, "Up early. Going fishing?"

Montago was a small man, slightly hunched, with a grizzled face like a much fought-over battlefield, but his black eyes sparkled.

"If it isn't young Genera… What brings you over here from cocaine paradise?"

"Now is that a nice thing to say about beautiful Tijuana, Montago?" Genera asked. "We are not perfect, but still there are good deeds."

"And it looks to me that you've done me one, bringing me a beautiful woman."

"Yes, none other than the daughter of our own Ahmal."

"May the saints preserve us—but they won`t. Ahmal may."

"This is Thea and this is her American brother Damien."

"I help no Americans... they're buggering our country."

"This bugger is escaping from the American police, Montago, and Ahmal wants to meet him," Thea said.

"Then that is different. So how can I help?"

"Take them across to Puerto Peñasco."

"That's about four hours... hard on the gas... which now costs..."

"Never mind what it costs, old man. They'll pay."

The old man got up and came to the side of the boat, peering down at them.

"When do they want to go?"

"Now."

"Not on this boat," the old man said. "They patrol the sea every day from their cursed helicopters. Going down there with this boat, they would think I was smuggling something."

"So you won't take them?"

"I have a panga, Genera. I'll take them in that."

"But that's an open boat."

"That's right. And looking down from their accursed helicopter, what will they see? ...Two people out fishing with an old guy steering the craft. A lot of our visitors do that. Go fishing down that way."

"Have it your way, Montago."

"For me, my way is the only way. But it will get you there, Thea."

"Ahmal will bless you for this."

"Gotta get the panga, though."

"Can Thea and her young man wait inside this fishboat?" Genera asked. He looked around but no one else was in sight. "Now, Montago."

Montago gestured them aboard and pointed to the below deck living area.

CHAPTER SIXTEEN

Peter Gregory was worried about the missing girl that had brought him to San Diego and Sam Schumacker. His main lead to the human trafficking gang, The Slavers, had disappeared. In fact, he was afraid his lead's disappearance might be permanent. That morning, his client Morton Schulman had phoned, furious over the lack of progress in finding his daughter.

And to top it all off, Peter's new girlfriend, Helen, had headed east to work with her publishers on her book and would be away for two weeks.

Peter phoned Sam. "That lead you gave me to The Slavers went nowhere. My client's given me ten days to find her, or he'll hire someone else."

"Sorry, Peter… but I've given you all the leads I have… Wait a minute… It's a long shot but you could try a guy named Chippo Domingo who's been on the inside and might help, given the right incentive. Here's his number."

"Thanks. How's the clone case going, Sam?"

Sam growled, "It ain't goin'. Thea and Damien have vanished. And the one lead we had to that woman… you know… Thea's mother? Nobody knows where she is—the Mexican police included."

"Weird," was Peter's only comment.

"It's weird alright, and maybe getting weirder. We know they went across at Tijuana, but then—nothing. Did they go Mexicali way, or down to Enseñada... and if so, why? As you know Tijuana is cocaine city so the gangs are into everything. My guess is that those two holed up there and they've got crime friends."

"I doubt it, Sam."

"Why am I not surprised? Go on."

"I think there's something else... something Thea's worked out... but don't ask me what."

Sam waited.

Peter went on, "I think maybe we should look more into Thea's mother, this Ahmal woman. I'm curious that there's so little information about her."

"Hmmm. You may have a point....This isn't one of your goddamn 'feelings' is it?"

"Might be."

"Fucking red power."

"What...?"

"Red power... shamans... you people are always drumming on about it."

Peter snorted, "Okay, Sam, have it your way. Right now my red power tells me I've got to take a leak. Then I'm going to drum up some good news for my client... somehow."

But dinner came without a break. Sam's lead, Chippo Domingo, didn't answer the phone. Peter left a message.

That evening Peter went over his notes yet again. There had to be a key to the door of his ignorance.

Then the phone rang. "Chippo here..." It was a gruff voice.

"I'm Pete Gregory. Sam Schumacker gave me your number... said you might help me."

"How?"

"I'm looking for a 17 year old girl from Vancouver. She was shipped across the B.C. border about April 20th or thereabouts."

"Asian?"

"No. white, black hair and eyes.... I'll email her picture."

"Might help. The date's more useful, though." Chippo grunted.

"So what can you give me?"

"Most likely nothing. But if I do get something, it'll be the receiver."

"The one who took the shipment?"

"You got it." There was a pause. "Did Sam tell you I charge heavy? Want to know how much?"

"No."

"Good. I'll phone you tomorrow night same time." He hung up.

Within five minutes the phone rang again.

"Hi. Is that Peter Gregory? The Mountie?" Peter recognized Danielle's voice.

"What can I do for you, Danielle?"

"I'd like to talk to you."

"We're talking."

"I think you know more about me than I do about you. And that doesn't work for me. Could we meet in the morning?"

"What time?"

"Say 10 o'clock."

After hanging up, Peter wondered why he hadn't said no. After all, he was no longer on the clone case. Danielle'd been a girlfriend of Damien's, but so what? Then he realized that, for some reason, he thought she might reveal something about Damien that she would not tell Sam—not willingly. And maybe now would be the time to explain that Damien was a clone, if she didn't know already.

DAMIEN

Something else he hadn't yet talked to Sam about was Arnold Head's mention of ayahuasca in his last statement. But Peter didn't know the right questions to ask, so in his spare time he'd been reading up on ayahuasca and cloning, two wildly divergent and complicated topics. Just how had Arnold Head made such a ground-breaking discovery so far ahead of his time? Peter figured the FBI people would be looking at it from too narrow a perspective. After reading for another couple of hours, he gave up, not having the biochemistry background needed to take it all in. He phoned Tom.

★★★

The next morning, Peter found Danielle in a booth in the coffee shop.

"Thanks for meeting me," she said as he slid into the seat opposite her. She was wearing a rich green t-shirt that hugged her body. She looked very young, yet alert, in charge of herself.

"Are you still on the case?" she asked.

"Let's say I'm on call." He paused. "Didn't you know that?"

"If you mean have I talked to Sam Schumacker the answer is yes. Sam told me about you—perhaps more than he meant to. I'm very persistent with questions."

"And I'm sure you are going to ask me a few."

She threw back a few strands of hair. He noticed that her skin had a faintly olive sheen.

"From what I've heard, and not just from Sam, you're somewhat... shall I say... unusual." She let the comment hang and so did he. "I'm referring to Thea," she went on, "who is herself unusual." Another silence..."Thea wasn't afraid of Sam. She was afraid of you, your prescience. That's what she told Tom. And I think that's the main reason she got into her car, picked up Damien and took off for Mexico."

There was another long silence between them. Her dark eyes shone.

"And you want me to help find Damien," he said quietly.

"Exactly," she said.

"You know he's a clone, don't you?"

"So I've been told." She suddenly grabbed his hand. "Listen, please... if he did that he didn't know what he was doing. He needs help... desperately. I think I know how to look for him... I mean what I have to find out in order to find him and I need you to help me."

"No you don't."

"Why do you say that?"

"If I found him I'd have to turn him over to the FBI."

She let go of him, sat back. "All I'm asking is that you help me to figure out where to look for him. I'd do the actual finding." After an uncomfortable pause, "You don't have to tell the FBI about your guesses, do you? Do you?"

Again she grabbed his hand.

"Do you love him, Danielle?"

Danielle loosened her grip, and her eyes wandered to the window as she thought about that question.

"Love is a big word, isn't it? I care about him, and I guess I believe in him." She frowned. "Look, I just want to help the guy. He's a friend. Leave it at that."

"Okay, Danielle. What can I do?"

"Work with me... come to Mexico even. I'd pay you your standard fee, of course, plus expenses."

"I'm afraid I'm expensive."

"In three weeks, when I turn 21, I come into quite a lot of money. I'm sure I can afford you." She paused. "I'm going anyway, Peter, whether you come or not." Then, with a whimsical look. "And you wouldn't want to see me down there all alone among those dangerous Latinos, would you?"

Peter was tempted.

"I have to close another case first, but I'll consider your offer if you come up with a viable plan. It will mean that I will have to stop assisting the FBI, of course. Your lovely distinction between finding Damien and determining where we *might* find him only means that you'd make a hell of a good lawyer."

Now she gave him a tiny smile.

★★★

It was getting close to 2:30 that afternoon when Peter found Tom in his lab, buried in notepaper.

"Sorry to interrupt you, Tom. But I need some help."

"So you said." Tom looked up at him. "Pull up a chair."

Tom looked somehow older than his years—depleted, with shadows under his eyes.

"I was kind of rude to you last night, and I'm sorry. But your being puzzled by Arnold's last statement is no big surprise. Parts of it puzzle me, too, and I'm trained in his field."

"Have you heard from the FBI specialists about this?"

"Yesterday."

"What did they want?"

"Me to explain to them the obvious: how Arnold could have come up with a method that worked as early as 1990 when no one else was even close."

"And…?"

"No idea. Arnold didn't explain it, just threw out some useless hints."

Peter pulled out his copy of Arnold Head's last statement from a side pocket.

"He says here that he found out how to clone himself with jaguar genes after using a special variant of ayahuasca."

"Yeah. Ahmal helped him with that."

"Ahmal?"

"Yes. I just found his journal from that trip. She took him to the jungle near Meridor, where they found the plant, then they went to Chiapas just across the border. It was a dangerous place then."

"Why Chiapas?"

"He says here that they took the ayahuasca to an old man. A brujo," said Tom.

"That's a Mexican shaman?"

"Yes. And this shaman told Ahmal how to prepare this plant medicine for Arnold."

"Really? I had no idea she was so involved."

"According to this, Ahmal did prepare the ayahuasca, and they—Arnold and Ahmal—had a ceremony, Arnold taking the drug and calling on Ahmal's Nahuatl, her jaguar spirit."

"Do you think this Nahuatl could have anything to do with Arnold's discovery of the formula?" Peter asked.

"I'm sure it does. But how's that going to help you, or anyone?"

"Did the FBI specialists ask the same questions?"

"I hadn't found the journal, so they don't know all this yet. From their perspective, though, the ayahuasca was just a recreational drug trip."

"And from your perspective…?"

"As you probably know, I went to Guatemala with Arnold some years later. I met Ahmal and Thea there. There was and still is something about Ahmal I can't figure out. I've always thought it's because she's a bruja. So I can't dismiss what Arnold wrote in that statement." He paused. "Nor could I explain it. Then or now."

CHAPTER SEVENTEEN

They set out into a brisk off-shore wind, soon letting line out in an attempt to catch corvina, the sea bass. Thea kept glancing skywards, though Montago cheerfully told her not to worry, that police air patrols were rare. Besides, if one did happen upon them, they would probably be left alone as he was just an old fisherman taking out a couple of tourists. Thea knew full well that his record with the police probably did not quite fit with the picture he was giving them.

"Come on, Montago… don't bullshit me. I've lived too long in Mexico for that. That other boat you use for smuggling on night trips across to Puerto Peñasco. You've probably been caught a few times, right?"

Montago grinned at her. "It is truly shocking how you see right through me. But I should not be surprised, since you are the daughter of the wondrous Ahmal. Yes, my beauty, I am not as innocent as I appear."

Thea giggled.

"But you will also know," he went on, "since you see right through me, that my many contacts in the region of Puerto Peñasco may be—no, will be—of great help for you and the young man." He looked at Damien, who was gazing listlessly out to sea. "By the way, I trust he does not understand the language."

"Not much. In any case, Montago, I know your contacts will be valuable and I thank you for them."

"Good. My main contact in the Puerto will see that you are driven south in a truck because that is the safest way. I'm guessing you are headed to Mexico City."

"Yes… Ahmal's people are there."

"And they will take you to her. For nobody knows where Ahmal herself is, now here, now there. The police go crazy trying to find her."

Suddenly Damien struggled with his rod. A fish had struck.

"Tell him to let it fly. Play it," Montago said.

Thea repeated this to Damien, but he ignored her, winding in astonishingly fast, but there was a sudden snap as the fish escaped. Damien threw down the rod in disgust.

"Doesn't your Yankee know how to fish?" Montago said.

"I guess not," she said. "He's not used to giving in."

"It's not giving in… it's playing the fish."

"Montago is sorry you lost that fine fish," Thea said to Damien.

But Damien shook his head and turned abruptly away. They were passing the little island called Los Carvo when they heard the distant thrum of a helicopter.

"Here is a straw hat," Montago said, handing it to Thea. "It belonged to a beautiful lady friend of mine," he added, grinning. "It will only make you look like more of a tourist because your beauty cannot be improved upon."

The helicopter passed to the north then swung toward them, dropping in altitude, until it was no more than 20 to 30 feet overhead.

"Look up at them and wave, and tell your friend to do the same, Thea. Mexicans never do that. Anyway the police just want to peer into my boat to see if I am carrying anything. They do this all the time."

Thea gave a broad smile as she waved, and after a shattering two or three minutes, the helicopter banked away, gaining altitude.

"The one who leaned out to look at us—we recognized each other. I know his father who was a smuggler like me. Anyway the boy gave me a little wave before they left. You can relax, Thea, and forget about fishing. As for me I am going to catch a nap. Ask your Yankee boy to take over the steering, and tell him to keep headed toward that point of land." Montago pointed to a spot barely visible in the blue haze.

They settled into their new positions, Montago leaning back with his hat down over his eyes, Thea and Damien watching the unending swell of the waves.

"Now can you explain things to me, Thea?" Damien said at last. "More about this organization that's helping us?" He hesitated. "It looks like I'm going to be dependent on them."

"Yes, you are, and so am I."

She was silent, thinking how best to answer his question.

"And your mother's involved with these people… how's that?"

Thea remained silent, gazing blankly at the boat's worn floorboards.

"You said the Mexican government is against this group, but hasn't made it illegal." Damien prompted her again.

"My mother's involvement is a long story, I'm afraid."

"We've got time."

Thea still hesitated, wondering where to start. "Okay. Mama was born into a village in the Petén jungle of Guatemala, where her father owned a small farm. One day the soldiers came and told her father that his hereditary land was being absorbed into a latifundium."

"What's that?"

"A large estate, often owned by an absentee landowner. And my grandfather now had to work for the estate, which would grow coffee for export. When he refused, they beat him into the ground with their gun butts, leaving him unconscious. Mama still remembers her mother's screams that day, though Mama was only five at the time."

"Where were the police?" Damien asked.

"What police? The landowners controlled the justice system. So, as soon as they were able, Mama's parents gathered their few belongings in bags over their shoulders, and led Mama and her brother Zingli, who was seven, into the jungle. They managed to survive in the jungle for a year and a half, until soldiers found them, took her father prisoner and repeatedly raped her mother—and Mama. Mama does not speak of this part, but I have heard her cry in the night. It was lucky that Zingli was off in the jungle or they might have made him into a child soldier as they did so many others."

"Oh my god! Who were these soldiers?"

"They were government soldiers enforcing the Guatemalan government's policy of amalgamating small landholdings into modern industrial farms. The CIA supported them."

"But your grandparents were hiding in the jungle at that point!"

"They had become part of a stubborn resistance movement. By then the government's policy had degenerated into a brutal campaign to break the backbone of this resistance, which was mostly Mayan. In fact, over 200,000 Mayans were killed during that time."

"That's genocide! So then what happened to Ahmal and her family?"

"Zingli crept out of the jungle and somehow cared for Mama and their mother, though he was barely nine years old. After a week their father returned, his face pitted with burn marks. Silently, he put together the last of their belongings and they went deeper into the jungle of Petén. Eventually, they joined a group of fugitives like themselves."

"I guess they were lucky he wasn't dead." Damien observed.

"Yes, but Mama said my grandfather was a changed man. He became a ruthless bandit leader, raiding haciendas many miles away and returning with the loot. The soldiers tried desperately to locate them, so the band was always on the move, following the jungle's animal trails. They were very successful until one day her father did not return home. His comrades said that he had been shot, rather than admit to my grandmother that he had been captured."

"Why?"

"It would have been better to die quickly."

"Oh."

"Mama was then twelve and her brother Zingli fourteen, strong enough to help load three mules with their household goods and the loot—gold and silver, precious jade and amber—that her father had hidden against this day. They made their way north serenaded by howler monkeys, who went silent only when jaguars were in the area. They stopped to bury some of the treasure in the jungle, hide some silver coins around Mama's and Zingli's waists and two or three small bags of gold coins around my grandmother's waist where they were protected by her ample dress. When they reached the Usumacinta River dividing Guatemala and Mexico, they stayed on the Guatemalan side because their father had said there were Mexican soldiers on the other who thought nothing of shooting the Maya. They found help in a jungle village called Lacandón, where they paid a guide with their last mule to take them across the border to a small Mexican town called Tenosique. There, they boarded an old and rusty train that clanked all the way to Mexico City."

"What a story! Were they okay in Mexico?"

"Pretty much. There was a Mayan community on the outskirts of the city. Grandma apprenticed Zingli to a metal worker and put Mama into a Catholic school for girls where she learned Spanish. Mama loved school and was soon getting very good marks. It was a good time for her."

"So when did she become a bruja?"

"Grandma noticed that Mama had some psychic gifts, so she took her back to Guatemala to meet her tribe's bruja. You see, the Maya believe that shamanistic gifts can be very dangerous if not properly controlled, which requires a great deal of training."

"But all this doesn't answer my original question. Who are these people who are helping us?"

"Two groups: the Zapatistas and the Savonards."

"The Savonards is your mother's group, right?"

"Yes, but she used to be a leader in the Zapatista movement, which fought against similar land reforms in the Mexican state of Chiapas."

"How did she become involved with the Savonards, then?"

"Well, she became convinced that no true change is possible without a spiritual revolution, so she founded the Savonards to pursue that goal."

Thea studied Damien, whose eyes were fixed on the distance as he steered the boat. She noticed his noble head, so like Arnold's, though not so large on Damien's more generous frame. Thea could not imagine a more beautiful man, and his uncertain future filled her with a deep sadness.

Damien glanced over at her. "So what's the relationship between the Zapatistas and the Savonards now?"

"We do cooperate with them on occasion."

"We? Are you a Savonard too?"

"Let's just say I sympathize with them."

"Ok-ay…So how does the whole spiritual thing work in the Savonards?"

"You sound like the spiritual thing bothers you."

"Only it doesn't mean much to me. You know me. I tend to stick with the physical dimensions. I'm not religious."

"Well…this is not really religion. A religion is a particular set of beliefs you have to accept. You can write down what those beliefs are. Our way is based not so much on belief as on practice. Some of it comes from the old Mayan way, where we enter and become part of the animal world."

She saw the frown mar his face. "Look, Damien, I'm an anthropologist. The whole of western science is built on a belief in rational thought that's supposed to be superior to the natural world from which we evolved. In a very narrow sense, that may be true."

"Go on."

"It's the old idea that for every gain there is some loss and vice versa. Well, in trying to cut ourselves off from our animal selves we've lost contact with…" She searched for the words… "a huge part of reality… the inner, buried non-human animal self."

He turned and looked at her with a small smile. "I should know that… being part jaguar."

There was a deep silence.

"You know, Thea, I've been thinking about this whole part jaguar business and it makes so much sense—I mean why I smell so well and can climb trees so fast and see in the dark and stuff like that. I never thought about it much 'til now, but at some level I've always wondered why I'm so very much better than anyone else at such things."

DAMIEN

"So you're naturally more in touch with the natural world than any other living human."

Thea was reminded of how her mother had always been so interested in Damien, and now, knowing her mother's role in his begetting, she suddenly realized why her mother had been so willing to assist Arnold. She remembered that, in the Mayan tradition, brujas were responsible for mediating between the human and animal world, often using powerful hallucinogens such as ayahuasca to become one with animal guides and open up whole new dimensions of power. And for the Olmec, the original culture of Mesoamerica, the primary animal the bruja called on was the jaguar because of its sheer physical power and prowess. Now, in Damien, this combination of animal and human had been achieved in the physical world.

"That's why," she said, breaking the long silence suddenly. "You have much to give us."

"Who is *us*?" he said abruptly, his smile gone.

She took a deep breath. "Savonards means 'the ones who know.' Mama developed the old Mayan tradition in a way that we hope speaks to the hearts of people today."

"All people or just Mayans?"

She felt the boat's sliding motion in the waves. "The aim is all people, very likely in different forms, but we start with the Maya because they are open to it and need it."

"And the Zapatistas…?"

"They are allies because they know that, for the Maya, a political creed has to be backed with spiritual strength. So, up to a point, they help us and we help them."

Damien turned to look appraisingly at her.

"I always knew there was a lot to you, Thea."

Suddenly, she was terribly afraid—for both of them.

CHAPTER EIGHTEEN

Peter Gregory's night was dominated by a dream that woke him sweating and twisting out of his bed. He was in a canoe with a young woman he did not recognize and they were paddling at the foot of a huge cliff in search of something—at first he was not sure what—and only when a withdrawing wave revealed the mouth of a cave did he remember that their whole mission was to enter and explore. There were many stories about the cavern's strange properties, but one stood out above all others: that if you got in and survived until the next low tide you would gain magical powers. What powers wasn't entirely clear except that you would live 20 years longer than the fates decreed. The woman explained that others had survived the cave's inundation at full tide and so would they. Peter knew that survival was less important than fulfilling the mission.

Then he saw that the cave was half exposed after each big wave thundered in.

"We've got to be in the next trough!" the woman cried out.

And somehow he managed it so that the next wave picked their fragile craft up and with an enormous sucking sound tossed it into the cavern. He was soaked, but they had made it, grinning at each other in the faint light from far above. But her skin drew tight over her skull and her eyes sank in their sockets till only the bones stood out, lipless teeth still grinning. Repelled, Peter jerked away, only to wake up rolling off the bed covered not in sea water but in sweat, yet still, inexplicably and horrifically, wanting the woman.

He sat up and looked at the clock: 2: 36 AM. Then he heard his cell phone, seeming to scream at him from his dream. He got to his knees and grabbed the phone.

"Yes," Who could possibly be phoning at this hour? "Yes?'

"Remember me? It's Chip." Peter tried to clear his mind. "It's about the girl."

"The girl...?" Peter was still thinking of his cave girl.

"The doll you're looking for. I've found her. You said she went missing about the 20th April."

"Yes!"

"I'm talking about the girl with a price on her," Chip said with some irritation. "$600,000."

"I need to verify you've got the right girl."

"At 102nd Street and Arnheim. Tonight. 4:00 AM. You can meet her then. Set up the money transfer to the account number I'll email you. You verify the girl's identity and complete the money transfer. When I see the funds in my account, you can take her away."

"That girl has to be unharmed."

"I wouldn't know." Chip hung up.

Peter pulled on his clothes and headed out to scout the location.

The meet was nerve-wracking, but amazingly for such a situation, everything went smoothly. Coco turned out to truly be Morton's daughter Claire, and Peter took her back to the two bedroom unit he'd arranged and had a doctor verify her basic health.

She was very thin but seemed remarkably in control of herself. Her hair and eyes were black and she had an even tan. There were dark circles under her eyes and tracks on her arms. She said nothing about her captors. Whatever had happened, she did not want to talk about it. Her father arrived by 11 a.m. the next morning, and after he'd left with his daughter, Peter phoned Sam.

"Your guy Chip came through, Sam. The girl is on a plane with her father headed for home."

"So, case over," Sam said, "which means you'll soon be headed home yourself."

"Not just yet, Sam. Remember Danielle?"

"Damien's girlfriend: sure I do—a good-looking young lady."

"Well, she wants me to help her find Damien." Peter waited for Sam's reaction.

"You mean she can afford you?"

"Apparently she can. She's coming into an inheritance."

"You in Mexico...? You don't speak a word of Spanish and don't know the country. And it's a different kind of Indian down there."

"I won't be working for you, Sam."

"Meaning if you find Damien you'll keep it to yourself?"

"She doesn't want me to find Damien, just help her figure out where to look for him."

"Meaning you wouldn't tell me where to look for him."

"Of course, you could always pay me more than she would. I might tell you then."

"No you wouldn't. She's got sex appeal."

"Not a candle to you, Sam."

"Anything to get back at a white man."

"You're not white, you're pink and gray."

"Thanks, partner. Keep in touch anyway. You might need help."

DAMIEN

"I'm sure I will. And if I don't tell you where to find Damien I might tell you where he isn't."

"God you're generous."

"Thanks, Sam. And I'll keep in touch. I do appreciate your helping to find my girl."

"Think nothing of it partner. Even if we've lost Damien for now, you were the one who put us on to him."

★★★

That evening, while Tom was cooking dinner, Danielle buzzed at his door. When he let her in, she laughed at his apron patterned with whales leaping out of the ocean

"Who gave you the apron?"

"He smiled, looking down at it. "Thea did. She said ... for me cooking was as tough as for whales to jump out of the water... but if I wanted an American meal from time to time I'd better learn how. She only cooks Mexican and Guatemalan dishes." He led her into the kitchen. "Actually I've gotten to like cooking. Do you want some of my attempt? It's not really American, it's a Yorkshire pudding."

"Thanks," she said. "I'd love it."

"And corn on the cob. We think corn's an American dish, but for the Mexicans it's basic and always has been. They call it maize. Have a beer?" He had opened one for himself.

"Sure." She stared at him. "The last time I saw you, you were in the dumps. What's the good news?"

"None really," he said. "But I reread Thea's last note to me." He handed the can of beer to her. "I'm certain that she didn't run off *with* Damien but *for* him. She believed the police were about to arrest the boy, and she had to save him. She's that kind of person."

Danielle thought about this, fingering her beer can. "I've talked to Peter Gregory, and I think he's going to come with me."

"Come with you? Oh yes, you mentioned going to Mexico in search of Damien. I still think it's a crazy idea."

"Maybe it is, Tom. Anyway, I'm going. But there is something I need to ask you."

"Shoot." He sat down at the kitchen table after turning down the heat on the stove.

"You first met Thea in Guatemala."

"Yes, at Tikal. She was with her mother, Ahmal."

"That was six years ago."

"That's right."

"Thea returned with her father and you to live in San Diego."

"Right," he said nodding.

"Tell me about Ahmal."

He frowned. "What do you want to know?"

She leaned forward a little. "What impression did she make on you?"

He spread his hands and frowned.

"Why does my question bother you?"

"Because... I couldn't figure her out. She was a small woman, about forty and magnetic. Maybe it was her eyes, the way she looked at me. But there was more to it than that. I'm a scientist, so I look for information I can verify. But what I was getting from her was..." he shook his head. "I don't have an explanation."

"Is it all that voodoo stuff?"

"Voodoo...?"

"You know, that she was some kind of shaman."

Tom reflected on this, turning the beer can in his hand. "Thea told me once that her mother seemed to sense danger... and that saved their lives more than once. She said her mother had many followers there too, that they are part of the ancient Mayan people." He stood up. "I think I'd better get that Yorkshire pudding for us."

He pulled a couple of plates out of the cupboard and served them, together with a small plateful of salad and corn.

"Why are you asking me all this about Ahmal?"

"I think you know why," she replied, chewing her food reflectively. "This is damn good, Tom."

"It better be—I cook it about twice a year."

"Please ask me to share it with you in six months when you cook it again."

"By that time you might have found Damien."

"I might have."

"If you can find Ahmal."

"Yes, she's the key. Thea is sure to get to her. Ahmal has a big following."

"You've been making enquiries."

"I have. It's a kind of movement she's the head of, the spiritual head. I have a couple of friends who live in Cuernavaca. The husband, Jim, is a political scientist and he knows about Ahmal and her movement. He says the government is worried about her because she has a lot more popular support than anyone wants to admit, even among the Ladinos. It's an undercurrent of the old indigenous spirit, so it's as much cultural as anything."

"But it's cultural, not political. Why would the Mexican government be worried about it?"

"I asked Jim the very same question. He went into a long lecture about the radicalization of the Zapatista movement."

"But that's not Ahmal's group."

"The government is worried that somehow the cultural-spiritual thing might... you know, mesh with the political movement and if so...it could end up being a revolution... not just a rebellion."

"My god, Danielle, you're way ahead of me. I wouldn't want Thea winding up in a goddamn revolution."

"That's why I've got to find them."

"And how can Peter Gregory help you?"

"He's a remarkably good detective. Sam Schumacker says he's pretty intuitive."

Tom drained the last of his beer.

"All I can do is wish you luck, Danielle."

"No, there's something else you can do."

"What?"

"Give me another helping of that Yorkshire pudding."

CHAPTER NINETEEN

As Montago had promised, a Savonard family at Puerto Peñasco had put them up for the night, then driven them down the coast, passing through the last of the Army check-points without trouble. In Puerto Peñasco, they had bought Damien a Mexican-style hat and trousers in khaki, and a small backpack for his stuff. With his tanned skin and black hair, he no longer looked typically American. Only his eyes were different, but then Thea had never met an American with yellow eyes like that either, so she'd bought him sunglasses.

When they arrived at Guaymas, they'd been handed over to their principal Savonard contact, Amornia, who was in her mid-forties with hair already turning gray. Now, Amornia was driving them in her old Ford jalopy through the countryside not far south of Guaymas.

"I'm only half Yaqui," she said referring to the Yaqui Indians who had once caused the Mexican government nothing but headaches.

"My Yaqui mother got screwed by a soldier and I'm the result."

She lived in Guaymas with her husband who owned a store selling mostly hats and sandals. He'd done pretty well by his standards and headed a local merchants' society, which sought to keep their area of town attractive and free of riff–raff. His major problem was his wife's commitment to the Savonards. While it brought him business from a few of the Yaquis hanging about, it tended to turn off the proper Ladinos, the more westernized and upwardly mobile mestizos. On occasion Amornia held meetings at night in the back of the store, but he stayed in their small house two blocks away, and never asked what went on. He'd heard that the Savonards were not well regarded by most people like him, and so the less he knew the better. Besides, his wife was not someone to be ordered about.

"I'm Catholic, of course," she said with an air of complete assurance, "but we Yaqui Catholics have our own Yaqui saints. You understand?"

"I'm sure I should know," Thea said.

"Well, I'll tell you. The Catholic church in Mexico is changing. The indigenous ways are influencing it. And we Savonards are a part of that."

"What will this do to belief in Jesus Christ?" Thea asked, wishing that Damien's understanding of the language was better.

"Strengthen it," Amornia said, "because Jesus himself is reborn as the Quetzal bird of heaven. He will truly become the God of new life." There was a pause. "Here, we're coming into the town of Yaqui."

They parked not far from the town center, where a celebration was taking place. Amornia beckoned them to follow her, then disappeared into the crowd.

"I don't get it, Thea—I mean, why we're here." Damien whispered to Thea.

"I'm not sure either. Amornia said something about celebration—Yaqui dancing and invoking their gods."

Amornia approached them, leading a grizzled old man with a strange headdress.

"Meet Chief Matos," she said to them.

He looked closely at Thea, then spoke in a low voice, but not in Spanish.

"He says that he is pleased to welcome the daughter of Ahmal," Amornia said, "whom he addresses with a special title. Do you wish to know what it is?"

"If I may..."

"He calls Ahmal the Cave Goddess, which is an ancient title of many meanings."

"Could you explain?"

"No... not now."

The Chief had turned, chanting to the crowd of Yaqui celebrators. They waved their arms over their heads towards Thea.

Thea spoke to Damien in a low voice, "Slip back out of this crowd. I never expected this. And it's not good."

Now the Chief moved from invocation to rhetoric, gesturing toward Thea, while Damien slowly melted back to the edge of the crowd. Soon a drumbeat was heard and people assembled around the dancers, all young men wearing cloaks of dried maize, coloured paper streamers flowing from their heads, gourd rattles in their right hands and chicken plumes in their left. Thea found herself in the center of this group with a special garland on her head. Beside her was the Chief.

"Are you American?"

Damien turned to see a small middle-aged man beside him.

"Yes," Damien answered.

"That pretty lady in the center is your friend. I saw you together."

"Yes?" Damien looked more closely at the man.

"I'm Mark... Mark Selman," the man said.... "From San Francisco."

"Pleased to meet you," Damien said.

DAMIEN

"And you're from…"

"Oh, from San Diego."

"Okay."

The drumbeat reached a crescendo then stopped. The crowd cheered Thea, two of the maize dancers lifting her on to their shoulders.

"Where are you headed?" Mark Selman asked.

"To Mexico City," Damien answered, wishing he could add, "nowhere I can be found."

"I'm surprised you aren't taking pictures of her." Selman nodded in the direction of Thea, who had been placed on a raised platform. She was being urged to speak.

Damien saw that she had been caught up in the excitement of the crowd, and had raised an arm for quiet. Then she began to speak, quietly at first, but her voice strengthened as she found her theme, gaining confidence.

"Do you follow Spanish?" Selman asked.

"Quite a lot, but I still miss some vocabulary."

"Want to know what she's saying?" He looked at Damien through thick glasses.

Damien nodded vaguely. He was beginning to wonder about this little man.

"She's talking about a group of people called the Savonards. It's a movement in Mexico, developed by the indigenous people but being taken up by some Ladinos. Of course it won't succeed; it's doomed like all these Mexican attempts to go their own way, separate from America."

Damien was alarmed. This man knew too much. Damien edged away, but the little man followed.

"Don't you want to know more about what she is saying?"

"Not really," Damien said. "You an American official of some sort?"

"You might say so," the man answered, staring at Damien. "And you? Her boyfriend? You're dressed more like a Mexican."

"Been doing some local shopping, obviously. And, I'm sorry, but it's actually none of your business."

Damien heard a cheer and saw that Thea was climbing down from the platform and looking around for him.

"Yes, I am an official, and I need to see your I.D."

"Get lost," Damien said, suddenly darting through the dispersing crowd toward Thea. He found her avidly talking to Amornia.

"We've got to get out of here," he said in a low voice, glancing backwards. "Some American official just asked me for I.D."

Thea's eyes registered shock. She spoke rapidly to Amornia.

"Yes, yes," Amornia said.

Damien searched the crowd behind him, but Mark Selman was nowhere in sight. Then he saw him, talking to a Mexican policeman and gesturing in Damien's direction.

"Gotta run," Damien said to Thea, and dashed away after the Chief and two of the maize-draped dancers. Thea followed him, and in a moment they caught up to the Chief, who listened to her rapid explanation. He then directed the two maize dancers to intercept Selman and the policeman. The Chief grabbed Thea's arm as Amornia caught up with them. Descending quickly down some stairs to one side of the plaza, they followed narrow winding streets through a maze of tiny shops and street vendors. Eventually, they entered a store selling hanging drapes and rugs, pushing through it to the office in the back.

The Chief stopped and took off his headdress, smiling reassuringly at Thea and Amornia. He sat behind the desk and took out a map to show Amornia where they were so that she could bring the car there after dark. Then they went into a suite of rooms beyond the office, and the Chief poured out glasses of tequila for all of them. They toasted the celebration in the square and he and Amornia launched into a conversation about families and local politics.

Damien turned to Thea. "That was too close."

"You're telling me," she said in a subdued voice.

"If you want to get into this Savonard thing, okay. But leave me out of it."

"You're right. I'm afraid I got carried away. It was stupid." She thought for a minute. "Who was that man?"

"An American official, he said. It felt like he was on the lookout, but he seemed more interested in my relationship with you, which is strange when you think about it."

"That depends, Damien. There's no American embassy or anything around here. So he might be some kind of federal agent, maybe CIA."

"Oh lovely. They'll certainly know about me."

"Probably not. You're not known for any political reason, and I think they usually don't pay much attention to criminal suspects. They're interested in the Savonards, insofar as they think it's political."

"That's a relief."

"We still need to visit the Huichols. I have to talk to the shaman. He'll know where my mother is or how to go about finding her."

"Is he a Savonard?"

"No. He's not interested in social movements. The Huichols have kept close to their pre-Hispanic beliefs. He's just been very close to my mother."

"It's your call, Thea."

CHAPTER TWENTY

They left Yaqui after dark, headed for a small suburban home in Tepic, where they met a sturdy six-foot middle-aged man, Gregorio del Corso, a Savonard who was friendly with the Huichol Tribe. Still in his dressing gown at 8 a.m., Gregorio greeted them hesitantly until he recognized Amornia.

"You made good time, Amornia," he said. "When I got your phone call, I thought you would take at least seven hours."

"We had a brush with the police earlier and had to get out of there fast. And I am not one to lag on the road. Meet Thea, the daughter of our renowned Ahmal, and her American friend, Damien. Ahmal very much wants to see these two."

"I'm sure that can be arranged. I am very honored to meet you, Thea... and to take you wherever you want to go. But first I imagine you need to sleep."

They moved into a fair-sized sitting-room.

"Thea and Damien want to eat, Gregorio, as they slept all night long while I drove. I'm the one who needs sleep."

"When I take them to meet Tzimbique, you can sleep here all day if you want," Gregorio said to Amornia.

"Have you talked to Tzimbique about this?" Amornia asked.

"Tzimbique doesn't use telephones."

"I wonder how he always knows what's going on."

"He's a shaman, Amornia. Anyway, make yourself comfortable... and help yourself to such food as I have."

★★★

Gregorio, Thea and Damien drove without hurry on a side road that angled up enormous clefts of rock into the Sierre Madre and the Huichol village where Tzimbique lived. A brief downpour turned the world into a haze.

"I'm beginning to realize just how important your mother is." Damien spoke from the back seat.

"She works through others. She's like a spiritual power within the movement. It's hard to explain."

There was a long silence.

"I have to ask you something, Thea," Damien said.

"I can guess what it is."

"What?"

"How's she going to help us?"

She looked back at him. He looked tired, but no longer so diminished.

She went on slowly, "I don't know. I am hoping she can help you gain insight into yourself—how to manage the predatory instinct."

Looking at the beautiful young man coiled in the back seat, she suddenly wondered what she was doing. This man, her gentle, brilliant half-brother, who was part savage beast that could be provoked into startling violence—who was he really?

As they angled higher, ridge upon ridge of treeless mountain ranges fanned out into the far distance. There was no sign of human habitation anywhere.

Gregorio seemed to read her thoughts. "There's more than a million square miles of wilderness. No wonder Cortez gave up conquering the territory as soon as he laid eyes on it. And to this day the Huichol people still feel themselves strangers in Mexican society. They're their own people, living in tiny communities the Mexicans call ranchos. They survive on small patches of maize, beans and squash... hardly any meat." He paused. "They are different from us."

"What exactly do they believe in?" Thea asked, "Aztec Gods or something?"

"No, no. They have their own gods, the forces of nature: wind, sun, earth, and Grandfather Fire. And there are female deities like Nakawe, Grandmother Growth."

He was silent for a while, focused on getting the 4-wheel drive vehicle over partial washouts from the heavy rains, though the rainy season was just about over.

"So what can you tell us about Tzimbique?" Thea asked.

"As you know, he's a shaman, or mar-akate as the Huichol call them. He's quite old and belongs to no community, just travels around on foot from rancho to rancho. He belongs to all the Huichol." There was a pause as they turned a sharp curve. "They believe he has special foreknowledge."

"Amornia said you were a teacher."

"I teach Sociology at the University. My PhD thesis was about the Huichol. That's how I learned their language. Six years ago I met Tzimbique, who told me much about myself that no one else could know—not minor biographical details, but basic make-up and destiny. He's a strange and remarkable man."

"Being university-taught, I'd have thought you spoke English."

"Oh, I do."

DAMIEN

"But you haven't spoken to Damien."

"I did not have your permission."

"Well you have it gladly. He doesn't speak much Spanish and would be happy to have someone besides me to talk to." She turned to Damien, but he spoke before she could open her mouth.

"This Tzimbique—how come he's the only person who knows where to find Ahmal? Is she on the run or something?"

Thea was startled to realize how quickly Damien was learning Spanish.

"Yes, Ahmal has been on the run all her life."

They had begun to descend from the mountain cleft into an unexpectedly green valley.

"Why is that?"

"Because governments fear and hate her," Gregorio answered. Ahmal is a shaman whose spiritual strength bolstered the rebel cause, first in Guatemala in the time of trouble, and then in Chiapas. After the Chiapas uprising of the 1990's led by the famous Commandante Marcos, the Mexican authorities became aware of her powerful influence and started to look for her, especially. The military eventually found her and tortured her for weeks with electric shocks. Do you mind me telling this, Thea?"

"No, Damien should know."

"Torture is standard procedure because it works." He paused making a sharp turn on a narrow road. "Except it didn't work on Ahmal. She suffered horribly, the weeks turning into months, until they realized Ahmal would die before she'd talk. So she was sent to hospital to recover."

"Why are you telling me all this, Gregorio?"

"So you will understand why the government has very good reason to fear Ahmal. They only sent her to hospital so they could start again on her. You see, she knew what nobody else knew: the location of the guerrilla units, the names and whereabouts of the leaders, the plans for operations soon to happen, the long-term strategy. I would say that she knew more than anybody, so they had to make her talk."

"Yet she survived."

"If the military knew why she had to be made to talk, the guerrilla leadership knew it too. So they launched operation Carrero, a daring raid in which about 300 guerrillas took over the hospital and freed her. She's never been found since by the police or military." The car turned tightly around another bend. "Or I should say she's never been arrested, because since those days she bowed out of the rebel army and became more a spiritual and cultural leader, founding the Savonards. She no longer had inside information on the rebels, though the military never appreciated the extent of her shamanic knowledge. The upshot, as the English say, is that Ahmal is the inspiration and power behind the movement, just like Mahatma Gandhi. What the authorities now really want to know is what she's up to, so they can derail her movement before it gains too much of a following."

"The thing I can't figure," Damien said, "is why this great lady is interested in me."

"No idea," Gregorio responded.

They drove in silence across the plateau's desert landscape.

"It makes no sense," Damien mused. "I mean what would she want with me, a guy hunted by the police?"

Thea looked quickly back at Damien. "Gregorio didn't know that."

"So what?" He shook his head vehemently. "It doesn't matter."

DAMIEN

"You are right. It doesn't matter," Gregorio said evenly. "We have many people wanted by the police in our movement. In many ways, the police are our enemy."

They entered a small village hanging on the side of a river.

"Here we will find Tzimbique," Gregorio said.

There were few people around on the drab street. The town seemed to be nothing but a collection of small huts. At one of these, set a little aside, Gregorio stopped the car. He opened the door and stood alone staring at the hut. A few people soon gathered around. One of these, an old woman, came forward. Gregorio raised his hat to her and spoke in her tongue.

"Hello, Grandmother. We're here to see Tzimbique."

"You are welcome," she said, her voice surprisingly young, "Tzimbique is waiting for you."

They entered the stone house, which had a grass thatched roof. Tzimbique sat on a sort of pallet, long thin legs folded under him. His face, too, was long, his gleaming head and chin and sunken cheeks streaked by wisps of white hair. His eyes were black and he did not smile. Gregorio gestured and they sat down.

"You have come," Tzimbique said, his voice a clear tenor.

"Yes, Tzimbique, and I have brought two visitors: Ahmal's daughter, Thea, and Damien the American. Ahmal wants to see him, though we do not know why."

"I know why," Tzimbique said.

On hands and knees he crawled to Damien until his face was within a couple of inches of Damien's. He stared into Damien's eyes, then poised on his knees, and pulled the young man's eyelids back, studying them. Damien was uncharacteristically amenable to this treatment.

"Open your mouth," Tzimbique said in Spanish. Gregorio started to translate, but Damien had already opened his mouth. Tzimbique reached into Damien's mouth, feeling his back teeth. He then closed his eyes and took Damien's head firmly between his hands. Damien was startled to feel the air change as Tzimbique entered a trance. Just when Damien thought he couldn't stand it a moment longer, Tzimbique opened his eyes, breathed on him, and let go.

"Yes, I know why," he said, but would say no more.

CHAPTER TWENTY-ONE

In Mexico City, Peter and Danielle took adjoining rooms in a converted nunnery built in the 18th century by a wealthy Catholic lady who had wanted to recreate the religious artistry of old Spain in the new world of Mexico. The spacious building surrounded a large open area, where the path for walking penitents passed among fountains and flower beds. Birds flitted among the herbaceous plants. During noon hour and early evening, piano music suffused the aromatic space. Peter felt that the religion responsible for such a place must have its merits.

Tables had been placed in this open area, and Danielle and Peter chose one not far from a fountain centered on frolicking concrete cherubs. They ordered margaritas.

"I've asked Jim and Alice Bernini to drop by. They're friends of my parents and they're coming from their home in Cuernavaca. You remember I mentioned that he's a political scientist at the University of Mexico and happens to know about Ahmal, or at least the Savonard movement she heads."

"I know nothing about it," Peter said watching two birds frolicking in the fountain.

She watched them too. "I think they're courting," she said.

"I think they're having a shower."

She stared at him, fingering the stem of her glass…

"You asked me if I was in love with Damien. Have you ever been in love, Peter?"

"Yes, very much in love."

"And…"

"She died of cancer."

"I'm sorry. She must have been quite young."

"She was."

"And she's been the only one?"

"The only one I've really loved."

"And the others…?"

"I don't regret a single affair, not that I've had many. I've certainly come to appreciate *woman* in the collective sense, though."

She laughed. "And does each one appreciate being appreciated as part of a collective!"

"You tell me." He smiled at her. "I'm sure that's how women also view me… simply as a member of the collective male."

She shook her head. "I don't. I mean, I experience the men I know as special… unique."

Danielle drank from her glass, looking over the rim at him. Then she lowered her drink. "You're not really making much sense to me, Peter. Your wife, when it comes right down to it, was just a part of the collective called woman, no matter how much you loved her."

"Except that to me she was *the* collective called woman…not just part of it."

"Beautiful… and it sounds like fiction."

"Maybe so… maybe love as I experienced it isn't real… maybe it's an illusion."

"Like the beauty of music is an illusion."

He thought about this, frowning. "I don't know. I can't believe that beauty is an illusion. But if it is, let's have more of it."

"Here are our guests," she said raising her hand to wave and standing up.

A couple in their early fifties approached them. They were evenly matched in height and leanness.

"Hello you two," Danielle said, "I haven't seen you in four years and you both look just as young and fit as you did then."

"But you've changed in these four years, Danielle," Alice said. "You were just a girl then. Now look at you: a beautiful young woman."

Jim nodded his agreement.

At the next table, perhaps ten feet away, two men who had little to say to one another were having dinner. At first glance, given their difference in age, they could be taken for uncle and nephew or employer and employee, the second being much closer to the truth, for the older man, in his forties, worked for Mexican Intelligence and the younger was a junior officer. Now and then they exchanged a few words but never even glanced at the next table.

Now into his main course and his second retsina, Jim was trying to explain how the Mexican government worked in relation to the Mexican population, most of whom were indigenous and very poor. His wife had already passed a note to him alerting him to the two men at the next table. But her husband paid no attention. He knew they were under surveillance and had been for years, but he preferred to ignore the implications. He was well known for his sympathy for the underprivileged, especially the indigenous people, and had written books about what he believed was the inevitable social revolution in Mexico. He knew that he was not appreciated by the authorities, who had sought to have him dismissed from his university position, so far without success. The President of the university had pointed out that Jim Bernini was a respected and much published American scholar, and that the government did not have the right to interfere in university affairs, unless they could prove unlawful behavior.

However, the constant surveillance bothered Alice. She was a painter and gloried in the colors of Mexico. Even after seven years in Cuernavaca, Alice was still entranced by the mysterious deep crags and green valleys defining the area. They had a villa high in the hills above the city. Jim drove to the nearby university for his three lectures a week, and they developed warm relations with artists and intellectuals in the region. For her, it was a good life, and she did not want to return to the U.S., at least not for quite a while.

But then she read about the discovery of the bodies of two Mexican political journalists, who wrote for the radical left. They'd been found by the side of the road, shot through the head. She and Jim knew them both; they had interviewed Jim, and written favorably about him. For the first time, Alice was really afraid.

She showed Jim the story when he was in the midst of preparing a lecture.

"I'm worried," she said. "These two were our friends. They were decent, principled men and now they've been murdered. Why? I mean has it come to this, that people with a social conscience are murdered for their beliefs?"

Jim set aside his notes with a sigh. "Alice, I understand. It concerns me, too. But…"

"Jim, you know we are being watched."

"Nothing new about that, Alice."

"Nothing new! Is that all you can say? If they're watching us, it means we're on their list of undesirables."

"The government says the act was criminal and they will find the criminals."

"You don't believe that!" She was all at once angry as well as afraid. "You sound like Don Quixote, just another duped idealist! My God, Jim…"

"Now wait a minute, Alice. Calm down. There are many, many good people out there, Mexicans, who criticize the government constantly. I don't believe it was government agents who killed them. I think it was certain wealthy individuals who decided to silence them. It's not the first time." He paused, looking up at her, trying to calm her. "Whatever else they were, those two were investigative reporters, and were probably getting close to uncovering something that certain moneyed people could not allow. It happens, Alice. That's the real world, I'm sorry to say."

She did not respond for a moment, thinking about the implications of what he'd said.

He went on, "They may well have found links to illegal drugs. It's a huge business in this country, as well you know."

She realized that he might be right, though she did not really believe it. Why would government agents be watching them? She knew he would point out that the government watched all kinds of people who opposed them, that it was meant to frighten critics into silence. The best response was to ignore them. Sooner or later they would give up and desist. She fervently hoped he was right, as she watched Jim explaining things to Danielle.

"Anyway," Jim said, looking up at Danielle, "I've lectured you enough on Mexican politics, and haven't even asked why you're here. I understand, Peter, that you're working for Danielle as a private investigator."

"Yes, I'm helping her locate someone. But she's the one to tell you about that."

DAMIEN

"It's someone I knew very well when I lived in San Diego," Danielle said. "A young man I care about who has disappeared in Mexico. He came with Thea, who is the daughter of Ahmal of the Savonards. I believe that Thea thinks her mother can help the young man."

"How...?" Jim asked, noting out of the corner of his eye that all conversation had ceased at the nearby table.

Alice dropped her knife with a clatter and made a lot of noise scraping her chair around and picking the knife up.

"You see," Danielle paused staring down at her plate. "I'm not sure, but I think he wants to leave the US for good and seek a new way of life. Maybe he's interested in Ahmal's special spiritual powers."

Jim and Alice glanced at one another. Alice placed her hand over Danielle's.

"I think I understand. But, really, what can this Ahmal do for your young friend?"

"Give him meaning in his life maybe." Danielle looked searchingly at Jim. "I think you know a lot about her and the Savonards."

Jim leaned back in his chair. "Yes, we know about her and the Savonards."

"But Danielle," Alice said loudly, "don't you know that Ahmal and her movement are opposed by the Mexican government? Your young man would never find refuge with her."

"Alice is right, Danielle," Jim said. "Ahmal's in constant hiding. She can't possibly offer your friend refuge."

"Have you met her?" Danielle asked Jim.

Alice loudly asked Peter about his life in Canada while Jim responded to Danielle.

Leaning forward and dropping his voice very low, Jim answered, "Yes, I have, once."

"May I ask why you met her?" Danielle also lowered her voice.

"I was preparing a paper on the indigenous people of Mexico. Since Ahmal was such a powerful influence in the movement I wanted to talk to her, and had a devil of a time finding her. Luckily I had a friend or two in the indigenous movement who helped me. I'd never have got to her otherwise."

"Please, tell me about it."

"It took place in the jungle area near the border between Chiapas and Guatemala. She was with a young commandant of the Zapatistas, and it was evident she saw herself in sympathy with them. She said that in order to understand the indigenous movement in Mexico you have to be aware of the forty year struggle of the Mayan people in Guatemala."

Alice kicked Jim's shin under the table but he paid no attention except to withdraw his feet. He rapidly wrote something down on a pad and Alice read it: *Everything I'm saying the government knows already.* He was silent for a moment, continuing to write. Then he turned to Danielle.

"You will never be able to meet Ahmal. You'll find, though, that San Cristóbal in Chiapas is a delightful town and well worth visiting. You'll like it and also the ruins of Palenque. Many tourists go there. I've written these and a few other sightseeing suggestions down for you. But forget about Ahmal. Nobody knows where she is, including me."

He gave the note he had written to Danielle. She read it swiftly and gave it to Peter.

Pay no attention to what I just said. We're being monitored by government agents. We need to walk in the park tomorrow afternoon. I'll come by your room around 4 PM. Okay?

Danielle nodded to Jim, smiled and they began talking about family news.

The two men at the next table soon lost interest.

CHAPTER TWENTY-TWO

The next morning, Thea and Damien's bus was approaching Xalapa near the Caribbean coast where the hot air was clammy and smelled of rotting vegetation. Neither had slept well on the bus and Damien was fed up with what seemed an unnecessarily tangled quest for Ahmal. Tzimbique and all his mumbo jumbo had irritated Damien no less than the way the old man had treated him as if he were a horse for sale. At one point, Damien had actually flung the old man's hand away from his knee, which had inexplicably delighted Tzimbique. In the end, Tzimbique had spoken at length to Thea, but it was not until they were on the bus heading for Xalapa that night that Thea confided in Damien.

"Tzimbique has told me who to contact next on our quest for Mama."

"I'd hate to have an urgent message for her," Damien responded ascerbically.

"But you, yourself, are the message." Thea shot back.

"I'm not a message, dammit. I'm a living breathing, feeling being!"

Thea took a breath, "Of course, Damien. Nobody's suggesting you aren't. But you are something more than the average, and that arouses the curiosity of those who know."

She turned away, trying to account for the apprehension that his flashing sunlit eyes evoked in her.

***

They had climbed the few steps to the Museum of Anthropology in Xalapa, when Damien stopped, staring. Thea, too, looked in wonder. At the entrance was a stone sculpture of the head of a man that was more than six feet in height and almost as wide. Around the forehead was wound some sort of band that was incised with symbols. The man's eyes peered from beneath his lowering brows, his nose spread wide, and his very full lips were open and turned down at the ends. The face exuded overwhelming power and control.

"If you will notice the symbols on the head band…" a woman standing nearby said to Thea in Spanish. Hearing the code phrase Tzimbique had given her, Thea looked sharply at the woman. She was tall and thin and had a slight stoop suggesting she was in her sixties.

"You look like your mother," the woman said more quietly to Thea. "Her beauty is on the inside as well as on the outside."

"Do you know where my mother is?" Thea asked abruptly. Like Damien, she was growing impatient.

"No. I was asked to show you this head, which is over 3,000 years old. We believe he was a ruler of the Olmec people who lived here, and that he was more than human."

"More than human…?" asked Damien. Thea looked at him in surprise. He was picking up Spanish much faster than she would have thought possible.

"Yes. More than human…. The headband represents the claws of a jaguar. Looking at him, can you think of him as an ordinary man, with those unblinking eyes and the very wide curled-down fleshy mouth?" She paused to consider Thea and Damien. "The Olmec believed that he was in fact a blend of man and jaguar." Thea stroked Damien's arm to distract him from staring at the woman.

"I have one other thing to show you," the woman said, walking through a doorway.

They followed her into a room where several pieces of sculpture were on show, and stopped in front of one that was titled, *The Lord of Las Limas,* and represented a youth holding in his arms a were-jaguar infant—part human, part jaguar.

"There are many of these combinations of human and jaguar in Olmec culture," the woman said, "but no one seems to fully understand the thinking behind it."

She was silent for a moment.

"That is all I was to show you. You are now to go to the sacred site of Chalcatzingo where you will meet your next guide. Here, I have written it down." She handed Thea a card. "If you want to find your mother you must go there. Goodbye. It has been an honor as always to serve Ahmal." She ignored Damien as she turned and left.

"Your mother," Damien said, "is telling me something I already know. Although I didn't know that it would feel as though I were meant to be here."

Thea took his hand and squeezed it.

They bussed west to Cuernavaca, beautifully nestled among mountains which led into the green valley of Morelos. There they checked into a small hotel built in 1530, not far from the palace of the conqueror of Mexico, Hernando Cortez.

DAMIEN

★★★

They ate a dinner of tortillas in a small café, having each finished a tequila. Walking down the darkening street back to the hotel, Damien held her hand.

"If I were hired by the police to try to follow us, I'd be going a little crazy." He smiled at her and she squeezed his hand.

Their room was small, with one double bed, all they were able to find in the vicinity. It wasn't a tourist hotel catering to Americans. The smell of tangerines filled the air. Since it was so hot, they both wore only their underwear, and stayed well away from one another.

That is, they did until later in the night, hearing distant thunder, she found herself in his arms and very aware of his maleness.

"We can't," she said. "Damien, we`re brother and sister." She pulled away.

"No, we`re not," he said.

"We`re half brother and sister..."

"Not even that," he said, moving closer to her. "How can we be half anything? If you mix blue and yellow you get green, a new color. If you mix animal and human you get a new creature, neither animal nor human. That woman called the mixture a were-jaguar. It's a new species. I'm a new species."

"Please...don't." He was too close. "I'm afraid." Yet her body yearned for him, and that scared her too. He pulled down his underwear to press himself against her. A kind of blackness suffused her... the feathered serpent K'uk'ulkan spreading his wings over her... and, in that instant of dark death, she experienced the nothingness which is everything. She rolled suddenly to the edge of the bed and sat up, hearing his predatory growl.

"We must not, Damien," she said quietly into the dark. "This is not for us."

She could hear and feel his struggle, the primordial force of it.

"Whatever else you might be, we still share our father's genes," Thea added.

After some minutes he spoke hoarsely.

"Have it your way, Thea." He turned his back to her.

Thea pulled on a t-shirt and curled up on her edge of the bed, as far away as she could get.

"You are no ordinary woman." Damien mumbled.

She thought about this.

"You are no ordinary man." She was silent for a bit. "I don't know what it is, Damien. I'm not sure I even want to know, but you're... destined for something more…"

He was silent.

Again she spoke out of the darkness: "My task is to set you on the right path... beginning with my mother but..." she could hardly believe what she was saying, "not ending there."

It was a long time before Damien murmured, "I still find it hard to believe any of this."

★★★

As instructed by their guide in Xalapa, they were picked up at 10 a.m. outside the palace of Hernandez Cortez. This time they were in the hands of a young man, Roberto Malaga, who said that he spoke good English if that's what they preferred.

"Relax and enjoy yourselves. It is not a long drive to Chalcatzingo, maybe two hours." Then he said: "Did you see the wonderful statue of Zapata, our leader?"

"We didn't even know there was such a statue."

"I am sure you, daughter of Ahmal, know all about the man, bless his memory. He fought to save Mexico, and lost his life—was murdered—by the owners of the haciendas."

Thea, as usual, sat next to the driver; Damien in the back because he liked to stretch out.

Speaking over his shoulder, Roberto continued, "You are American and may not understand Mexican history, nor will I go into it, because you can learn all you need from Ahmal's daughter. I just want to say one thing. What Zapata started in 1910, the revolution of the people of Mexico, is still going on but it is under the surface, and takes many forms, including the Savonards. The outcome is inevitable. In the end Zapata's cause will triumph and Mexico will regain its former glory."

"I guess you mean the glory of what Thea calls its pre-Columbian past... before the Spanish conquest," Damien said, a little piqued at the way all these Mexicans seemed to assume he didn't understand anything.

"In those days before Columbus discovered the New World," Roberto said, unperturbed, "over twenty million people lived here in splendid cities. It was not Spanish swords but smallpox and tuberculosis that destroyed our civilization. Now we are a mixed people and we can withstand disease, so we want to recapture the power which once belonged to the indigenous people, those who are now crushed under the heel of global capitalism."

In the back seat, Damien rolled his eyes. Thea changed the subject as they drove on through the blossoming trees, whose scent filled the car.

"I don't know much about Chalcatzingo,"

"What do you know?" he asked.

"My mother always believed it was an especially sacred site, and took me there once when I was a girl. Frankly, I didn't think much of it compared to the great sites like

Monte Alban and Palenque. But my mother had a different idea. Do you know why we are going there? Or should I ask?"

The young man looked at her sideways. She found him handsome, though he was a small man.

"No, I don't know why we are going there," he said in his perfect English, "but I have heard that Chalcatzingo has a secret. No doubt Ahmal will tell you about it. The place is centered on twin towers of rock, each about 300 meters high. Those natural towers were the temples of gods who lived in them. Don't ask me which gods, there were so many."

"This was Aztec stuff?" Damien asked.

"No, no," Roberto said, "this was about 2,000 years before the Aztec, around 700 B.C. The archaeologists call those people the Olmec. They're supposed to be the ones who gave birth to the whole pre-Columbian culture, from which sprang all the other cultures of Mesoamerica like the Maya, the Mixtec, the Toltec, the Aztec, and so on."

"Roberto," Thea said. "You speak with an American accent."

"I was educated in the States. My father worked up there. He was a specialist in irrigation systems."

"But you came back to Mexico."

"Yes, with my parents. They bought a fruit ranch over in Guerrero. I went into teaching English to Mexican students."

"How do you know Ahmal?" Thea asked.

Roberto swerved to pass three children riding bicycles.

"I met her entirely by accident. Over in the Yucatán during the lighting ceremony at the Temple of the Warriors at Chichén Itzá; I went with a girlfriend. Her mother was a priestess in Ahmal's cult of K'uk'ulkan."

"I know something about that," Thea said.

"Of course you do," Roberto said glancing at her. "Anyhow, my girlfriend introduced me to her mother who was staying in a small hut off the site. It so happened that Ahmal was with her in the hut. I knew she was someone special. Later my girlfriend's mother asked me if I would act as a courier for Ahmal. Of course I accepted. She is helping the cause of Zapata."

"So where are we going?" Damien asked.

"To the rock face of the mountain called Cerro Chalcatzingo to stare at a carving which will puzzle you as it has puzzled archaeologists."

CHAPTER TWENTY-THREE

Roberto led them along the rock-strewn path to the foot of Cerro Chalcatzingo, an imposing rock crag which dominated the valley along with its partner Cerro Delgado. Thea remembered the impression they had made on her when she was a girl of ten. She'd found them threatening, though her mother thought otherwise, telling her that certain powers lived in them, especially the rain god Chaac, without whose help the people who lived in the valley would die. Properly worshipped, Chaac would see to it that after the long dryness the rain would fall on their maize crops, causing them to flourish. When the Spaniards had come, her mother said, all the carvings were destroyed, the shamans burnt at the stake, and drought brought an end to human settlement in that valley.

Years later, when she was fourteen and they were living in Mexico City, Thea had attacked her mother on the subject.

"That primitive old society was disgusting," she said, repeating her Catholic school training. "Ignorant people thinking the gods needed human blood to make the crops grow!"

Ahmal said nothing in response, but moved her to a non-Catholic school. Later, Ahmal explained that she did this so that Thea would receive the broader education she needed to adapt to the modern world. But Ahmal also saw to it that Thea spent time with a woman shaman she respected.

The woman, whose shamanic name was Xquik, was a Yaqui Indian committed to the Toltec Way. She said the Toltecs had left central Mexico about 1,000 AD to establish a new society far away in the Yucatan where they worshipped the god K'uk'ulkan, which was the Mayan name for Quetzalcoatl, the feathered serpent. The Toltec built most of the fabulous temples of Chichén Itzá, co-opting the Mayan culture by using Mayan craftsmen to adorn their temples, though usually with Toltec symbols.

Xquik explained to her young charge why the gods of the Toltec and the Maya were of such vital importance. Thea remembered those lessons well. The mistake of modern science and technology, Xquik said, had been the failure to learn from the indigenous people how to connect and work with nature's vital, dynamic forces. She taught that the human brain can open directly to these natural forces, working with them to effect change. But this skill can only be achieved by learning to follow the ancient ways.

"So the gift of blood will release the rain," young Thea challenged.

Xquik stared at her.

"You just said," Thea persisted, "that it's possible for humans to influence nature if we learn to connect our mental and physical selves to nature's dynamic forces."

"Yes," Xquik said.

"So, the gift of blood can release the rain."

"Correctly done, yes," Xquik said.

"I don't see the connection. I mean blood and rain are two completely different substances. I don't see how they connect."

"Because you miss the point... Your life depends on blood moving through your system. So to release your blood by cutting your arteries means your death... surrendering your own life... the same thing with the cloud formed by moisture. It does not give up its moisture until the pressure becomes so great that it must do so. So the shaman finds a connection between the release of blood and the release of rain, making the release of blood *cause* the release of rain."

Thea shook her head in bewilderment.

"But how," she said, "can the one release cause the other? I don't see it. Rain doesn't happen because a god gives the order."

"Not normally, that's true. But *if* a god gives the order it happens."

"So we're back to the gods."

"The gods are the connections between things, connections created by intention. The shaman knows this, knows how to make intention turn into connection. Connections have physical power, like electrical connections."

Thea thought about this, then shook her head.

"I happen to believe," Thea said, "that the physical and the mental are totally different. No connection."

"Tell me how your brain works," Xquik said. "Is it physical or mental? There has to be a crossing-over between the mental and the physical, a real working connection."

"Back to connections."

"Back to connections. Shamans know how to make them."

And that was it. Xquik presented a way of thinking that both puzzled and fascinated Thea. She remained skeptical, yet uncertain. For one thing, whatever she recognized about the rationality of science, she was influenced by her mother. What could explain Ahmal's knowledge, not just of plants uncharted by science, but of events to come?

★★★

As they moved up Cerro Chalcatzingo, Thea felt again the lunge of fear she had experienced at ten years old. She tried to pretend her fear was simply due to the formidable size of the great tower of rock.

They climbed slowly, then Roberto pointed upward. Carved into the rock just above them, Thea could make out the image of a woman sitting half inserted in a niche. The carved woman was fabulously attired and held an object in her arms. Her headdress was extraordinary, but most curiously, she looked at a world swirling with twisted forms which emanated from her own form. Outside her niche, rain was falling from banks of clouds and plants were growing, frozen in the rock's stillness.

"We don't know," said Roberto, "whether she is a shaman or a goddess, but she has power, for it is she, the experts believe, who brought on the rain." He paused. "And those elegantly twisted forms represent the power she has sent forth to get Chaac, the rain god, to respond. He has sent her the rains she requested, and brought life back into the world."

"So what is she holding in her arms?" Thea inquired.

"Nobody seems to know for sure," Roberto answered, "but some think it represents the world tree, which was an important symbol to the Olmecs and Maya."

"Mother brought me here when I was ten," Thea said to Damien, "but she never showed me this carving. I wonder why. Obviously it was important."

"It is important," came a voice from below.

Thea looked down to the base of the rock and there stood her mother. She had grey in her hair and her face had aged. But her black eyes shone.

"Hello, Thea," Ahmal said, her voice stronger than ever. Thea clambered down the slope and they embraced. Then her mother smiled at her and nodded.

"You are almost too beautiful," Ahmal said. Then she looked at Damien, "You have brought the young man."

Damien spoke, "I've heard a lot about you. May I call you Ahmal?"

"Please do," Ahmal answered, looking closely at him. She turned to Roberto. "Good-bye and thank you, Roberto. I hope they did not ask you questions you could not answer."

"I do not envy you, Ahmal. They wanted to know everything, especially that daughter of yours." He gave a little wave and headed down the trail.

"Do we not need his car?" Damien asked.

"Roberto told you to bring your backpack, didn't he?" Ahmal said. "That's all you need. You're coming with me." She smiled at him. "Surely that does not surprise you."

They followed her on a narrow path they had not seen before, which skirted the back of the Cerro Chalcatzingo. There was no sign of life other than some small cacti and the flies buzzing among lifeless threads of grass. After a few miles, Ahmal stopped and pointed a couple of hundred yards further on to a few buildings, simple wooden structures clustered around a water tower, which surprised Damien.

"Where's the water in this desert?" he asked.

"You will find out," Ahmal answered, and trudged on.

As they approached, Thea made out a low rambling building with a workshed and a makeshift garage housing an old Ford truck. A middle-aged man emerged from the

DAMIEN

house. He was lean and hard-boned, wearing sandals but no hat.

"Greetings, Ahmal," he said in Spanish. "I was expecting you earlier. I suppose your daughter and her friend want something to eat." For indeed it was approaching dinner time.

"Sometime soon, Giberto," Ahmal answered. "Would you show the young man to his room?"

"Yes," he said in English. "Come along then." He beckoned to Damien.

Damien followed Giberto through the front door. Ahmal and Thea passed through double doors directly into a sitting-room. Thea was surprised at the size of it.

"We have meetings here," Ahmal said, then walked through another door into a small bedroom. "Here's your bedroom. You've had a long journey. Do you need anything?"

"I think I'm good, thanks." Thea hugged her mother again and was reminded that her mother had never really been the hugging sort.

Ahmal looked deeply into Thea's eyes, "You've been travelling closely with Damien, and he's a powerfully attractive young man."

Thea started. "You can't think I've been sleeping with my own brother!"

"The gods would be tempted, and you're only human."

"Mama!" Thea exploded, remembering the scene in the bedroom in Cuernavaca. Angrily, she turned her back on her mother, pulling stuff randomly from her bag.

"I bring him all this way, and this is the thanks I get," Thea fumed.

"I do thank you. You know how much we need Damien, Thea. He alone can awaken the Mexican people as well as the Mayan. Right now he is our one hope to reinvigorate the race, to bring the ancient heritage to life again."

"Mother," Thea said, turning again and shaking her head vehemently, "you're giving me a speech already. Damien's only one young man—and a pretty confused one at that— for God's sake!"

Ahmal reached up and gently covered Thea's mouth with her hand.

"So was Eve's Adam only one young man, but he brought forth the human race. We need Damien's seed, Thea."

She lowered her hand.

Thea stared at her mother, stupefied. "You mean... because he's part jaguar?"

"That boy's jaguar blood, Thea, is due to me. I found it for your father—I found the leaf and told him how to do it."

DAMIEN

CHAPTER TWENTY-FOUR

Sam Schumacker had been working practically round the clock on the tree murder case, so he was exhausted and relieved when his wife Ruthie finally came home from her holiday, looking younger than she had for years. She didn't talk much about her trip, but when she did, her eyes shone. She was at that age when women change. He remembered his mother calling it Change of Life, when the woman becomes incapable of conceiving a child. That, he'd always thought, was surely a negative experience for a woman. So this didn't explain his wife's strange blossoming. Then, it occurred to him that she might have met someone who aroused her romantic longings. He'd certainly tried that when they were much younger. Sam in those days had sported a moustache which she'd said reminded her a little of Clark Gable, the movie idol in *Gone with the Wind*. Well, okay. He'd play Clark Gable for her, and damned if he didn't try, which was one of his first big mistakes. She soon said that it wasn't Clark Gable she'd fallen for, that was just a joke. Clark Gable was on the screen well before she was born for God's sake. No. It was Paul Newman and he didn't sport a moustache.

This was the problem, Sam reflected—he'd never quite got it right. Romantically, that is. He wasn't a wine and roses man, yet he'd proved he was a damn good detective, and he'd hoped she'd appreciate that, but he very much doubted it. She had soon let him know that his occupation did not appeal to her. In fact, it came between them. He was always being assigned to some case that led him to "God knows where," working hours that no reasonable healthy human being should be called upon to serve. "Why didn't you get a sensible job?" had become something of a refrain. There was very little social life among police detectives. Ruthie was pretty well left alone to create her own social life.

In spite of it all he loved her. And he hoped she loved him, even a little. They'd had many a laugh together. That was one good thing. She had a sense of humor, mischievous and naughty at times, and so did he and that was a real plus in their marriage. So he'd made a joke about how she was blossoming after her time away and looked many years younger, as she had when they were courting, and he hoped the guy was as good looking as he himself once was. But instead of being amused, she began to cry. And with that, he realized that she had in fact met someone else.

Suddenly he despised his detective vocation. Yet again it had led to a discovery he did not want and did not know what to do with. If anything, he wanted to fall on his knees and ask her to love him but he would never do such a thing—never. That was his curse: he had to live with himself, the twenty-four hour a day detective. He lifted his cell and called Tom.

"Hi Sam.... What can I do for you?"

"No word from Thea?"

"Nothing..." A pause, "You got something?"

"We got a report from the CIA. An agent in Guaymas says he talked to a young American who fit our description. Putting it together, he's sure it was Damien Head. He said they talked during some kind of Yaqui festival, and then this young American walked away to join a beautiful woman. So it sounds likely this was Damien and Thea."

"Didn't this guy follow them?"

"He tried but some Indians blocked him off. He's sure they did it deliberately. The young American disappeared into the crowd. He thinks they must have left town that night... probably headed south. Damien and Thea could have gone straight down the coast or over to Mexico City through Guadalajara."

"I'll bet it's Mexico City."

"A beautiful place to look for anyone among a mere 21 million people." Sam said wryly. "We have another report, though."

"Go on."

"Mexican Intelligence reported listening in on a conversation between two American couples in Mexico City. The older couple was known to them, and they overheard the younger woman being called Danielle. This conversation was in a famous old convent converted into a hotel."

"So do you think that was Danielle and Peter?"

"I do. Ahmal's name came up."

"No surprise there." Tom commented. "So we have both the CIA and Mexican Intelligence on the alert for Damien and Thea?"

"We do." Sam said. "I expect that Danielle and Peter will head down to Chiapas, since Mexican Intelligence believes that Ahmal is there somewhere. Peter will be in touch."

"You'll let me know, won't you?" Tom asked.

"Certainly."

"I sure hope Danielle and Peter find them first," Tom concluded.

★★★

Jim Bernini, Danielle and Peter were chatting as they walked through the park near the hotel. Bernini knew that Mexican Intelligence agents were lurking nearby, but he was pretty sure they wouldn't be overheard, although there were few people in the park that Monday afternoon.

"I have to give a lecture at 5 p.m. so I haven't long to talk. As I mentioned, actually getting to meet Ahmal is difficult, to put it mildly."

Danielle nodded. "Can you help us?"

"What I need to tell you is that Mexican Intelligence is probably onto you. As you know, they were eavesdropping at the table next to us yesterday. I don't know how much they overheard, but if they figured out that you were asking about Ahmal, they'll be tracking you too, because they've been trying to find her for a long time. She's less of a priority than she used to be because she's not so political, but she's still a person of significant interest to them. So you'll have to be careful. I have lost track of her completely, I'm afraid."

"Oh," said Danielle in disappointment.

Bernini took her hand and said paternally, "But you shouldn't waste your time chasing after people like her when there's so much to see in Mexico."

Danielle felt the paper that Bernini put in her hand as he said in a lower voice, "Memorize this and destroy it. Mention my name when you call."

They chatted inconsequentially about tourist destinations until Bernini took his leave to give his lecture.

When Peter and Danielle got back to their hotel, Danielle looked at the slip of paper Bernini had given her. On it was a woman's name, Francisca della Lamarna, with a phone number and address in San Cristóbal , the second largest town in Chiapas. They both memorized the number, then tore up and flushed the paper down the toilet.

★★★

When Sam opened the door to his house that evening shortly after seven, he immediately felt troubled. For one thing, there was no smell of cooking, though Ruthie usually expected him home around seven. She was nowhere in the kitchen, which showed no sign of food preparation, nor in the living-dining room. He climbed upstairs and found her sitting in their bedroom on a chair beside her dressing table. She had her purse in her lap.

His heart sank. "What is it, Ruthie?"

"I'm leaving you, Sam."

A long silence followed. Off in the far distance a siren wailed.

"We've had 23 years together and that's long enough. At last, I've found someone who makes me happy... and wants to make me happy."

Sam could find no words.

"All you've ever really cared about is your police work... I was here to cook your meals, keep your place clean, and share your bed... which hasn't been much fun for the last few years. I've had enough, Sam. Our love died, and at last I've found love again."

She stood up.

"I've left my new address in the desk downstairs. And I think I've cleared out all my stuff. Of course we'll need to talk about the house and other things later."

"I don't believe this," he mumbled.

"And you're supposed to be the great detective, knowing everything. Well, get used to it. I'm not your

Ruthie Schumacker anymore. I'm changing my name back to Ruth Dearborn."

"You can't just leave me like this." Sam breathed heavily. "Didn't you like any of it?"

"How could I?" She said. "Your wife was the FBI and she got all the attention."

"Please, Ruthie, please don't. Don't leave me. Please"

"Why do you say this now? I am leaving you. I've left you." She walked out of the room and down the stairs. He heard the front door shut. Feeling tears on his face, he waited. Her small car puttered away down the street.

CHAPTER TWENTY-FIVE

Giberto showed Damien which of the lower two bunk beds was to be his. Damien was surprised to see that the other three were in use, though unoccupied. Giberto pointed to the bed above Damien's, then to himself.

Damien heard a woman's voice singing outside.

Giberto pointed to Damien's bunk.

"You... sleep now."

"Sleep in the afternoon?" Damien asked in surprise.

"Yes, now."

"Why now?"

Giberto stared humorlessly at Damien. "Tonight we busy."

Damien instinctively didn't like Giberto, and liked being ordered around by him even less. But that bed looked inviting.

Giberto left and Damien stripped down to his shorts, for it was a warm day. For a few minutes he lay listening to the woman singing, and heard another woman's voice join in. Unaccountably, he felt happier than he had in a long time. The shock of what he might have done in San Diego had faded like a bad dream which he dismissed for the moment.

Damien came drowsily to the warm surface later, thinking of his father in his wheelchair in his solar aquarium, face turned to the sun. He missed the old bastard, missed sparring with him. Damien wondered what Father was doing, what he thought about Damien's having left so suddenly, why he'd not told him about his cloning. Why would he hide it like that? Maybe he should call him when he got up… And Damien drifted off to sleep again.

At 8:00 PM they woke him—two young men in jeans, sandals and T-shirts. He followed them to the large kitchen centered on a dining table, where Thea was with a middle-aged woman who seemed to be in charge of cooking. The two young men disappeared beyond the kitchen.

"Everybody else has already eaten, Damien, so we're having our evening meal together. Mama said she will join us for dessert."

"Whatever," Damien said, smiling at her.

Thea tried to return the smile but did not quite succeed.

"What's wrong, Thea?"

"No, no, nothing. I mean after all, I found my mother."

Thea realized that he wasn't fooled, but she didn't know how to explain her discomfort. She had no idea how he would react to her mother's plan for him.

Damien touched her hand. "Mothers can be difficult, and she's a particularly powerful one," he said sympathetically, thinking of Eden and her rule of Arnold's household.

They sat down and were served a dinner of tossed tostadas, delicious tortillas topped with beans, chicken and guacamole. As they finished, talking mainly about Roberto's views about the Zapatistas and the need for a deep change in Mexican society, Ahmal arrived bearing two large cups filled with pulque, the pre-Columbian drink made from the agave cactus called maguey. She poured a little from one of the cups into an empty cup for herself, gave the other two to Thea and Damien, and sat down.

"This is to celebrate the arrival of my daughter, Thea, and of you, our visitor from America, Damien. We expect a new infusion of life from you, Damien, being the creation of such a father."

They drank to this. Then Damien, putting his cup down said, "Speaking of Father, I'd like to phone him tonight."

"Yes, let him know we're okay," Thea chimed in.

"That might not be such a good idea. His phone may be tapped. We can get a message to him through my channels, if you want to prepare one in the morning." Ahmal responded smoothly.

After another drink of pulque, Damien observed, "I think, Ahmal, that you are interested in me because of my human-jaguar genes."

Ahmal nodded.

"Yes."

"But I'm not sure how I can help you. In fact, I think I'm a liability. I'm wanted for murder, you know. I can't believe I did it, but that doesn't seem to matter to the American police."

Ahmal did not answer, so he went on.

"I couldn't have come here without Thea's help. Anyway, I came looking for refuge," he paused, tapping his fingers on the table, "but I think I may be more trouble than I'm worth. If you think so, I'll be on my way. Just tell me which jungle to get lost in." He finished off his cup of pulque. "I don't know what's in this, but it's powerful. Where does it come from?"

Ahmal poured him another cupful. "From the maguey plant, a type of cactus. It was discovered by a woman hundreds of years before the Spanish came with their guns and their priests." She got up, moved behind him and gently massaged his stiff shoulders.

"Young man, we can offer you refuge. All we ask in return is your cooperation in our celebrations honoring our society. We seek to bring it to life again... to restore the living power it once had. Will you do this for us?"

"Of course," Damien said "But I don't see how."

"You will soon see and you will find yourself fulfilled in a way you never imagined possible."

"Sounds great," Damien said, definitely feeling the effects of the pulque.

"Oh, it is. Now follow me." She released him and he rose, following her through the far door into a pantry lined by fixed cupboards from waist height to the floor. Each cupboard had a door knob. Ahmal grasped the last two of these and twisted them one way, then the opposite way, and to Damien's astonishment a six foot section of the cupboard swung open revealing a flight of stairs leading into the darkness below.

"This is a big improvement," Ahmal said, "over the usual hole in the kitchen floor disguised by a floor panel. And the deception does not end here, as you will soon see. Follow me."

She took a large flashlight from a cupboard above and started down the secret stairway.

"Isn't Thea coming?" Damien asked.

"Not tonight. Come along, Damien."

Damien hesitated, looking back at Thea, who shrugged. Then he turned to follow Ahmal down into the darkness. In a moment he stood beside her.

"Now watch." She pressed a button on the side of the stairway, and the cupboard above swung shut while lights came on in the passageway. Ahmal switched off her flashlight.

"Clever," Damien muttered.

"And necessary," Ahmal said.

They walked down a long passage that bent slowly to the right, then wound a short way to the left to another sharp right hand turn into a large storage area. Here Ahmal stopped. She reached up to a small crevice near the corner, but merely to point it out to Damien, then unclipped a remote control from her belt and directed it at the crevice to open another section of the wall. Damien was impressed to see that the false wall looked exactly like the large and irregular pieces of limestone that composed the entire corridor. As they stepped into the next passageway, the wall sealed behind them.

"We only have about half a kilometre to our destination." Ahmal said lightly.

Damien was beginning to like Ahmal. She was not the misty-eyed True Believer he had expected her to be.

The corridor opened into a natural cave which wound on, here and there growing in width and height. They passed through two caverns which Ahmal said were close to 30 feet high, and finally came to one with a much higher ceiling and widely separated walls.

Ahead of them stood several people wearing traditional Mesoamerican dress. Three were young men, one at the back and two at the sides of a strange looking seat which Damien later learned was made of the wood of the sacred Ceiba tree which represented the Mayan World Tree, from which all life grew. Draped over the throne-like seat was the skin of the sacred jaguar. The young men wore only loin cloths, their oiled upper bodies covered with strange designs worked into the skin, their heads resplendent in snake skins and eagle feathers.

Damien began to seriously wonder what he had gotten himself into, but he was very curious.

"You will now, Damien," said Ahmal, "let these attendants dress you in preparation for the ceremony."

DAMIEN

The two attendants bowed and moved respectfully toward him. For a moment, Damien wanted to stop them, but the pulque seemed to have dulled his defensive instincts. Damien was amused to find himself floating happily, observing his attendants working swiftly. They replaced his street clothes with a jewelled snake belt around his middle and folded in a richly ornamented loin cloth. He looked around for Ahmal, and was both relieved and anxious to see that she had disappeared while he dressed. Next, the attendants helped him put on a waistcoat decorated with jade pendants. Finally, he donned a headdress which was filled with jaguar hair and festooned with iridescent green, blue, purple and red quetzal feathers. They slipped onto his feet some beautifully ornamented sandals and he was led to the throne where he sat down. He felt weird but strangely comfortable. Perhaps it was the pulque. This was definitely an adventure, he thought to himself.

Now Ahmal appeared before him in a long bejeweled garment and held out to him a small cup, beckoning him to drink. Reverberating through the cavern came a trilling that sounded like flutes, but not of a type he'd ever heard before. And then he saw them, five swaying young women naked but for scant strips of animal skin shifting alluringly over their gleaming bodies.

They danced closer to him, and one knelt to offer him a small cup. He looked down at her glistening brown skin and leaned forward, nostrils distended to drink in her scent, but was recalled to himself by a tiny bell tinkling on Ahmal's costume as she took her place behind him.

"Drink, Damien... For you are the jaguar man returned to us and we must honor you... Drink."

He smiled to himself and drank, though the liquid was bitter.

"And these maidens are given to you. They are of the earth and seek new life through you who possess the jaguar power."

Her voice had become compelling, songlike, and he floated, engulfed in her radiant power. He rose from his throne overcome by desire for the maiden before him. She led him toward a curtained bower and, as he entered, he took her into his arms.

★★★

After three in the morning, Thea woke up, hearing the cooing of doves outside. She was deeply disturbed, thinking of Damien. Had she brought him all this way merely to serve as her mother's stud animal? Bile rose in her throat and she stumbled outside. The moon was full, lighting the desert around. So Damien was fucking some wenches. So what? Better that, than being arrested for murder and sent to prison.

In fact, the whole situation was utterly absurd. Twenty years ago no one had even thought hybrid animal-humans were possible. Yet here was Damien. It was as though the most fantastic science fiction had become a reality. Who knew what monsters might rise? She thought of her favorite poet, W. B. Yeats, who wrote in *Second Coming*:

"When a vast image out of Spiritus Mundi
Troubles my sight: somewhere in sands of the desert
A shape with lion body and the head of a man
A gaze blank and pitiless as the sun,
Is moving its slow thighs, while all about it
Reel shadows of the indignant desert birds.
The darkness drops again, but now I know
That twenty centuries of stony sleep
Were vexed to nightmare by a rocking cradle,

DAMIEN

And what rough beast, its hour come round at last,
Slouches towards Bethlehem to be born?"
Thea crawled back into bed and shut her eyes to the
moon, but sleep would not come.

★★★

Ahmal went off with Giberto in the truck the next
morning, so Thea didn't see her until midafternoon, when
she found her on the patio and sat down in the remaining
chair. Ahmal was sunk in reverie, but composed herself to
address Thea.

"Your young man did very well for himself."

"I'm sure he did," Thea said, not wanting to know
the details. "But I don't understand why you're doing it
this way. I mean with these girls from the district. Soon
the world will know, and your cave will be swarming
with police."

"I know." Ahmal said. "Which is fine with me... the
police will be happy to have found my hiding place: the
long lost cave of Chalcatzingo." She smiled. "And I'll
be long gone. After another night or two like the last at
least ten of my selected girls are going to be pregnant
by Damien."

"A little beyond the power of shamans," Thea said drily.

"Exactly," her mother said. "But through my direction and Arnold's genius we've succeeded where the
shamans failed."

"You planned it this way."

"Of course. As the gods decreed, the jaguar man has
come and is creating a new race—"

"With ten pregnant girls?" Thea interrupted sarcastically.

"Starting with ten pregnant girls.... It is enough."

"You mean," said Thea angrily, "you will have him fucking hundreds of girls in some other fucking cave!"

"Thea, you're getting upset," Ahmal said mildly, "He will be worshipped as the man-jaguar god he is. This is the only way to do it. Believe me, these young women found that he was no ordinary man. And that news will soon be broadcast everywhere."

Damien appeared, looking fresh and energetic.

"Looks like you enjoyed your night!" observed Thea dryly.

Damien smiled playfully at her.

"Sit down Damien. I've been waiting to get you both together. I have very sad news." said Ahmal.

Damien settled languidly into his chair.

"I can't get a message to your father. He's dead. He shot himself." Ahmal explained solemnly.

"No!" Thea exclaimed. "Shot himself?!"

Damien and Thea stared at one another. Thea shivered. After a beat, Damien cleared his throat to ask, "When?"

"A week ago."

"Oh my God! That must have been the same day we left," Thea cried, remembering how upset Father was after their last conversation, feeling a wave of guilt that she had just left him like that. Her composure crumpled as tears forced themselves silently to the surface.

Damien leapt up and began to pace lithely from one side of the patio to the other as if caged, suddenly in a fury. How could Father do this? He creates this mess and now he opts out when it gets tough! What'd he expect, making me part jaguar? There'd be no help from him now. Damien suddenly realized how much he'd depended on Father, always there, supporting and challenging him. He'd been subconsciously counting on Father helping somehow even from so far away. And now Father was gone. Gone!

DAMIEN

Something twisted inside and Damien wanted to rage, to cut and slash and burn. He turned on Ahmal.

"That's the real reason you didn't let us call him last night, isn't it? You knew, didn't you?" He loomed over her.

"That's not important now," she responded calmly. "What is important is helping you both to come to terms with this, and you, Damien, with who you are."

Damien snorted and strode off.

Thea looked at her mother through her tears.

"I can't believe you," she said, and got up to leave, stumbling slightly on the edge of the patio.

The rest of the day passed numbly. Dinner was subdued, everyone gathered at the long table speaking quietly, casting sidelong glances at Thea and Damien, who sat at the far end, Thea barely touching her food. Damien didn't eat much either, then got up to pace again. Ahmal approached him gently, touched him on the sleeve.

"It's time," she said.

"Time for what?" growled Damien.

"To go below."

"Now? After all that's happened?"

"What better way to honor your father than by perpetuating his genetic legacy?"

"Ah, more little were-jaguars!" retorted Damien sarcastically. But he allowed himself to be led down the dark tunnel.

Thea watched them go, then excused herself and returned to her room. She thought sleep would never come as she stared at the dark slashes of the wooden beams in the gloom of the ceiling. Oh, she missed Tom tonight, his gentleness, his voice, his warm body. Sleep took her over finally, a great leaden keel weighing her down with no sails to bear her forward. Shouting woke her too soon in the morning and she looked out her window to see the cook run into the yard, completely distraught.

"Giberto, Giberto is dying! That American did it!"

DAMIEN

CHAPTER TWENTY-SIX

Peter and Danielle flew from Mexico City to San Cristóbal de las Casas in Chiapas, a town of about 130,000 which was 7,500 feet above sea level. It was here that the Zapatistas first struck in 1994. Danielle immediately phoned Francisca della Lamarna, the contact Bernini had given them. A carefully modulated female voice answered. Danielle explained that they were tourists and their friend Jim had suggested they contact her. After a long pause, Francisca agreed to meet them in an hour, just inside the entrance to the *Na Bolan*. They had heard of this coffee bar, where Lacandón Indians had gathered during the Zapatista uprising.

Inside the entrance way, they spotted Francisca by the grey braid and blue glasses she had described. A patrician woman in her mid-forties, Francisca was reading a newspaper and enjoying a coffee at the window ledge. They took the stools next to her and looked out the window at passers-by. Without looking up from her paper, Francisca spoke unaccented English with quiet authority.

"To meet your next contact, Fernandez Templico, catch the 1:00 PM bus tomorrow to Mizol Ha, Highway 199."

Then she casually sipped her coffee as though she had not spoken, and indeed Peter had not heard what she said.

"We have to take the bus to Mizol Ha at 1 pm tomorrow to meet a guy named Fernandez Templico," Danielle told Peter as they left the coffee bar. She was sorry not to have another day in the pretty little town of San Cristóbal with its squares and fine old colonial buildings. They decided to make the best of the time they had.

The next morning, they headed for the bus station. Peter found himself thinking about the night before. He had paused at her door to say goodnight when she took his hand.

"Come in for a last drink?" She said, looking archly up at him. "Okay, Inspector?"

Inside, he said, "I'm not an Inspector anymore."

"So the Mounties fired you for this?"

"For what...?"

"Consorting with the ladies, I'd guess."

He decided to see how far she would go. "How did you know?"

"I don't really. But I'm getting to know you."

"Oh oh..."

"Oh is right... Because I can see the look in your eyes... Especially when you say goodnight at my door."

"Well, you're a very attractive woman, Danielle."

"Well?" she asked, moving seductively close and trailing her forefinger down his chest.

"...But I can't."

"Why? Oh," she placed a finger on his mouth. "Because... you're supposed to be working for me..."

"Yes, and..." Peter found himself somewhat distracted.

"You're really a bad character," she said, unfastening the top button of his sports shirt. "Amazing how long they let you stay on in the Mounties."

"Well, you see, while I was there they appointed a new Superintendent... and it was a woman," Peter said, gently moving her hands away. "And I was in a relationship then, as I am now."

Danielle pouted prettily. "So that's why she fired you."

"Actually, I quit."

"How sad," she murmured, "for the Super."

As they arrived at the bus station, Peter brought himself back to the present and they climbed onto the bus. At Misol-Ha, they had little time to be impressed by the 100-foot high waterfall, for they were immediately approached by a boy of about sixteen. Without speaking, he handed them a note with Fernandez' name on it, then led them down a jungle trail which branched into a smaller trail then, it seemed, plunged straight into the jungle, though the boy still knew exactly where to go. Finally, they came to a small rather broken-down hut with a bench outside occupied by a man in his fifties, with a small beard touched by grey. He stood up as they approached, holding out his hand.

"I am honored to meet friends of Professor Jim Bernini," he said in stilted English. "My name is Fernandez Templico. I have met and talked to the Professor on three occasions when I visited Mexico City, and wrote to him once. He says that you are seeking the whereabouts of Ahmal, our spiritual leader. Please sit down," he said, indicating the bench.

"I apologize for the complicated path to me, but it is necessary in these days." He shrugged wryly. "Now, please describe yourselves."

"Yes," Danielle said. "We understand the need for caution. I'm Danielle Deneuve, an American citizen, and this is Peter Gregory, a Canadian private investigator, formerly an RCMP detective. I hired him to help me locate a young American, Damien Head, who's wanted by the FBI. He came across the border with his half-sister Thea, who is Ahmal's daughter. We are sure that Thea will seek her mother's help for Damien." Danielle glanced at Peter before continuing. "Actually, I believe that if Ahmal helps Damien, she will put not only herself, but the cause you all stand for, in greater danger. The FBI will be pressuring Mexican authorities to find this Damien. They have reason to worry about him."

For a few moments, Fernandez stared out into the jungle.

"The last thing we want is an American felon jeopardizing our cause. It makes sense for us to help you get this man out."

"So how do we get to Ahmal before Thea does?" Peter asked.

Fernandez smiled. "I see that it is true the Mounties waste no time getting their man."

"I am no longer a Mountie," Peter said.

"No, but you think like one," Fernandez said, then he turned to Danielle. "The problem, as always, is knowing where Ahmal is at any given time."

He thought for a moment. "I have to tell you that there is a certain amount of—I won't say conflict, exactly, but tension, between our political Zapatista movement and the more spiritual Savonards. Besides, Ahmal is rather demanding." He carefully examined his hand. They were capable-looking hands. "I don't blame her really, after the total hell she went through in prison. Anyway, it is a problem. She contacts us, not the other way around. That's the rule. But we can try to send a message and hope she'll reply."

"How long will it take?" Peter asked.

"I cannot say." Fernandez spread his hands in a gesture of resignation.

Danielle shifted impatiently on the bench, "But we cannot wait indefinitely."

"Well, there may be another way. I can arrange for you to meet Ramón Gutterriez, our Zapatista Commander. He may get a faster response from Ahmal—if he's willing to help you."

★★★

Damien struggled along, choking in the desert heat. He had heard that it was possible to get a milky liquid out of the cactus, but he did not even have a pocket knife and staggered blindly on. One thing was sure—he would not go back. In his mind's eye, he still saw the figure of the man Giberto shaking him increasingly violently, shouting at him to get up, and then Giberto was tumbling across the room and hitting the opposite wall with a terrible cracking sound. Damien had fled the house, wearing only the shorts he slept in. The heat scorched his bare torso and feet unmercifully, and even though the midday sun was long past, he knew he must find shelter soon. He found himself thinking of the eggs benedict and fresh-squeezed orange juice that Eden had so often made for him. He'd be salivating if his mouth weren't so dry. He missed her gentle touch and her soft blue eyes. What would she be thinking? He knew that she would never believe that he had killed Catherine. He didn't either—except now, what had he done to Giberto? And this time he remembered what had happened even though he hadn't been fully awake when it happened. He looked up miserably, noticed a wall of rock a mile or so off and stumbled toward it, all his mind now focused on reaching that one shady goal.

What he did not notice, could not, because of the gradual rise and fall of the land in the distance, was a truck with three men in it. They had been busy extracting the sap for pulque from wild maguey plants, and having taken all they could carry, were headed back to their encampment in the mountainous wilderness of Guerrero. They were members of a guerrilla band, once much larger in numbers, which had rebelled along with the Zapatistas of Chiapas.

These three couldn't believe their eyes when they saw a practically naked man crossing the road 100 yards further on. They honked, and Damien turned at bay like a startled animal, then took off across the desert.

Suddenly realizing that he had been hearing and smelling the truck for a while, all that Damien could think was that it was pursuing him—that he had killed that man at Ahmal's place and these people had been sent to capture him. He stumbled on as fast as he could through the arid brush. Glancing back, he saw that they were following him and shouting. He knew he must not give in—must escape—and if he hadn't stepped on a low-lying cactus he might have done so. But he fell, his foot pierced. Then the three men were around him. One of them came close, talking to him. He grabbed the man's leg, biting deeply into it. There was a yell and then blackness.

PART THREE

CHAPTER TWENTY-SEVEN

The old man had waited at the edge of the jungle for more than three hours, and he was tired. Dr. Anton Bresagi knew that he was to meet a New Being, but had no idea what form this being would take.

Dr. Bresagi was a retired Astrophysics and Cosmology professor at the University of Mexico who had been startled when he began having strange visions in his mid-seventies. The psychiatrist he consulted attributed them to early childhood experiences. Unconvinced, Bresagi turned elsewhere for help. Eventually, he heard of a famous old lady named Oranga, who was said to possess great powers. He found her in a small town not far from San Cristóbal surrounded by her devotees. She recognized that he had the shaman's gift and helped him to understand and develop his power. She taught Bresagi about the Mayan star system and calendar with its prophetic ascendancy. Strangely, Bresagi found that much of his new knowledge made sense in the context of recent scientific discoveries like entanglement, the phenomenon in which a change in one particle might instantaneously be experienced in another particle even as far away as a distant galaxy. So Bresagi, whose ancestors were from Yugoslavia, had become a shaman in the Lacandón region of Chiapas.

For some time now, Bresagi had been receiving power-fully clear messages from the galaxy about a New Being who was to appear on any one of three consecutive days during the eighth hour on the Mexican side of the Usumacinta River, near an old ruin which was a small part of a huge sacred temple site called Yaxchilan.

This was Anton's second day of waiting, but no one had appeared. Tomorrow, he would try again for the last time. He was about to take the boat back to Oranga's place by the river, when he felt a presence. He turned around but saw no one.

★★★

After two days of searching for Damien in the brush-land west of Chalcatzingo, Ahmal called a halt to the hunt. Giberto was recovering in hospital. Thea sat out on the patio, unable to speak. Ahmal joined her.

"Damien is very strong, Thea. He will survive."

Thea could not bring herself to answer.

"He will survive because he has to," Ahmal said. "He is a special being—beyond any of us."

This was too much. Thea turned her anger on her mother.

"Special! I know what you mean by special," she said. "It was an orgy, wasn't it? An orgy of fucking so you could spread his seed around. It's all so... so puerile!"

Ahmal stared over the vast sloping land rimmed by the mountains of the Sierra Madre.

"It was not merely his seed I wanted, though of course that will help. But, yes, the orgy, as you call it, was impor-tant. Those ten young women will tell their friends about what it was like, that this Damien is no ordinary man. Word will travel fast and multiply."

"But it's so... degrading. Damien is not merely some wild animal!"

"He is that, and more. Even you know that there is truth in the ancient Olmec lore about a powerful spiritual connection to animals giving astonishing strength and energy. Just look at the Jaguar Temple at Tikal and the snake-bird Quetzalcoatl.

"But mother..."

"Listen, Thea. We began to lose the source of our strength when the Aztecs moved away from the jaguar to foolishly rely more and more on human sacrifice to satisfy the Sun God. Then we lost it altogether when Cortez came and sought to put an end to the cult of the jaguar and Quetzalcoatl."

"You really, actually, believe this?"

"Yes, I do. And I thought you did too. Otherwise, why did you bring Damien to me? He has made the jaguar alive again among us," she paused. "Now we regain our vitality. Revive our nation."

Thea stared at her mother in astonishment. Perhaps Ahmal was right. Perhaps Thea had unconsciously obeyed her mother's will. The woman amazed Thea.

★★★

The next morning, Thea was sitting at her desk writing a letter to Tom when her mother came in without bothering to knock.

"We have news," she said, "about Damien."

"News? Has someone found him?"

"Have you heard of Ramón Gutteriez?"

"The Zapatista leader, you mean?"

"He is holding Damien prisoner."

DAMIEN

Thea whirled around. "What! Prisoner?"

"Apparently, the Guerrera Zapatista band found Damien in the Sierra Madre desert and took him prisoner. Somehow they figured out that Damien had been with us, so they passed him on to Ramón."

"You must know Ramón."

"I do. He's both friend and foe."

"They're a guerilla group. Wouldn't Damien be a liability? Won't they just give him back?"

"To answer that you have to know the politics, Thea," her mother said. "Meantime, our movement, the Savonards—"

"You mean your movement. You're the leader."

"As it happens, yes. But hear me out. As you know, we sympathize with the goals of the Zapatistas but not their violent methods. And we think that the US would be quick to prevent any kind of communist revolution in Mexico and Central America. The Cuban solution would not be allowed to work here."

Thea nodded.

Ahmal went on, "That's why our solution is so much better. We change minds with persuasion, not force. We appeal as much to non-indigenous poor people as to the Maya and other native groups. So our appeal is really to the whole of Mexico except for the rich."

"And except for the Mexican government. Anyway what has this to do with Damien?"

"Everything... believe it or not word has got around about Damien being our man-jaguar ruler, the one we've been waiting and preparing our people for."

"How did that happen so fast? I mean..." but words failed Thea.

"Damien's the one, Thea, and now the Zapatistas know it too. And let me say that what you called the orgy in the cave two days ago—well those ten young women all declared that Damien is no ordinary man... and that news has spread like wildfire."

"My God..." Thea could only shake her head.

"Gutteriez," Ahmal said, "now has possession of the most important acquisition of the Savonards and can use him for their purposes."

"Not to wage peace, but war."

"Exactly... using Damien to force us to support their militancy... even though that is anathema to us."

Thea could only stare at her mother. She'd brought Damien to her mother for refuge and now he was a political pawn.

CHAPTER TWENTY-EIGHT

Fernandez Templico's directions led Danielle and Peter to Palenque. There, they rented a jeep for the drive to Boca Lacantún, where the great river Usumacinta winds frantically before curving gracefully into Guatemala. They arrived at dusk to discover that Boca Lacantún was hardly more than a small collection of shacks, the largest of which was a post office in which a man in his mid-forties sat in a rickety chair behind a shelf-like desk.

Peter nodded to him and, upon learning that he was their contact, shoved Bernini's note across the desk. Carlos read the Spanish note with care, then peered at Peter and Danielle, who was looking at the posters on the wall.

"You want Tarada," he said. "I call him. You wait outside. He'll take you."

Danielle interpreted for Peter and they headed out into the sun's glare.

Tarada turned out to be a small man, Peter guessed in his thirties, with sharp observant eyes. He wore a green hadja which came down to his knees, and a band around his head rather than a hat. He read the note and then studied the two in front of him.

"Do you speak Spanish?" he asked.

Danielle answered. "I do; he doesn't. But I am the one the note refers to. This man," she nodded at Peter, "is my helper. I employ him."

Without answering, Tarada turned his back on them, took a few paces along the wooden walkway and spoke quietly into his cell phone. The call lasted longer than Peter expected, Tarada saying little. At last he turned to them.

"Very well. Please follow me."

So they followed him past dusty huts with chickens and patches of maize and sometimes a few squash until he stopped at the door of one hut and spoke to an old woman inside.

To Peter and Danielle, he said, "Too late to go now. You sleep here. In the morning, we go."

Danielle looked at the dusty floor of the hut and the wizened old woman's gap-toothed smile, then shrugged and nodded. After a dinner of maize cakes, Danielle and Peter looked at the sleeping pallet on the floor.

"After you," Peter said graciously.

"Not exactly romantic, is it?" Danielle gave him a look and lay down fully clothed. Peter chose the far side of the pallet and turned his back to her, resting his head on his arm. Though they slept uneasily, Danielle was snuggled up to Peter's back when Tarada reappeared at 6:30 the next morning. Peter looked at her quizzically.

"Well, you seemed safer than the cockroaches," she mumbled, rubbing sleep from her eyes as she sat up in her wrinkled clothes.

Tarada led them down a narrow trail enfolded in the thick growth of the jungle. They walked close to 40 minutes, passing several side trails. Sweat dripped down their backs as they came to a small clearing where a dozen or so armed guerillas swiftly surrounded them. Danielle shrank against Peter. Then the guerillas recognized Tarada and Peter knew they were close to their goal.

★★★

Damien paced the cave floor. His four guards had escorted him through the guerilla barracks which backed onto this cave where he was imprisoned, and now they watched his every move. They were fit young Mayans, used to the hardships of jungle life, and totally committed to the Zapatista cause.

Damien thought about his interview with Commander Gutteriez. He had been stunned to discover that they were holding him for political reasons. The idea that he was the Mayan man-jaguar god was more than a little much to swallow. First the adventure in the cave with Ahmal's girls and now this? These people were nuts. And they had a thing for caves.

Damien listened to the gurgle of the stream that ran beside and dove beneath the cave wall, upon which a few electric lamps created deep clefts of light and shadow. The sound of the water changed as it went underground, but he suddenly realized that he could hear another change deeper in the hill where the stream must come to the surface again.

He knew he would have to escape, but he did not wrestle with the problem of how to do so, knowing the solution would come to him unbidden. He sat down, wondering if this tendency to act without thought or planning when under threat was an attribute of his jaguar nature. He thought it probably was. And this troubled him, remembering how his father had shouted at him about the three boys he had roughed up so badly. Father. He

DAMIEN

could not imagine Father taking his own life. The image of Father dying morphed into Giberto hitting the wall across the room. Damien fervently hoped Giberto had survived, even if he was a jerk. Damien missed Thea and wished he had not had to run away. With her was gone his last link to home. Was it barely two weeks ago that he and Danielle had been playing tennis and fooling around? And only a month ago, he'd been talking to Catherine in Chemistry class—he still could not accept that he could have ripped her throat out with his teeth and stashed her in a tree. Speaking of nuts. He thought again of his father, the great Dr. Arnold Head—brilliant geneticist! Theoretically, he was identical to Arnold but for his jaguar genes, but he—Damien—would never have done to anyone what Arnold had done to him. How could he cope with this predator within? How could he learn to manage it? He wished he could talk to Father about this. He curled up on the cave floor.

Yet somehow, knowing the truth about himself helped. Deep down, he'd always known he was different. He experienced things so vividly, like the smell of leaves and animal hair. Now he understood why his hearing was so acute and he was so incredibly sensitive to smell, why he tracked others by their odor without even thinking about it.

Thea had said he was superior, mentally and physically—a kind of superman—but he didn't want to be that different. Why couldn't he just live a normal life? Damien fell asleep on this thought. Zynta whirred into his dreams, hovering close to him with her vibrant colors and minute body. He was overwhelmed to see her again because he remembered crushing her months ago. In wonder, he stretched out his hand to her. But she changed, the delicate wings morphing into the coils of a snake. In shock, he recognized the Mayan god Quetzalcoatl, but even as he did so, her eyes turned yellow, like his own, and he found himself looking at his jaguar self.

His jaguar self. There was no escaping it. He turned onto his side and felt the cold rock pressing into him. And then he was furious. With his situation. With himself. If they thought he was a god—by God!—he'd use that. If he really was superior, he could get out of this. And he would. Noting out of the corner of his eye that two of the guards were asleep, Damien rose from his bed and moved swiftly over to the other two guards, who were playing cards near the entrance. They looked up, the quicker one reaching for his gun.

"Don't waste your time," Damien said. "I can move faster than you can fire that." And he kicked the gun across the room. The guard yelped and cradled his dangling wrist. His companion leapt to his feet, but Damien grabbed and broke his gun arm, hurling him at the cots where the other two guards were just waking up.

"Everything you've heard about me is true, and more," he hissed. "Let me go or risk your lives."

Damien smashed the guard with the broken wrist to the ground, and almost in the same movement, leapt after the ones on the cots. Just as one rudely awakened sleeper was swinging his submachine gun round, Damien grabbed him by the neck and smashed his head against the other, rendering them both unconscious—or worse. The guard with the broken arm was on the ground, pushing himself backwards with one arm as fast as he could.

Damien growled, "Tell the others what you've seen here, what happens to those who oppose me." And he clouted the side of his head, knocking him out.

In the silence that followed, Damien became aware that his foot was sore where the thorn had pierced it. He looked at the heavy wooden door that led out to the barracks, then at the stream. He moved to the spot where the stream flowed out of sight beneath the cavern wall and listened again. Then he stepped into the stream and held his breath as he ducked underwater. He let the current sweep him along, emerging as he had hoped into a cavern where he could breathe before being sucked into another subterranean tunnel. He would stay with this stream until it released him or he died in its depths.

★★★

Tarada spoke to one of the guerillas, who stepped aside to make a cell phone call while Peter and Danielle waited uncomfortably. Then the soldier beckoned them to follow through the ramshackle buildings to what looked like an office. A man with a Fidel Castro-type beard and moustache and piercing black eyes stepped forward to greet them, exuding a powerful aura of command even though he was short and compactly built.

"I am Gutteriez, Commander of the Zapatistas," he announced to Danielle's breasts. He led them into a makeshift office, where he sat down behind the desk.

Peter wasn't surprised that the Commander was interested in Danielle, though he didn't much like it. Danielle was wearing a khaki ensemble which was in no sense attractive, but somehow failed to diminish her large brown eyes, dark brown hair, perfect skin, and breasts pressing against the fabric of her workshirt.

The young aide held a chair for her. Gutteriez read the note from Professor Bernini which Danielle gave him.

"Yes," he said in accented English, "several days ago I received a letter from your friend, Professor Bernini. I have great admiration for him, having read his recent book, *The Mexican Dilemma*. Of course I had already met him and agreed with his views, which were remarkable for an American. He is no ordinary man. So I am naturally curious to know the purpose of your visit, and that of your companion." He nodded in Peter's direction.

"Peter," Danielle said, "works for me." She looked at Peter, "And is an excellent assistant and guide. We are here, Commander, to ask you to help us find a young American by the name of Damien Head, who is a personal friend of mine."

"I suppose you are aware," Gutteriez said, "that this friend of yours is wanted by your FBI and our Mexican Police."

"Yes, I am. I assure you it is a false charge."

"And are you also aware that, whatever the truth of it, this Damien Head is supposed to be..." he searched for the appropriate words... "extra-human, not an ordinary human being?"

Danielle looked at Peter in astonishment, then back at Commander Gutteriez.

"Is that what people are saying?" she asked carefully.

"You may be sure of it," Gutteriez said, "many say he is nothing less than a man-jaguar god returned to the Mayan people."

"You're kidding!"

"I'm afraid not," Gutteriez responded.

Peter had a thought, "Does this have anything to do with the Savonard movement?"

"Indeed it does," Gutteriez said. "Being American you might have difficulty understanding the importance these Savonards attach to the appearance of this Damien, who ushers in a new age in which the indigenous peoples will return to power in Mexico and Central America."

Gutteriez shrugged, "I do not believe this non-sense, of course. I am committed to armed struggle—to revolution—as Fidel Castro was committed. That is the only hope for Mexico."

"This really complicates things. We think Damien has gone to Ahmal for help. Can you help us find her?" Danielle asked.

Gutteriez paused, then asked, "What exactly is your interest in this young man? What do you hope to accomplish by finding him?"

"I intend to take him away from all this, beyond legal and political reach."

"And can you do this?" Gutteriez shifted his gaze to her eyes.

"Yes, I have the means." Danielle answered.

Gutteriez looked at Peter, who nodded.

Studying them both, Gutteriez took a long breath, "It so happens that this Damien has come into my hands."

"You have him here?" Danielle leapt up. "He has him here," she repeated, beside herself. "But how is that possible?"

The Commander smiled, clearly pleased with the effect of his news.

"Señorita," Gutteriez said quietly. "Please, I cannot tell you how it is that he came into our hands, only that he is here. We are glad that you have come to us, and I will now explain why."

Danielle recovered herself, and sat down. "Where is he? Can I see him?"

"In a moment. But I want you to promise me, Señorita, that you will take him out of Mexico, never to return." He studied her reaction.

Danielle stared at him in amazement.

"It is terribly important," Gutteriez continued, "that you do this, not just for me but for the sake of my country. To try to resurrect the past and return to the worship of ancient animal gods is just madness, and it must, Señorita, *must*, at all costs, be prevented. As you are his friend, his close friend, he knows you, and will be overjoyed to see you. He will be glad to be rescued from us, believe me, as you will see. So, you will do this? You will take him out of Mexico? If not for the sake of Mexico, then for young Damien's sake? Will you?"

She pushed herself back from the table and stood up.

"Of course." She paused. "I promise you."

Gutteriez stood up. "Thank you. And now you will see your young man. He is in good health, I assure you, but necessarily imprisoned, for we could not risk losing him."

"Imprisoned? Then I imagine he'll be more than glad to leave with me."

An aide opened the door at the back of the room and they descended some stairs to a large, very thick wooden door. The aide knocked on the door without response. He looked to the Commander for assent, and then unlocked the door and pulled it open. Almost on the threshold lay the body of a young guard with a twisted wrist. With a terrible oath, Gutteriez pushed his way into a scene of horror, finding two guards next to the cot, one with his neck broken and the other deeply unconscious. The fourth, on the floor with a badly broken arm, was just returning to consciousness.

There was no sign of Damien, though the aide searched the cave thoroughly.

DAMIEN

CHAPTER TWENTY-NINE

Swept along the subterranean channel, Damien held his breath as he had so many times in underwater swimming events. Now, though, he had to protect himself from the jutting rocks in the narrow stream. For a couple of panicky moments he got stuck, but managed to wiggle free, tearing his shorts. Then the passage widened and he was able to take deep breaths of the moist air as the current bore him rapidly on. At last there was light, and then blinding light, and he realized he was being swept toward an opening. He gripped a rock against the powerful pull of the stream, then inched towards the opening. Huge tangled trees rose thirty or forty feet away. Wedging his feet and hands against the sides of the cleft, he peered over the edge, seeing the water spilling down a cliff face which bottomed out on a pile of shale that disappeared into the jungle thickets. Water racing around him, he hung on with all his strength, knowing that his life was balanced on this gleaming edge. Yet somehow, this extremity exhilarated him, slicing like a sun's ray directly into his core.

Fixing his feet hard against the bottom edge, Damien used the force of the current and his own raw strength to eject himself from the waterfall's mouth. He flew clear of the cliff face and landed with a crash in the pile of shale, which gave way, careening him into the thick brush of the jungle.

★★★

After Sam phoned Tom twice without success, he went to Tom's place but found no one there, which worried him a little. So he rang Eden's bell and after a moment she opened the door, and smiled.

"Please come in, Detective Sam."

He was glad to see that, despite the tragedy she had suffered, she was looking a great deal better. She wore a light green dress that suited her plump curves, and her blond hair was attractively pulled back. He noticed, too, that the house was clean and tidy, transformed from the day of the tragedy.

She asked him to sit down. "I suppose you want to ask me about the papers I gave Tom."

He knew nothing about such papers.

"For several days," she went on, "after Arnold... I was in a state of confusion. I think I forgot my own name."

"And the papers?"

"I found them one day in a bedroom cupboard. Why I had them, Lord knows. It was scientific stuff. So I handed them to Tom."

Sam said nothing.

"Is that what you came to ask me?" She asked.

"No.... but thanks for telling me. I wanted to ask you where Tom is. He's not answering his doorbell, either at the house or the lab."

"I know. I guess he's mourning. Losing Thea has been a terrible blow to him."

"Do you think that's it?" Sam paused, thinking. "You're sure he's around?"

"His car is there, as you must have noticed, being a Detective." She smiled at him, and he felt a surge of warmth. How he had missed this making fun of his profession since his wife had left. Of course, he had noticed the car. But he was still troubled by Tom's non-appearance.

"It's lunchtime," Eden said, "just about. I'd very much like to make us both sandwiches if you'd care to stay on for a bit."

Sam found that he did want to stay on.

★★★

Danielle lay on a cot in Gutteriez' office. She had not spoken to Peter since entering the cave. Gutteriez paced the room.

"Commander," Peter said.

Gutteriez stopped. "Yes?"

"Does that stream in the cavern exit to the outside? Maybe Damien's body is there."

Gutteriez looked interested.

"I think that's likely," he said. "I know the land falls away on the other side of this ridge down to the river."

Gutteriez went over to a map on the wall and pointed to the contour lines so that Peter could see what he meant.

"The stream probably ends somewhere along here." Gutteriez' fingers traced along a line. "I think it eventually descends to the Usumacinta. That's a good idea, Peter. It would make me very happy to find Damien's body."

Gutteriez turned to the aide, "Find Pedro. He knows the land around here best."

So they set out, following the trail to the Usumacinta River, then branching off to fight their way through the jungle's undergrowth until they saw the drop that Gutteriez had identified on the map. From the edge of the jungle, they looked up past a large bank of shale at water tumbling from the mountainside perhaps forty feet above them. Climbing with great difficulty over the loose shale, they arrived at the bottom of the cliff, but a body was nowhere to be seen.

After gazing gloomily around, Gutteriez spoke, "I don't believe anybody could survive a drop like that. So that means—"

"His body must be stuck in the cave somewhere," Peter said.

Ignoring Peter's interruption, Gutteriez kept speaking, "—this New Being of the Savonards is dead, thank God."

Danielle had fallen into a deep sleep when they returned to Gutteriez's headquarters.

"Would it be okay to let her sleep a little longer?" Peter asked, nodding toward Danielle. "I would like to visit the river. Pedro said it would take about two hours there and back."

Gutteriez nodded.

"The only people you will see down there are the dope smugglers who come across from Guatemala in their pangas."

Peter grinned at Gutteriez. "I'll be sure to buy some of the best!"

Gutteriez smiled broadly. "How else do you think I'm going to win this war?"

The walk took less than an hour. The embankment was deserted except for one old man walking towards him.

"Hello," the old man said, looking unusually closely at Peter.

"How did you know I speak English?" Peter asked.

"You look like an English-speaker."

"May I ask where you learned English?" Peter asked. "You speak it very well."

"Reasonably well. I'm a scientist, born in Yugoslavia and educated in England at Cambridge."

"But you are here in Mexico."

"I'm a retired Cosmologist from the University of Mexico. Now I am in Chiapas. The Mexican government thinks it owns the state, but it really belongs to the Maya."

"You really think so?" Peter asked, noting the clarity of the man's slate-grey eyes.

"Yes, the soul of Chiapas, at least from San Cristóbal east, is Mayan."

Peter did not respond. There was something odd about this old man walking here just now on the bank of the Usumacinta River.

"You are not just an American, are you? You have Indian blood," the old man said.

"Blackfoot. From Canada."

"And you are not walking on this bank of the river for the view."

"No sir," Peter said, "just as you are not here for the view."

The old man searched Peter's eyes.

"I'm here," Peter said, "looking for an unusual young man. I think he escaped from Commander Gutierrez's cave. I need to talk to him."

"You will not be able to talk to him," the old man said, nodding toward the river. "I saw him swim to Guatemala."

"So you saw him climb out of the river?" Peter asked.

"Yes."

"You seem to know a lot about him, Sir."

The old man nodded and started to walk on.

"He will bring about a great change, but you will not hear of him for some time. And when you do..." He did not finish but slowly continued walking, vanishing around the next bend of the river.

DAMIEN

Peter stared across the Usumacinta River at Guatemala. The light brown waters bore sediment from mountainous border between Mexico and Guatemala to the Gulf of Mexico. On the Guatemalan side, the jungle rose high, thickening as it climbed. At the spot where Peter had been told that Damien had climbed out of the water, the tallest of all the trees rose straight to the sky, a rare *Ceiba* tree, sacred to the Maya, joining earth and heaven. It was called the Tree of Life.

CHAPTER
THIRTY

Thea drove her mother to a tiny house on the outskirts of Ocosingo, a town about a hundred miles along the road from San Cristóbal towards Palenque. Ocosingo had been a center for the rebel forces of the Zapatistas during the uprising of the nineties, and had suffered for it. Mexican troops made sure of that.

"Oranga is getting close to a hundred, but she is still a woman of very great power." Ahmal said.

"Is she a Savonard?" Thea asked.

"No. She has no interest in social causes."

"Then why is she important to you?"

"I met her after I escaped from Guatemala. Though she was just the local bruja, she took me deeper within the Power than I have ever been. But my work for social justice was of no interest to her. This is where we parted."

"You mean to say you haven't talked to her since then?"

"That's so."

There was silence between them. Two days ago, Thea had decided to go home. She could do no more to help Damien. When she told her mother that she was leaving, Ahmal had asked to be driven to Ocosingo to see this old bruja, Oranga.

Oranga was not only a hundred years old, but a tiny ball of a woman, looked after by a girl of thirteen.

"Hello, Ahmal," said the tiny ball. "I understand you brought this New Being into the country."

"Yes. Oranga. Actually it was my daughter here, Thea, who brought him to me from the United States."

Oranga stared at Thea. "I see. And I see that your Thea has some power too, but seldom uses it."

Thea felt a flood of warmth from Oranga.

"Unfortunately," Ahmal said, "this new New Being, as you call him, has been captured by Gutteriez, and we have heard nothing more."

"Then it's time you heard more. He escaped from Gutteriez."

"He escaped?" Thea cried. "But how?"

"Anton the Astronomer can tell you."

Stooped, white-haired, and with slate grey eyes, Anton came in and sat next to Oranga.

"Anton, this is Ahmal of the Savonards and her daughter Thea who brought the New Being to Mexico. Tell them about your meeting with him," the old lady said.

"I received a message to wait for a New Being by the banks of the Usumacinta River. On my last day, I was about to give up when I heard the howler monkeys go quiet the way they do for jaguars. I turned and saw him standing there, wearing only torn shorts. Tawny and lithe, he moved forward, giving the impression of springing off the balls of his feet, though he was only walking; magnificent, like Adam must have looked to Eve.

"Who are you?" he asked in Spanish.

"Anton."

"And why are you here?"

"Waiting for you." I replied in English.

"Why?"

"I received a message telling me of a New Being."

Damien looked skeptically at me. "Explain."

"A New Being connected with the sixth transformation of the world. According to Mayan tradition, our world is mediated by cosmic rays emanating from its galaxy. It has gone through five transformations and is about to enter a sixth."

"So you received a message about the coming of a New Being from the galaxy?"

"Yes."

"Bullshit! It would take more than a lifetime for messages to travel to this planet, even transmitted by light."

"Well, you're quite wrong," I said calmly. "You're forgetting that, in quantum physics, distance is no problem for entangled particles or particle fields, no matter how separated."

"And you're an expert in decoding galactic messages?" Damien asked.

"You see," Anton continued quietly, "the identity that binds our world to the galactic center has not changed from the moment of its first formation to now, though we travel farther and farther from that center."

Damien was quiet for a moment, then said, "I misjudged you. This idea that I'm a New Being is hard to accept, though I'm entangled alright, and it is true that I am part man and part jaguar. Did you know that?"

"No, I did not know what form you would take."

"I can tell you that it has done nothing but get me into a lot of trouble. Far from being a step forward in evolution, it's a step backward, resulting in a guy who can't control his violent instincts. New Being—I'm sorry, but I'm anything but. An old being is more like it. So old, I'm primitive."

"Yes. Primitive. And the first of your kind. Hummingbird, Quetzalcoatl and jaguar."

Damien paused uncertainly, looked wonderingly at me, then turned and dove into the river, not surfacing until he was well out from shore, swimming with powerful strokes.

Anton stroked his chin, looking into the distance as he told his tale. "I saw him, finally, a small figure climbing up the far bank and plunging into the Guatemalan jungle." He shifted a little.

"And that was it."

Oranga, enveloped in her chair, nodded her tiny grey head.

"But Guatemala?" said Thea. "Petén is mostly jungle. Can he survive there?"

★★★

After their night with the Zapatistas, Danielle said nothing as they hiked back to Boca Lacantún where they had left their rented jeep. Only after they'd driven halfway to Palenque did she speak.

"We have to go after him."

Peter took a while to respond, then asked, "Where?"

"Guatemala. You said that's where he is."

Peter decided there was no point in arguing with her. She was on a quest.

"I can't go with you. I'm overdue in Vancouver. By the way, you owe me. Quite a bit."

He had to bring her back to reality. She looked gloomily out the window.

"You never took me to him."

"Oh yes I did, but Damien decided to leave us behind, after killing two young men and grievously wounding two others."

"They were probably brutal with him."

Peter could only shake his head.

They drove on toward San Cristóbal de las Casas, passing many mangled shacks by the roadside. Beyond, cattle grazed upon land owned by beef export companies. Peter didn't imagine that the local people got much work from those companies. Danielle was quiet all the way from Palenque and up the steeply winding road to Ocosingo. Finally, she spoke as they were leaving Ocosingo.

"I'm sorry," she said. "You're right, Peter. I'll never find Damien, especially now that they'll only want to kill him." She began to cry again.

★★★

Damien worked his way through the jungle, needing food but seeing nothing other than the odd bird flitting by. And then he did see something—a small lizard on a large palm leaf. Almost before thought, his hand whipped out to snatch the reptile. He twisted off its head and consumed the inside, being careful to avoid the potentially poisonous skin. The taste was surprising agreeable, so when he found another, slightly larger lizard, he ate that too.

Light was beginning to fade when Damien burst out of the jungle onto a trail where three young women were picking berries. They were startled, staring at him with fear and then curiosity when they saw he was unarmed and practically unclothed.

"Hello," he said. "Is your village nearby?" And then he remembered that they spoke no English. Each was dressed in a tunic-like, colorless piece of cloth that hung down to her knees. He tried again in Spanish. After a moment of excited chatter, one nodded at him, then they all started down the trail. Damien followed, careful not to catch up.

Their village surprised him by its size. People of all ages gathered around him as he followed the girls to an open area before a large thatched structure. An old man rose from a squat to greet Damien in halting Spanish. Everyone was dressed in sandals and garments similar to those of the girls. Clearly Damien was an object of some surprise, this young man in torn shorts appearing out of nowhere.

Damien remembered Thea telling him about the Lacandón Mayans, who had several small communities in Petén, the state on the Guatemalan side of the Usumacinta River. A middle-aged man wearing the standard tunic but distinguished by a cloth head-piece came forward and greeted Damien. He had with him a woman who spoke fluent Spanish, asking him where he came from.

Damien explained that he was American and wanted to go deeper into Petén, gesturing toward the east to emphasize his point.

The woman translated for the chief. The headman then beckoned toward the hut and Damien followed him in, and was in turn followed by the young woman who had nodded to him, and an older one who Damien guessed was the headman's wife.

They sat on matting inside, and the young woman offered baskets of tortillas and fruit. Damien helped himself. He told her his name was Damien, and she repeated it. Then she told him her name, which sounded like Yonchin. She smiled at him. She was very attractive.

After a moment she reached forward and stroked his arm.

When the headman and his wife left the hut, Yonchin closed the door.

CHAPTER THIRTY-ONE

Sam rang the bell at Eden's place on Saturday morning. He carried a large bouquet of flowers of many hues. She opened the door wearing a housecoat, hair loosely falling around her shoulders. She was not expecting him, and obviously embarrassed, yet pleased.

"Why.... Sam!" After just a moment's hesitation, she opened the door wide. "Come in, Sam. I was just doing some housework, but I am glad to see you."

He entered, wondering if his timing was a little out. He felt she liked him, but you could never be sure with women, could you?

She turned toward him in the kitchen. "Your timing is right," she said smiling at him as if she read his thoughts. "I was just about to make a pot of coffee. Now I'll make it for two."

She admired the flowers, leaned forward, and kissed him lightly on the cheek.

★★★

Danielle opened the door to her La Jolla apartment, weary from their long journey, even though they had stayed the previous night in San Cristóbal. Peter carried in her luggage and she turned to him.

"Thanks, Peter. You did your best and now it's over."

"I'm sorry we didn't find him, Danielle, but at least we found out where he had been and where he went."

She shook her head, and he felt her bleakness.

Peter was heading back to Vancouver. It was time to shake off the jungle and the figure swallowed in it.

"Just remember, Danielle, that Damien has terrific resources of mind and body. I think he'll be alright."

She looked at him. "You really think so?"

"Yes. He's remarkable. He'll come out on top." They hugged, Peter kissed her forehead and left.

Danielle stood for a long moment looking at her luggage, still determined that one day she would find Damien.

★★★

Holding the front door open, Sam stared at Peter as though he had just risen from the dead. It was a little past nine in the evening.

"Am I dreaming?"

"No, Sam it is me... Just flown in from Mexico, and headed for Vancouver in the morning."

"And the girl—I mean Danielle?"

"She's home."

"So Damien got away."

"It's all in your e-mail, Sam. I'm here to ask about Tom. I phoned and there was no answer, so I called Eden but she had no idea where Tom was; hadn't seen him for a week. She said you were there, that you visited her."

Sam smiled broadly. "I sure did."

"C'mon, Sam. Are you telling me there's something going on with you two? Of course, now that your wife has gone, why not?"

Still smiling, Sam asked. "Do you want a beer, Peter?"

"Sure do."

Sam went into the kitchen and came back with a couple of cans of Budweiser. Peter thought he looked younger somehow, that there was even a spring in his step.

"Good for you, Sam." He drank a slug of beer.

"Don't worry too much about Tom," Sam said. "I mean he's become something of a recluse. But I managed to get him to open his lab door for me. Tell you the truth I was a little surprised to see he hadn't shaved in at least a week. He told me he'd been totally focused on finding how Arnold created Damien. He's sure he has the answer. But there's a downside to it, at least from the way I look at things. He managed to find out just what kind of ayahuasca Arnold took. So he found a local source and took a dose himself. He said he was in another world for three days. And…"

There was a long pause.

"And what?"

"And he got the answer. He said it was pretty weird and he didn't want to talk about it."

"Yeah, but…." Peter thought about it. "How does he know it's the real answer, the one Arnold found?"

"I asked him that too."

"And?"

"He just said it won't be very long before he finds out. Maybe in a few months."

Peter thought about this. "Then will he let the secret out?"

"I asked him that too. And he said, "when I have the baby in my arms. Not until then.'"

"We live in amazing times, Sam."

"Amazing is one way to put it. Bloody crazy is another." He frowned into his beer can.

"Well, I`m headed back to Canada, where we think that to have babies you first have to have sex. We`re such a simple people, almost primitive—especially we Injuns."

Sam grinned at him and handed him another can of beer. "Take it slowly, Chief," he said.

★★★

Thea let herself in the front door and walked into the living room. It was after nine in the evening on a Tuesday and she knew Tom was expecting her soon, but the house felt empty. She checked the study, the kitchen, the bedroom, tripping over dirty socks and aware of the smell of old coffee. It was unlike Tom to work in his lab till late, but she went to check, and there he was huddled on one of his stools, writing. She was shocked at the sight of him. He was unshaven, his hair long and disheveled. He looked up at her. "You've come back," he said hoarsely.

"I've come back."

She put her arms around his neck and kissed him. "And I love you."

Tom's eyes were a little bloodshot. "It's funny. I knew you'd come back to me. I understood, Thea. You wanted to get Damien beyond the reach of the law."

"Yes, and I think he's there now. He's on his own, and that's what he wants."

"And you're back." Tom took Thea in his arms.

After a long embrace, Tom looked soberly at Thea.

"I talked to the lawyer. Technically, I believe you're not guilty of evading the law, Thea. Damien hadn't been charged with anything when you took him to Mexico for a visit. What happened after that was beyond your control."

"I'm *so* glad," Thea said, then kissed Tom deeply.

After another long moment, Thea looked around.

"Your lab is a bit of a mess, Tom. That's not like you."

"I've practically lived in here."

"A special project?"

"I think I have at last cracked Arnold's code. And if I have..." He paused, looking hard at her. "I'm going to produce an engineered clone, just like he did."

She drew back from him. "Don't do it," she said. "Tom, you mustn't."

He looked at her blankly. "Why not?"

She could not answer at first, unable to believe he didn't see why not.

"Thea," he said, "this is a great step forward. By what we've set in motion, the human race can be perfected—made healthier and more intelligent."

"Are you sure?"

"No, I'm not sure." He turned to look at the trees outside. "But isn't that... hasn't that always been how it works—I mean how science develops—out of uncertainty? Half the time we don't really know what we're doing, we have to feel our way. Then..." He turned back to face her. "Suddenly, we turn a corner and we are looking at something we didn't know was there. A whole new vista opens up." He was quiet, staring down at the formula he had developed. "I think I've found out how to do it. Please don't stand in the way."

The phone rang and Tom switched on the lab speaker. "Hello."

"It's Peter. I just phoned to say good-bye, Tom. I'm headed for Vancouver in the morning."

"Guess who's with me right now."

"Thea?"

"How did you know?"

"I didn't know. I guessed. Tom, I want to tell you something."

DAMIEN

"About Thea or Ahmal?"

"No. It's about Damien."

"Go ahead."

"I think you're trying create a hybrid clone like Arnold did.... Am I right?"

"Sooner or later it's going to happen, Peter."

"Damien left a trail of dead and wounded in Mexico, Tom. What Arnold released into the world wasn't an improved man but a monster. And he's alive and free in the Guatemalan jungle. Think about that... Good-bye Tom." And he was gone.

Tom turned to Thea. "I think Peter is overreacting. He calls Damien a monster."

She touched his arm. "Tom, I spent a lot of time with Damien. In one way he's a young adult trying to understand himself, and that's very human. But provoke him and then he becomes something else—not human." Thea studied Tom, seeing the struggle he was having.

"Yet you're the one who rescued him."

"I am. I thought Ahmal could help him, but I was wrong." She sat down on the stool next to him, and put her hand on his knee. "How did you figure out the formula?"

"It's not just a formula, it's also a method. It was the plant that helped me to do it, the Ayahuasca."

"Yes."

"It took me right down into itself—myself—there was no distinction."

His eyes were distant, absorbed. His voice trembled. He was not quite the Tom she had known.

"I was afraid," he said.

"Yes."

"The plants know."

"Yes."

"They know, Thea."

CHAPTER THIRTY-TWO

Damien stayed six weeks in the village with Yonchin, the young woman who had attached herself to him, and learned her Mayan tongue, which was spoken throughout much of Petén.

The village contained over 300 people who lived in thatched dwellings, each family having their own plot for maize, squash and grapes. Yonchin was one of several young women in the village who were single—that is, until she met Damien.

Yonchin had never seen a man like Damien, so lithe and strong and complete, somehow, yet with an edge that she could not resist. She stroked his chest, trailing her fingers past his manhood and down his long thigh, admiring the muscles flexing under the skin, and giggled as he turned to her yet again. Losing herself in him, she knew deep within that she was no longer alone, that she would go with him when he left, for she knew he must leave.

For his part, Damien had never experienced love as Yonchin taught him: the delight of anticipation, the pleasure of slow seduction, the simple joy of just being together. When he was with her, he wanted to be touching her. As he gained proficiency in her language, he became aware of her surprisingly dry wit, deep knowledge of the jungle and its healing plants, and insatiable curiosity about the world beyond. Her gentle care of him was a balm to his troubled soul. He ended up telling her everything, finishing miserably with his fear of his jaguar self, his fear that he might hurt even her, his anger that he couldn't just be a normal human—or a normal jaguar. Yonchin listened quietly, snuggled up against him, never withdrawing even when he admitted his freakishness, only loving him. Damien had never enjoyed such happiness with another person.

Damien did not offer to help with the cultivation of crops, but quickly proved skilled at hunting, often going out with Juarez, an older and experienced hunter. Once, when they were out in the bush, Juarez suddenly put his finger to his mouth in a shushing gesture, then pointed to the undergrowth near Damien. Half-hidden was a black jaguar. Juarez put his rifle to his shoulder and moved slowly closer, motioning Damien to get out of the way.

"Don't shoot, Juarez," Damien said, not moving. "He only wants to sniff me."

The jaguar circled closer and closer to Damien, head down, nose working, until he was less than a foot away. Juarez kept his rifle trained on the animal, noting to his surprise that his hands were trembling.

"No, Juarez," Damien said softly, "Don't."

The jaguar licked Damien's lower leg and slowly backed off, then quickly turned and disappeared into the jungle. Damien nodded to Juarez.

"Thank you," he said.

Juarez's account of the incident raced through the community. Already the villagers were aware that Damien had unusual abilities, but this incident with the jaguar was truly extraordinary.

Yonchin herself was a little uncomfortable with the way that the jungle held its breath and the howler monkeys went silent whenever she and Damien walked there. It made her nervous that there was a jaguar nearby; gradually, she got used to this, finding solace in Damien's lithe protection. She felt his rawness, knew and admired his savage soul as much as his gentleness.

Then the trader appeared on his three month round bearing news and goods such as tools, hair brushes, cheap glasses, and colored pens for writing. From him, the villagers learned that a New Being had made an impossible escape from the cave prison at Gutierrez's headquarters and swum across the Usumacinta River into Guatemala. They weren't slow to surmise that Damien was that being.

Yonchin told Damien what was being said about him. The next day Damien explained that he had to go deeper into the Petén. Otherwise, he said, the Guatemalan military would sweep down on the village and arrest him, and probably the Chief and elders too, for offering him sanctuary. The village elders concurred and made a show of sending Damien on his way.

Damien and Yonchin prepared, packing food and other essentials into a shoulder bag. They went to her grandfather, an elder of the tribe and a healer who had travelled on foot through much of Petén. He gave them his old compass and demonstrated how to use it with the map to reach a very remote village.

"You head straight east," he said, "for about 80 kilometers until you cross a trail which is more like a track, wide enough for a horse-drawn cart. Then you change your compass bearing to almost exactly north-east. After maybe 20 kilometers on that bearing you will come to a river which is not much more than a stream, called the Lagarto. Cross this and continue for 50 kilometers on this same compass bearing to another track, which is not much used. You should avoid it because it ends at a small village called Pozo Guayacan. One cannot be too careful, because the military can be found anywhere these days. Head due north through the jungle to find the river Candelario for yourself."

"Here," he said pointing to the map, "near the river you'll find Shimara's camp."

"You call it a camp, not a village?"

"Yes, and you will find out why when you get there. The military is after Shimara's group." He answered Yonchin's inquiring look. "Don't ask me why, my child. You know that the Guatemalan military have been hunting us down like vermin for more than 60 years." He turned to Damien. "I hear you are gifted, so that even the black mamba follows you. Perhaps you can help our people. You can start by looking after my granddaughter, who tells me she is going with you. Yonchin is a good girl, and gifted also. I wish she would stay with us. But she has a mind of her own. May the gods help her."

"I have told her," Damien replied, "that she would be safer with another man, that I am not suitable, always on the move, living a dangerous life." She snuggled close to him. "But you see, she doesn't listen." Damien put his arm protectively around her.

"And never will," the old man added. He turned to go. "Remember me to Shimara."

★★★

After five days, they reached a rapidly moving river which had to be the Candelario and followed it for several hours. They stopped where a small stream joined the river and removed their sandals, dangling their hot feet in the cool water. Lying on the grassy bank, Damien sensed a presence, looked at the jungle's edge and saw a jaguar, not a black one this time. It lay on its stomach, its yellow eyes watching him. He sat up.

"We have a friend nearby," he said.

Yonchin looked and jumped to her feet. "It'll attack, Damien. Dive into the river!"

But Damien shook his head.

"It won't attack, though it may follow us," he said.

Yonchin stepped carefully closer to the river. "I think we'd better go," she said, her voice quavering, "and hope it doesn't follow."

She noticed that when Damien stood up, he made a strange hand motion as if beckoning the jaguar. Yonchin clambered still closer to the river's bank, Damien accompanying her. To her astonishment, Yonchin saw that the big cat was following a few meters away, though it didn't seem to be stalking.

Even though Yonchin trusted Damien, her childhood training took hold. She tried to make Damien realize the danger, "You cannot trust a jaguar. People of the jungle know this. They will attack anything—anybody."

"Don't worry, Yonchin. She's only going to follow. Remember Juan's story? It was true. Jaguars like me for some reason. Watch."

Damien turned and walked slowly up to the jaguar, which stopped and crouched down.

"Damien! Please!"

He stepped closer until he was less than a foot from the big animal, then crouched down also and extended his hand.

Yonchin's curiosity began to overcome her fear as the jaguar gently licked Damien's hand. He said something in a low voice and the big cat stood up and nuzzled Damien.

"You see, this cat just wants to be near me. Far from wanting to harm me, we connect."

DAMIEN

And now the animal came with Damien as he slowly walked towards her. Yonchin saw that the big cat's eyes were exactly the same colour as Damien's, and in that moment she fully accepted all that Damien was.

"You're alright. She knows your fear and won't walk too close."

"I don't understand this," Yonchin murmured, wrapping her arm around his waist and snuggling close, "but like me, even the big cats—" for she dared not mention the gods, "choose you."

Damien understood the significance of Yonchin's comment. He knew that, historically, the Maya believed that certain leaders were chosen by the gods and this divine link was vital for the well-being of the race, especially in times of war. To the Olmec who were the original Mesoamericans, divinity was symbolized by the jaguar, which represented not just animal power, but the solar power which gave life to the earth. The thrones of the kings were covered with jaguar skins. Often, from birth, important people were raised with elongated jaguar-like heads, and if jaguars ravaged young virgins, they were believed to give birth to were-jaguars. Damien's reverie was interrupted by the strong smell of rifle oil and unwashed bodies and he went on the alert, touching Yonchin to warn her.

Three young men armed with rifles rose before them as they moved warily over a small hill.

"Stay where you are," one said, pointing his gun at them. Then a look of amazement came over him. "That's a jaguar!" he shouted, seeing the animal slinking back into the jungle. "That jaguar was following you!"

"I know," Damien said. "She is my friend, and you will not harm her."

The young man was lost for words.

"It is true," Yonchin said. "He is Damien and the jaguar licked him."

The young man was round-eyed with astonishment.

"I am from the village of Taunkin and my grandfather, the healer, used to visit your village. This man," she said referring to Damien, "escaped from the Mexican army and seeks refuge here."

Stealthily they surrounded him, studying him.

Finally, one of the young men said, "I think our leader had better decide about you."

He sent one of the youths to report the situation. Then they settled down to wait, the two remaining young men looking nervously over their shoulders at the jaguar eyeing them through the undergrowth.

About three hours later, the camp commander, a woman in her mid-thirties, arrived with ten armed guerrillos, three of whom were young women. Commander Shimara wore her hair bound back from her strong square face and khaki clothes loose on her attractively lean body. Her grey eyes surveyed the two visitors and then she turned to the guerrillo who had reported the arrival of the strangers.

"Where is this jaguar?"

He pointed to the jungle's edge.

She turned back to the visitors whose Lacandón garments seemed completely out of place.

"So you expect us to look after you."

Luckily she spoke the same Mayan dialect. Yonchin answered, "My grandfather Oatomako said we should come to you to escape the military police who are after my friend Damien."

Shimara looked at Damien. "Why are they after you?"

"I may have killed some soldiers when I escaped from Commander Gutteriez." Damien said calmly.

Shimara looked sharply at him, then at the animal in the jungle.

"And the jaguar?"

Yonchin looked distinctly uncomfortable. "I cannot explain it. But this jaguar licked and nuzzled him and he talked to it."

Shimara grunted, and turned to Damien. "We've heard rumors about a guy who made an impossible escape from Commander Gutteriez... and walks with jaguars. You seem pretty young for all that."

"I am young and I have much to learn," Damien said, yellow eyes steady on hers. "But perhaps I can be of some service."

Shimara stared at Damien.

"We do not live in safety and if it is safety you want, I would advise you to move on."

"Safety I do not expect ever to have again," said Damien, "but my half-sister is Mayan and I sympathize with the cause."

"You realize that we live in encampments, moving every few days."

Damien looked at Yonchin, who nodded assent. "We wish to help," he said simply.

"You are here now. Let's sleep on it and talk tomorrow." Shimara responded.

The jaguar shifted in the undergrowth.

CHAPTER
THIRTY-THREE

One night turned into a week, then two, then three, as Damien and Yonchin settled into camp life, learning about guerilla warfare and survival tactics. After the first week they found out that soldiers had smashed Shimara's baby, gang-raped and shot her, and left her for dead when they razed her village four years ago. Shimara miraculously survived the unprovoked attack, but she was irretrievably radicalized and would stop at nothing to bring down the government that supported such brutality. In the second week Damien and Yonchin realized that Shimara was trading in drugs to finance her guerilla warfare. In the third week, Shimara made plain her attraction to Damien.

Shimara had been watching Damien closely, assessing his abilities and his usefulness to the guerilla unit, and discovered to her surprise that she was quite overwhelmingly attracted to him. Since her ordeal at the hands of the soldiers, she'd had no compunction about using men to her own ends, but then none had really interested her. Her observations of Damien told her that he was a powerful potential leader and she would have to be very careful how she handled him. Then again, welcoming Damien to her bed would put Vincenze, her overly ambitious sometime lover, into his place.

Yonchin was actually looking a little the worse for wear. The life of a guerilla was hard enough without having to satisfy Damien's insatiable needs, much though she enjoyed them when she wasn't too exhausted. So when she observed Shimara's interest in Damien, Yonchin was surprised to find herself a little relieved. She was confident of Damien's love and glad of another outlet for his physical needs. Her period was late, she was more tired than usual, and feeling a little nauseous in the morning, so she was beginning to believe that she was pregnant, in spite of their precautions. She'd need to tell Damien soon.

★★★

The attack came just as dawn lit the sky. Led by Colonel Affray of the Special Forces Division, the soldiers plunged into the forested encampment, shooting as they came. Yonchin and Damien's tent was riddled with bullets. Next door, Damien held Shimara tightly while he dug into the soft ground with tremendous speed and then lay still as bullets smacked through the supply tent they were using for their rendezvous. The attacking forces swept on as ordered, guns blazing. It was a massacre.

When the troops had passed, Damien cautiously lifted the edge of the canvas and peered out. He heard the rumble of a vehicle, but no one was in sight. He touched Shimara, who lay still, breathing heavily. He ran his hand over her body and found the wound in her chest.

"I'm dying," she whispered, coughing bloody foam. "Go to Popol Vuh. First hut. Our link there—Pepe Chan Bol—only I know. Take my ring to show him. It makes you new leader. Tell him… what happened." She breathed hoarsely for a minute, and he knew she was gathering her last shards of strength.

"…betrayed… Vincenze Garcia. He's threatened by you—and he was on patrol. He'd do anything to lead, stupid idiot." She choked again. "Shoot him." She coughed blood. "Sorry, jaguar man… Sorry." Her breathing became more labored. She suddenly gripped his wrists. "Password, only leader has password. It's your name, Nah T'subi'— Special Being or Chosen One. That's why I knew it would be you. Give Pepe that word and the ring. Remember: drugs are allies, weapons to bring down the Yankee world. Now go. They will be happy to find me… dead."

Clutching his khakis, Damien crawled under the edge of the canvas and over to his and Yonchin's tent. He found her corpse on their blood-spattered mattress, bowed his head into her chest and cried. Tears streaming down his face, Damien grabbed his emergency bag, heaved Yonchin's still warm body over his shoulders and crawled for the jungle.

As usual he had set their tent away from the others and close to the thick jungle, in the hope that his jaguar friend would stay nearby. And she had stayed until the shooting, then melted into the deep forest. When Damien had crawled some distance into the thick vines, he climbed a tree and stashed Yonchin's body where no other predators could reach her. Then he put on his khakis and pulled out his compass and map. He could hear shouting and the occasional shot from the encampment. He knew they would be searching for Shimara, and would widen the search when they found her headquarters empty.

Swiftly he opened the map and found Popol Vuh. Getting there was slow going, screams and gunfire fading behind him. At last his jaguar joined him. He welcomed the animal, stroking her head and making the deep throat sounds that she liked. Then he continued on his way, the jaguar by his side.

DAMIEN

At last he came upon a jeep trail of the sort frequented by adventure tour companies. Damien kept to the side, ready to be enfolded by the jungle if he heard traffic coming his way, and his jaguar friend melted further into the jungle. After an hour and a quarter's walk he came across a small trail marked with a half hidden sign: Figurines and Carvings, with the name Pepe Chan Bol beneath. Less than a hundred paces in, Damien found Pepe's shed where he lived and worked. Pepe was sitting on a bench outside, diligently carving a small piece of wood. He was somewhere in his fifties, with a scraggly greyish beard and short, sturdy body. Damien paused, almost overwhelmed by the peacefulness of this scene after the horror he had just experienced. Pepe looked up.

"Hello," he said. "Are you interested in original carvings?" And then he paused, studying Damien. "Somehow I do not think so."

Damien squiggled the ring from his finger. "I am to show you this."

"What's happened?" Pepe said looking sharply at the ring and then at Damien.

"The encampment was ambushed before dawn. Shimara was killed, and also I think most of the others."

Pepe set aside the carving, peering searchingly at the young man in front of him. "Shimara… dead?"

"Shot. At dawn. She said Vincenze Garcia betrayed us."

"I know of him. He was often with her."

"No longer," Damien said. "And she gave me this ring to show you."

"Why you?"

"My name is Nah T'subi'."

There was a long silence. Pepe stared at Damien. At last, he said: "Do you know what you are saying?"

"Yes." Damien turned his head and then pointed to the jungle just beyond the clearing, not fifty meters away. There sat his jaguar, ears up, looking with full attention at Damien.

Pepe took off his glasses so that he could see what was in the distance. He stared, unbelievingly.

"You?" He finally asked. "You are the Chosen One? You?"

"Yes." There was another pause. "Shimara told me to kill the traitor."

Slowly Pepe came to himself, and nodded. "Yes," he said, "you must do that."

"And you will help me, Pepe. You know that any survivors will be gathering at Popol Vuh. Vincenze will be among them because he was out on patrol when the soldiers came. Get him to come here."

"Okay," Pepe said. "He will be looking for the link."

"The link?"

"To the drug cartel. For this the army will reward him handsomely." He shook his head sadly. "It was Shimara's only fault, her weakness for handsome young men... like you."

He turned on Damien suddenly, pulling a knife from nowhere. "Have you ever killed a man?"

"Yes." Damien said calmly, catching Pepe's wrist and forcing him to drop the knife. Looking Pepe in the eye, Damien released his wrist.

Pepe picked up the knife and put it away. "We'll see."

Pepe looked at the jaguar still seated at the jungle's edge. "I will not be here when Vincenze comes. He will come alone expecting only me, but he will have troops at the road. Get out of here fast after you're done."

Pepe gestured to Damien. "Now come inside and I will instruct you on what you must do to contact the Cartel and gain its full support," he said, looking up at Damien, "young as you are."

★★★

Vincenze appeared the next morning about nine and knocked on the door. Damien opened it and waited in the shadow for Vincenze to step in before he punched him hard in the stomach.

Vincenze fell to the floor, gagging.

"What!" he gasped. "You!"

"Yes, me. And I will have your handgun," said Damien, ripping the shirt and holster from Vincenze's chest. "Now," he said, "you will listen."

But Vincenze hurled himself at Damien's lower legs. Damien cupped one hand under Vincenze's right shoulder and pulled him to his feet.

"Shimara died in agony, as you no doubt know by now. But before she died she asked me to take command and to kill you."

Vincenze, who regarded himself as an expert fighter, swung fiercely at Damien, but found only empty air.

Damien hit him hard on the chin, knocking him out. Then he carried the limp figure out the back door, down a short pathway to the edge of the jungle, dropped him there, and gave a high whistle. Within a minute the jaguar stood beside him. Damien kicked the inert figure in the ribs, and the jaguar wrapped her jaws around Vincenze's head, her fangs sinking deep.

When army personnel eventually came looking for Vincenze, they found the house empty, and finally discovered his half eaten corpse at the back edge of the property. They concluded that Vincenze, searching for Pepe, had gone into the back area and been attacked by a jaguar. They were right.

DAMIEN

CHAPTER THIRTY-FOUR

Following the instructions given him by Pepe, Damien visited a restaurant in the western part of the town of Flores, an area which tourists are warned to avoid because of the lawless youths wandering the streets. But the youths are not in charge there. The real criminals are the lords of the drug cartel called, "Manna from Heaven."

The restaurant looked run-down, with a few thick wooden tables spattered with coffee stains. There was also a smallish counter with four tall chairs. Damien handed a note from Pepe to the young man behind the bar, who studied it, looked up at Damien, then turned and went into a back room. He returned followed by a middle-aged man with a slight limp. Damien handed him another note of Pepe's. He was gestured into the back room and the man introduced himself as Mario. The younger man took up his post at the door, hands clasped in front.

"You come introduced by Pepe and wearing the ring of command. What do you want?" asked Mario abruptly.

"As Pepe may have told you, Shimara died before she could introduce me to your organization. I need you to brief me."

"But this is strange. You are very young and very American. You do not belong here. Yet the jaguar follows you and you are rumored to be the Chosen One." Mario looked warily at him, the tension grew and the young guard's hand hovered near his holster.

"I too am pursued by the law." Damien said.

"This I know. For the murder of a young woman in America and many murders since. You're a dangerous and impulsive outlaw, not a man to be trusted with command."

"I do not believe that I killed that girl, and the other murders were for survival. Shimara knows—knew—my value. I do not need to prove it to you."

"You fled; you are guilty."

"That's no proof. Have you never been falsely accused? My Yonchin is dead. Shimara is dead. I have no love for the government. You need me."

The older man shook his head. "That is not enough. You must be committed to our cause."

"What cause? You deal drugs."

A vein in Mario's temple pulsed. "To a greater end."

"What greater end? Drugs just destroy people."

"So do bullets and bombs."

"And your point is?"

"We've been shot—mowed down by the thousands—for trying to prevent the so-called developed world from taking our metals, our oil, our forests, our crops, our labour, and our lives."

"So you have the rebel army. That I'm offering to help with."

"But money is now the strongest weapon. With money we can fight back, buy back our land and businesses, buy votes in Congress, underwrite rotten mortgages. Billions of dollars in drug profits poured into destabilizing the economies that have made our lives hell."

"That's fiendish!"

"Says the murderer from a wealthy home!"

They faced off. Then, Damien consciously took a deep breath and leaned back slightly.

Mario said, "The drugs are just a means to an end. We know that. We don't want to actually destroy America. We want to cut it down to size. We want a fair deal."

"A fair deal," Damien said. "I'd like that too."

★★★

Damien spent four months in a training camp in the wilds of Belize near the Yucatán, where there were no Mexican or Guatemalan armed forces. Headquarters were underground in a system of limestone caves which stretched for miles. He and the other young people being prepared for leadership spent eight to nine hours a day learning combat; at least three or four of those hours were in the jungle. He was surprised at the sophistication of the weaponry, including RPGs for bringing down helicopters. In the evening, those from different linguistic backgrounds were tutored in Spanish and English. They slept under the stars at night. Including himself, they were thirty-six, of whom eleven were women. Damien spent only the first two nights alone.

On the last day of their training they met in a large cave, greeted by three training supervisors and a commander from one of the cartel's forces operating in the Yucatán. The commander talked for over two hours about the realities of the drug trade, explaining that each guerrilla combat unit is run by a cartel member who is in constant communication with headquarters regarding the movements of government forces.

At the end of the session, each participant was met by a representative of the cartel to which they were assigned. A female commander was approaching Damien when he heard a voice from his left, "Not her, Amigo, though she is beautiful."

It was Mario, whom he hadn't seen for months.

"Sorry to interrupt," Mario said in Spanish, "but you must come with me. You did very well, I'm told—one of the best—even in Spanish. Did you make love, too, in Spanish?"

"When making love, Mario, there is no language."

"And now we go where there are no beautiful women, sorry to say."

Damien grinned at him. "And why would I want to go there?"

"You will find out."

They emerged from the cave, and walked down a narrow jungle trail to a clearing where a helicopter sat. Greeting the pilot, they climbed in, and were soon airborne.

"We would not chance this in Mexico, or even Guatemala, but in Belize it is a different matter."

In less than twenty minutes they descended on the roof of a mansion on the Honduran coast.

"An important man wants to meet you. He is Mexican, originally from Oaxaca. He's on that deck down there."

The three men sipped strong Mexican coffee in a wide-windowed room which seemed to shake slightly under a buffeting wind from the Gulf. Their host was Domingo Savarano, a man in his mid-forties of medium height with brown eyes unusually flecked with blue, and hair slightly silted with grey. When he shook Damien's hand he held onto it and stared deeply into the young man's yellow eyes.

"So you are the one," he said in his deceptively gentle voice.

"The one?"

"Yes, the one everyone talks about."

"They must mean someone else."

"No. They mean you. I have heard a lot about you—how you escaped from Gutteriez's cave after killing or disabling your four guards though you were unarmed. And then how the old man Anton met you on the bank of the Usumacinta and recognized you as the New Being. How you swam like a shark across the river and disappeared into Guatemala. How you were welcomed by a jaguar and lived in a Lacandón village. How you went into the jungles of the Petén and found that marvellous woman Shimara, and executed her traitor. And how the women love you. All the signs are there."

He stopped, waiting.

"Who are you?" Damien asked.

"Ah. Well, you already know my name. Now, for my function in life: it is to guide the various groups, the cartels and their associates, into a functioning and effective single force working for a single cause. I'm a kind of Chief of Staff. That is the reason I have brought you here. Because you will play a vital role in my plan of action, if you are capable, as I believe you are." He said these last words with great emphasis. "Young as you are, hardly more than a boy, you fit the image of the great Mayan leader who took command when he was very young. But mere ability is not enough. You must stand for something that is precious beyond dispute." His grey eyes measured Damien. "From now on you will have a special name: Nah T'subi', which means chosen one."

Damien could take no more and stood up restlessly. "Stop right there. There is nothing supernatural about me. I'm just a byproduct of my father's scientific ambition."

"We know," Savarano said. "But at the same time, you are the first of your kind and you do fit the prophecies."

Damien could not help his upsurge of feeling. "I can't help that. I can see how my jaguar god image can benefit your cause and I can see why you need the drug money to further this cause, but I cannot see how bringing down the American economy will lead to a better world."

Savarano beckoned Damien to sit down again.

"Stopping economic exploitation will lead to a better world, though," Savarano pointed out. "Principled Americans naturally think selling illicit drugs to teenagers is a disgusting practice, and it is, but they choose not to see the economic exploitation in the developing world that supports their way of life."

He sighed and reached for a glass of water.

"Let's get to the main point: why I have brought you here. You will be my military commander. You will command a superbly equipped battalion together with air support. An experienced officer will help you plan and direct operations. You will report directly to me."

"I see what you're up to," said Damien after a moment. "These special missions will be highly publicized, and my leadership as the 'Special Being' will soon galvanize public opinion in Mexico. I will become your hero."

"That's it," Savarano said. "So long as you remember."

"Remember what?"

"You have been taught to obey, and you will obey."

"Of course," Damien said and then added, "Sir."

Savarano smiled. "Good lad."

Damien looked out the window, wondering what he'd gotten himself into.

CHAPTER THIRTY-FIVE

"Hi, Sam," Peter Gregory said. "I'm up here in Dawson City, heart of the Klondike, to protect the Mayor. He thinks that he is about to be kidnapped and held for ransom. Anyway, I got a call from Danielle before I left Vancouver. She tells me you're going to be married—to Eden no less. That's great Sam. She's a fine woman."

"Probably too fine for me, Peter. But thanks."

"And how are things going for Thea and Tom?"

"They seem happy. Thea managed to talk Tom into putting off his attempt to create another clone using Dr. Head's method. But one of these days, I think he's going to try it anyway. He knows if he doesn't, somebody else will."

"Have you heard anything about Damien?"

"Yes. He's led several attacks in Mexico, most recently on a big rally for the President. It's in all the papers down here. He goes by a funny name—Nah T'subi'. It's Mayan; means the Chosen or Special One. But the word is he's no Mayan."

"It's Damien for sure."

"What makes you so sure?"

"I met an old man at the Usumacinta River who'd seen a young guy in shorts come out of the jungle and swim the river—unfazed by the crocodiles. I think it was Damien. The old guy called him the Chosen or New Being."

Sam gave a sigh. "Okay. Chosen or New—whatever. At least he's not our problem now. Probably he'll be gunned down soon by some Mexican military goon. And good riddance."

"You have any cases you want my help with?"

"Not right now. But if I find any more bodies in trees, I'll let you know."

"I'm asking because Danielle wants me to come down there and take her into Guatemala to find Damien. She says she knows a way to save him. She's going down there with or without me."

"It'd be great if you did come down here. I can even offer you a spare bedroom in our new house."

"You've bought a new home?"

"Sure. One of those mortgage failures."

"Lucky man. Up here we've never heard of a mortgage; we just build our own homes out of logs or animal skins or snow."

"That's another world. Hey!"

"What?"

"A message just came through that Commandante Nah T'subi' has just attacked a military base near Tlaxcala, forty miles outside of Mexico City. What the hell is going on?! Gotta go." The line went dead.

★★★

They landed their helicopters in the middle of the town square. The firing remained heavy for perhaps fifteen minutes, after which there was no more resistance from the few government troops and police.

With a few of his men, Commandante Damien Nah T'subi went into the City Hall and up to the first floor balcony. There, facing a gathering crowd, he ordered the revolutionary flag raised. It was a green flag centered by a black panther. Standing next to Louisa Patrone, another revolutionary leader, Damien grasped her hand and they raised their arms high. The people responded with cheers. Then he spoke excellent Spanish into a microphone.

"Soon," he said, "the people of Mexico will be free and will live with the prosperity denied them while the nation's wealth went to the favored sons of the few. We will restore this country to its people." There were cheers.

Then Louisa Patrone spoke. She was thirty-seven years old and a seasoned fighter. She'd been brought up on a farm by a Mayan mother and a Mestizo father. When she was twenty, she'd married a young farmer, Raoul, whose parents owned a small plantation in Guatemala. So when his father died, he moved with Louisa and their newborn baby girl to Guatemala and the family farm. Sometime in 1989 the killing resumed. Raoul's father had been careful during the earlier periods of violence to pay off the commanders of the government forces, but Raoul knew nothing about this. So one morning on a rainy day, troops broke into the farmhouse, shot Raoul, bayoneted the baby, tied and raped Louisa, and left her for dead.

For a while Louisa had worked with Ahmal but, finding the Savonard preference for non-violence unacceptable, she became an officer in Gutteriez's revolutionary force. Before long, Louisa realized that the only forces that could and did outgun the government troops were those of the drug cartels. Through a woman friend of the Sinaloa Cartel she met Domingo Savarano, who offered her a position as assistant commanding officer of a battalion in which about half the combatants were young women. The officer in command was Damien, who was proving himself superbly effective in action. She'd heard his title of Special Being and made fun of him, but he didn't seem to mind

Last night, Damien had invited her into his tent to discuss the next day's action plan. He was seated on his cot in shorts, for it was a hot summer night. Holding a map, he rapidly went over the plan which had been worked out the previous day. But then he suggested a change in the operation which took her completely by surprise. The enemy would not know what had hit them.

And Louisa realized that she didn't know what had hit her either, because quite suddenly she was more than interested in this young man, and he looked very young indeed.

"Oh, yes," she murmured, putting her hand on his lower arm as though to move the map to see it better.

Damien needed no further prompting. In a moment, his lips were on hers as he ripped her shirt off. She would never forget that night. For a long time after the rapes, she could not have sex, but with time she had the odd careful affair. But the next few hours with Damien were on a different dimension, an erotic plane she had never reached before. When the love-making was finally over Louisa, too, was sure Damien was special.

And in her speech, Louisa did not neglect to remind the crowd that this victory in Tlaxcala was due to Damien's brilliant leadership. Louisa and Damien had just turned to go inside for a final briefing after the speeches, when a young officer hurried up to Damien.

"Mexican Army Group 11 has helicoptered three hundred troops just north of Tlaxcala and another six hundred are coming in trucks. They'll join the first group in less than an hour."

"Good," Damien said. "I expected them."

"But there's also a relief force of at least six hundred coming in from the south, near Puebla. So we'll be surrounded."

"I expected that too."

"Did you really?" asked José, the experienced officer Domingo Savarano had appointed to advise Damien.

"Yes. They've been trained on military textbooks. So it's easy to figure out what they're going to do."

"And what do we do? We're very few."

"Yes... sixty-three to be exact."

"So we'd better get out of here before it's too late." In agitation, José turned to give the order.

"José!" Damien's voice of command stopped him. "Remember old Pedro? The one you didn't want to include in this raid? He's got a secret passageway under his house where we are all going to hide right now while the government forces waste a lot of ammunition moving in."

"But then we're trapped."

Damien smiled at Louisa. "Only until the attack of the twelve hundred troops we have in the hills beyond."

José looked stunned. "You mean you've encircled the encirclers?"

"That's it, and we attack from the centre as soon as the perimeter is fully engaged so the Mexicans get shafted inside and out. We'll teach them what war can be when you use your brains and throw away the textbook."

José stared at him. "You're crazy."

"Crazy works," Louisa said.

There was a knock on the balcony door. Damien opened it to Pedro of the drooping white moustache.

"Are you coming?" he said. "Everybody's at my place. We're ready to go."

"Go ahead, Pedro. We're coming."

At Pedro's, they waited as the last of the armed men and women silently descended to the cellar of the house, stooping to squeeze through the hole in the wall and follow the passageway. Pedro slipped in after Damien and slid a panel across the opening. He turned to Damien.

DAMIEN

"If you looked at this wall from the other side I doubt you could make out the aperture."

Damien smiled.

"You did all this yourself?"

"I have many talents," Pedro said, "most of them unused. My mother told me I could be a great man. But when I asked her what I could be great at, she didn't answer. Come along, Commandante."

So they went by flashlight through forty-five feet of twisting tunnel, crawling on all fours to the main cavern, which was more than ten feet in height and provided a wide open space.

"This is where I hid my drugs," Pedro said. "It provided more than enough space. It was by pure chance I found the cave, and I doubt there is another one like it. But in Mexico you never know."

"Well, we're lucky to have you, Pedro, and your many talents. I think your mother was right and you will be remembered as a great man."

Louisa took Damien's hand. "I've brought sleeping bags. It's 10:00 PM, so we have to be up in six hours. I want to remember these six hours."

"I think we both will," Damien said softly.

★★★

The Mexican army commanders assumed that there would be at least a hundred enemy insurgents occupying the town, and that they would either escape by helicopter or fight it out. Either way, the soldiers expected an easy victory providing good press for the government cause.

They were completely unprepared for being themselves encircled, and they retreated toward the centre of town, fighting hard, only to discover their backs exposed to insurgents flooding from below ground. The Mexican army simply fell apart, many laying down their arms and others fleeing to tell the tale of Nah T'subi. Over 600 Mexican troops were killed and four attack helicopters shot down. Damien ordered the execution of several top officers who had been taken prisoner. This last action shocked everyone, even his crime bosses. And yet, to the public, the Tlaxcala battle had rapidly become a symbol of the power of this Special Being, spoken of in hushed tones everywhere.

CHAPTER THIRTY-SIX

They met in an abandoned farmhouse not far from Ocosingo, once a center of Mayan power: Ahmal, Oranga, Anton the Astronomer, and Commander Gutteriez.

Gutteriez, whose slight stoop betrayed his age, began, "Danielle, that American woman who was looking for Damien last year, is coming back with her private detective to look for Damien again. She wants to take him out of the country, into hiding. Do you think they could persuade him to leave?"

"I have my doubts. I've asked Damien to meet with me, but he has not responded," Ahmal said.

Gutteriez observed, "Damien is a deadly young man, and on top of that, very intelligent and resourceful. No ordinary unarmed man could have overpowered four commando guards and escaped from that cave as he did. Now he is the military commander for Domingo Savarano, the drug coalition Director, and has access to virtually unlimited funds and all the latest military hardware. Domingo believes he can control Damien, but I am not so sure."

Ahmal added, "His exploits—I should say his victories—have made him important to the cartels, but that's nothing beside his public image as a triumphant Special Being who promises a new dawn for Mexico."

Gutteriez looked at Ahmal, "You were involved with him from the beginning, were you not? You must know his weaknesses."

Ahmal looked down.

"I did help the American doctor get the information he needed to create Damien."

"Create him?!" Gutteriez asked in astonishment.

"Yes, he's a clone; a copy of the doctor's human genes plus a few jaguar genes for strength and speed. He truly is the first of his kind. And I believe his seed will revitalize the Mayan people."

"Then this is worse than I feared," Gutteriez said heavily. "If even an intelligent woman like yourself believes this nonsense."

Ahmal thought but did not speak of the ten women who had all become pregnant by Damien in those two magical nights when Thea first brought him to her.

"But I did not anticipate such a situation as this," she added.

"That explains why Damien is so extraordinary, of course." Anton said. "But doesn't Damien's destabilization of the regime further your own revolutionary aims, Commander Gutteriez?"

"To a degree, yes. But Damien is controlled—so far—by the cartels, who want only money and power. We Zapatistas seek to bring power back to the people." Gutteriez responded.

"As you know, I believe in spiritual not military revolution," Ahmal said, "but this man-jaguar warlord dangerously combines ancient myth with brutal reality and seems to have no moral compass. The damage he could do to our countries and our cause is incalculable. He's out of control."

"And he must be stopped," stated Commander Gutteriez. "In my view, there is only one way." He looked around at the others.

No one spoke. Ahmal's heart raced unexpectedly, though she was not an excitable person. She swallowed, and said, "I don't believe he can be persuaded to go into hiding as Danielle desires. It has gone too far."

"If we imprison him, he becomes a martyr, and we can't have that." Gutteriez pointed out. "He must die."

Old Woman Oranga lifted her tiny head. "We will anger the gods. They sent this Special Being to us."

Anton the Astronomer nodded. "In fighting under the drug lords this young man does not cease to be a Special Being. The powers of the galaxy have marked him as their own... to carry out their destiny... their goals for the earth. We can do nothing about that. Any attempt to kill him must fail."

"To the gods," the Old Woman said, "the wars of humans mean little—crime and criminals are phhttt." She made a gesture of dismissal with her hands. "What matters is surrender to the gods. They want our lives, hence this sacrifice of blood."

Though Ahmal had learned much from Old Woman Oranga, she did not believe that the gods actually thirsted for human blood. When the Aztec priests tore the hearts out of sacrificial victims, it was not the blood that mattered but the total submission to the will of the gods.

"If you two are right about Damien and the gods, all any of us can do is follow our destinies, however they intersect with Damien's." Ahmal said sadly.

★★★

Ahmal and Gutteriez met the following day to plan Damien's removal.

"It must look like an accident, or he will be a martyr." Gutteriez noted. "And he must be surprised, or it will become an ugly fight."

"We need to find a time when his guard is down," agreed Ahmal. "Your point about preventing martyrdom is important."

Gutteriez mused, "He's not afraid to capitalize on the ancient myths. Could we somehow take advantage of that?"

They paused, contemplating their task. Ahmal looked out the window at the distant hills, the encroaching jungle, and the well in the yard, chickens pecking in the dust and an old yellow dog lying in the shade.

"A cenote celebration like the one at Chichén Itzá!" Ahmal exclaimed. "It's perfect. Damien can be thrown into the well, the bravest and most powerful warrior offered to the gods, whose sacred sacrifice means he will not die, though we will never see him again, just as in ancient times."

Gutteriez added, "We can make it look like an offering made *by* Damien of himself, not an offering *of* Damien."

"We should do it at the traditional cenote in the selva espinosa. It's narrow and very deep, impossible to escape and not well known to tourist cave divers."

Gutteriez settled down to working out the mechanics of the event, so that, while seeming to make an offering to the gods, Damien himself would be plunged into the roughly 75 foot depth of the well to certain death. And the water at the bottom of the well would still taste as pure as it always had, despite the many offerings over the centuries, due to the swiftly running stream at its base.

Ahmal communicated with Savarano, to arrange cooperation of the Savonards with the renowned Nah T'subi' in the ancient celebration.

★★★

Six days later, Damien took a helicopter to Savarano's yacht off the coast of Belize.

"The Mexicans are so anxious to catch you," Savarano said to Damien, "that I couldn't ask you to my house. Every road to my place is being watched. And they have made a deal with the government of Belize whereby they can search my house whenever they want. I think I know the man they paid off, and he will not have much time to regret it."

Damien smiled. "I didn't know you could be like that. You speak so mildly, and you're so, well.... civilized."

Savarano tipped his head back and laughed. "So you thought you were safe with me."

"Well... I hoped so."

Savarano became serious. "I wish it could be so. Really... You're like the son I always wanted. Instead, I have three daughters."

He smiled again, and then the smile vanished. "But we are not here to discuss what we would like; only what we have to do to stay on this merry-go-round."

He paused and sat down, pointing at a chair nearby.

"You've become important to us, as I'm sure you know, but to a degree we hadn't anticipated. Your symbolic value to the people as the Special Being has become as important as your warrior value."

He took a sip from a glass of water on a small table beside him.

"Maybe even more so, and that creates a problem for us. Your Special Beingness has the power to transform the country, making you our Trojan Horse in the political world."

He paused taking another sip of water, then was silent for a moment, looking down.

"I've heard from Ahmal, leader of the Savonards."

Damien looked up.

"Yes, you know her, of course. You wouldn't believe how that little fuckfest at her hideaway spawned a tornado of lustful speculation throughout the country. Wonderful! Don't misunderstand me—I don't trust this bitch Ahmal. She's too clever, and has got everyone believing she's a pure peace lover."

Damien grunted.

"So what does she propose? ...That you start your political life in a grand way that glorifies the indigenous heart of Mexico, with you, Nah T'subi', being the centerpiece. Got it?" Savarano seemed to actually want a response this time.

"How?"

"But you don't get it. How can you? She wants to use you for her cause, to transform you into a symbol of peace. I know what you are going to say, so say it."

"I can't afford to go public. I'm a wanted man—wanted for murder. She must be crazy."

"Why crazy?"

"To think I would go for that."

"But you will go for that, and she knows it."

"Are you serious?"

"Totally... Now listen to me." Savarano stood up and walked slowly around the room, stopping in front of Damien. "She knows that whatever your achievements are, we made you what you are now, and you accepted that, even going to school to learn the art of war. Without us you would still be a fugitive or—far more likely—facing the death penalty. So you're going to do what we tell you." He stared at Damien.

"And what's that?"

"You'll disguise yourself in Mayan traditional ceremonial costume and go to this sacred event at the cenote. You'll be protected by our men and one of them will hand you a bag containing the offering as you come to the edge of the sacred well. When the signal is given, pull out the offering, hold it high for a photo op, then drop it ceremoniously into the well. After that, board the helicopter and come here to celebrate. Do you understand?"

"What do I throw into the well?"

"You will find out when you do it. I'm sure that it won't bother a young killer like you."

DAMIEN

CHAPTER THIRTY-SEVEN

Peter sat across from Danielle in the crowded café, trying to understand why he had agreed to come on this crazy quest for Damien. The fat fee Danielle was paying was nice, but Peter realized that he was fascinated by Damien. Although the lad was exceptional in many ways, the real mystery was how the jaguar and human elements could coexist in one being.

That old man by the river who had told Peter about Damien's escape and vanished, mumbling something about Damien being a Special Being who would change the world, could easily have been dismissed as just another case of dementia, but Peter knew better. In a strange way the old guy made sense, all the more so because he was a scientist. Let's accept for the moment, Peter said to himself, that Damien wasn't just Dr. Head's scientific achievement. Could there have been a greater power at work? What were the odds that an obscure Mayan girl like Ahmal would play such a major role in Damien's creation or herself become a powerful spiritual and political leader? What were the odds that Damien would return to her, that he'd escape the FBI and CIA, survive the jungle and a massacre by the Mexican military to eventually become a drug cartel military leader worshipped by the people of Mexico and

Guatemala? If the gods didn't have a hand in all that, Peter would sure like to know who did.

A man was standing beside their table looking down at them.

"Hello," he said in reasonable English, looking at Danielle, "I am Emmanuel and I believe you wish to meet someone."

"Yes, we do," Peter said, looking at his watch. It was 2:00 PM, so this must be General Gutteriez' man. Realizing that their best chance of finding Damien would probably be through General Gutteriez, Peter had called the private number Gutteriez had given him the year before.

"Just follow me."

Emmanuel led them to a parked car in the lane, and they drove off, turning and doubling back unexpectedly to avoid being followed, eventually ending up on the highway to Ocosingo.

"The Commander is expecting you at 3:00 PM, and we have a little way to go. I believe you have already met Commander Gutteriez," Emmanuel said. He was a man in his early forties, small but not squat. His command of English suggested that he was well-educated.

"We met him over a year ago," Peter replied.

"Yes, when you were looking for Nah T'subi'."

"He was only called Damien, then," Peter couldn't help saying. As he watched the passing landscape, Peter began to think of their journey thus far.

In Mexico City, they'd stayed with Danielle's friends, Professor Bernini and his wife, who were sad because they were returning to America. They felt that Mexico was rapidly turning into a narco-state, where corruption and violence ruled. They regarded Damien's rise to eminence with cynicism, as an example of how criminals subvert youthful talent. Despite the best efforts of its President, the

US, they felt, was also in trouble, but at least it could still be regarded as basically a lawful country struggling to live by its democratic ideals. After all that negativity, Peter and Danielle couldn't wait to say goodbye.

Danielle's spirits didn't lift until last night at the hotel in San Cristóbal. From the street the hotel looked old and dingy, but inside it opened onto a garden of flowering trees and a large fountain in which innumerable tropical birds were bathing and chirping with wild joy. Their room opened onto this Eden, which reminded them of the lovely converted nunnery in Mexico City. They had a Margarita each, then another, and talked late into the night about the cultural effects of cloning. Eventually they had stumbled to their rooms and slept.

"Have you given up talking to me?" Danielle asked, casting a sidelong look at Peter.

"No, just thinking about last night's conversation," Peter grinned at her as they were driven into a gated residence outside Ocosingo.

Emmanuel identified himself to the guard, and they were led upstairs to an office room where Gutteriez sat. Rising, he shook their hands and invited them to sit down.

"I suppose you know why we are here, Commander," Danielle said.

"Are you still hoping to get Damien out of the country?" Gutteriez had clearly not lost his fascination with Danielle's breasts, especially now that she was wearing a light summer top.

"Yes." Danielle said, "I think Damien is working for the drug cartels only because he has no alternative, but I can offer him one—if I can get to see him."

"Can you help us with that?" Peter asked.

"Believe me, if I could help you I would." Gutteriez spread his hands in a gesture of helplessness. "But the

DAMIEN

cartels have reorganized themselves in a way that defies all hope of communication."

"All hope?" Peter asked.

"For anyone outside their organization... yes."

"Do they never communicate with anyone else?"

"Only when they initiate it."

There was a pause. Peter leaned forward.

"I want to emphasize something my employer said," Peter nodded in Danielle's direction. "What she has in mind for Damien is his disappearance forever from the world scene. He will no longer be a problem for you or the Savonards, because he will be gone for good."

Gutteriez rubbed his hands, thinking hard.

"There is a possibility," he said slowly. Then he stood up and began to pace, struggling with his words. Peter could almost feel the thought waves emanating from his brain.

"There is a possibility," he repeated, looking at Peter "Do you know what a cenote is? No? It is a well, but in a dry country like Mexico a cenote is not just a hole in the ground filled with fresh water. It is sacred, and sacrifices have always been made at wells to give thanks to the water god. The cenote at Chichén Itzá, for example, has absorbed many sacrifices, including human ones, over the centuries."

He stopped pacing to look hard at Danielle.

"Now in five days there is to be a special ceremony at a cenote in the selva espinosa—the spiny forest. Disguised in Mayan traditional dress, your friend Damien will be making a ceremonial offering."

Danielle looked triumphantly at Peter.

"Yes," Gutteriez said. "But remember, you must tell no one else. If the word gets around, his helpers will know, and he will not appear. If you can persuade him to accept your plan for his escape before he makes his offering, then it may be possible to save him. Otherwise…" Gutteriez spread his hands and shrugged sadly.

"Oh thank you!" Danielle exclaimed. "Don't worry, we won't tell anyone anything. Thank you!"

"If he agrees," Gutteriez said, "you'd better have a helicopter close by to get him far away and fast. The cartel men around him will kill him before they'll let him go."

"Do you have any suggestions for how we get close enough to him?" asked Peter.

"You'll need to figure that one out yourselves," said the General with a thin smile.

After Danielle and Peter had left, Gutteriez phoned Ahmal and told her what he'd proposed to Danielle and Peter.

"This way if they get Damien to agree to go with them, he'll be shot by his own people. They'll do our job for us."

Ahmal took this in. "Good for you, Commander, I just hope it works that way."

★★★

Peter came suddenly awake, aware there was someone at the door. He stumbled to it, peered through the hole to see Danielle and opened it to let her in.

"You okay?" He mumbled.

"Not really." Danielle moved to the window to stare at the slim light of dawn growing in the sky.

"What's wrong?"

"I couldn't sleep thinking about Damien. I can't believe that he's really going to be there on Friday."

"Yes… but you might find him changed from what you remember. He's older and… well… experienced."

"I know. I expect him to be changed. But not… essentially."

DAMIEN

"Danielle, you said you have a place to take him where he'll be safe. Where is that?"

"It's an island off the coast of Turkey. It's very small, but I own it, so there's no one else. I'm sure he'll be safe there."

"Do you think he'll be happy all alone like that, though, even if you're there?"

There was silence between them.

Peter got up and hugged her.

"I thank you for all you've done, Peter. And I've grown fond of you. But..."

"I know." He wanted to say more about the danger, the likelihood of failure, but he could not.

She turned to him. "You think this is crazy, don't you?—the whole quest to save Damien... and you're probably right, but I have to do it."

She turned to stare out the window again. "I know you don't understand, and never will, really. But this much I will say. To me, Damien is a god. He is like the sum of powers mental and physical. That's what he is—I know it—truly a sun god." She turned to Peter again. "And here's what's amazing to me. He's a clone of a human and a jaguar, which is like going down the evolutionary ladder, isn't it? The way we were... before we evolved into humans. I thought a lot about it, Peter. And I've studied it too. After all, I'm an organic chemist and I know something about genetics. The fact is, with one exception, Damien is not a reversion to the animal ... that is, less than human—no. He's brought the animal back up the ladder. He's added it to us."

"What do you mean? How?" Peter asked.

"In our evolutionary progress we've lost much of our animal selves. So our sense of smell doesn't compare with animals. We used to sense a pressure change that meant a tsunami, but modern humans have lost that ability as well as many other ways of knowing and sensing. Damien has recovered all that without any loss of intelligence. So he's superior to us, more complete, and that's why we can't tolerate him."

"But, Danielle, he's also retained the hunting abilities and the instincts of a jaguar."

"You mean his acceptance of violence."

"Yes."

"I agree. To us, this is a problem." She frowned. "And yet..."

He waited. She looked at him. "Human progress has always depended on violence."

"You're serious."

"Yes, I am. Think about it."

CHAPTER THIRTY-EIGHT

The celebration at the cenote took place at sunset on Friday, hosted by the Savonards in the name of Chaac, the goddess of rain. It was Ahmal's first public appearance in several years, and was attended by representatives of three major Mexican news chains and two national television networks. No government representatives were invited and none appeared, with the exception of several federal agents.

Ten minutes before the celebration began, a helicopter landed in the setting sun's golden light on the field close by, and a group of tough-looking men emerged. In their center was Damien, dressed in golden robes and holding in his left hand a magnificent plume of multi-colored Quetzal feathers, symbol of royal authority.

Not far away was another helicopter, from which Peter and Danielle now emerged. They had no attendants. Gutteriez had assured them that he would arrange for his men and the Savonards to cooperate in getting them safely to their helicopter. Their plan depended entirely on Damien recognizing Danielle and being willing to listen to her.

The M.C., a member of the Savonard Directorate, began the proceedings by introducing Ahmal. Ahmal spoke to the crowd for several minutes, reminding the people of their pre-Columbian heritage, the richness of their culture, and the importance of maintaining the spiritual traditions that made their culture great. Darkness was falling as she finished. She took the torch from her podium and handed it to her assistant, who lit the three fires around the cenote. She walked round its five and a half foot diameter, stopped opposite Damien in his golden robes, raised her offering high and then let it drop down into the dark depths of the well, hearing the faint splash echoing upwards. Then, selected Savonard and Zapatista leaders came forward and made their offerings, which were chosen to represent the ancient culture of Mesoamerica. A group of Savonard singers sang a haunting song of long ago, mourning the loss of what had been, and celebrating its imminent return.

In the meantime Peter, holding Danielle's hand, edged closer to Damien until stopped about five feet away by one of his guards. Peter stepped back behind Danielle, who took out a small flashlight and held it to illuminate her face, smiling coyly at the nearest guard who allowed her to edge a couple of feet closer, Peter following on her heels in the darkness.

"Damien," Danielle called quietly.

Several people looked around in surprise and annoyance.

"Danielle!" Damien was stunned to see her, remembering quite suddenly the sandy smell of their California beach and her warm skin. He edged closer to her and gently touched her cheek.

"What brings you here?"

"You... Damien... You bring me here."

He stared at her. "What for?"

"Come with me Damien, we have a helicopter here. And I have an island where no one will ever find you."

Damien looked at Danielle in wonder, her fresh face untouched by the horrors he'd seen, her simple faith that her wealth could protect one such as him, and his heart twisted. His cartel guards surged between them, moving him closer to the cenote to make his offering. He looked over his shoulder at Danielle.

"This is no life for you, Danielle. Go home!" He steeled himself, remembering Yonchin's bullet-ridden body, and turned away.

"Damien! Please come! Save yourself!" Danielle cried frantically. But she got only angry looks from the crowd.

Several of the Savonards, young men who did not look like delegates, pressed closer to the Special Being, jostling with his own guards and the thickening crowd.

The M.C. announced, "And now Nah T'subi' will make the final offering."

A cartel guard handed Damien a large bag, and stepping up onto the very edge of the cenote, Damien reached into the bag. He felt human hair. He hesitated, then grasped the hair and pulled out the severed head of the Minister of Armaments of Mexico, who had been assassinated the night before. Steeling himself for the second time that night, Damien lifted that spiteful face high over the edge of the cenote.

"I dedicate the head of this tyrant," he said loudly in Spanish, "to the Mexican people's fight for freedom." Cameras flashed. Then he dropped it.

The head hit the water with an audible splash. Then, there was a roar, the crowd surged and the young Savonards took advantage of the moment to shove Damien hard off the edge of the cenote. He fell without a sound into that pit of darkness.

Into the stunned silence, the M.C. cried, "Oh my God! Nah T'subi' has sacrificed himself as of old, the bravest and most powerful warrior, to the gods!" And he raised his arms high in the light of the fire.

DAMIEN

Damien's cartel guards, beside themselves with fear and rage, pulled out their guns and shot the M.C., then rushed for their helicopter while shooting indiscriminately into the crowd. The night descended into chaos.

★★★

Danielle wept through much of that night in the small, rather dingy hotel nearest the cenote. She and Peter had been able to get away in the helicopter, but she hadn't wanted to leave Mexico until she knew Damien's fate for sure.

By the time the police arrived at the cenote, the drug cartel gangsters had melted back into the night. Ambulances took away the dead and dying, while some of the Savonards, including Ahmal, stayed on, flashing lights into the cenote as though to reassure themselves that Damien was really gone. At last they departed in their bus, singing songs about liberation. Peter knew that at some point the next day the military police would try to retrieve the Minister's head and Damien's corpse. He phoned Gutteriez to confirm the timing; the aging Commander, whatever his ineffectiveness in military combat, had an extensive intelligence network.

Peter and Danielle had a simple breakfast brought to her room, and Danielle ate in silence.

"I need to be there when the police go down into the cenote today," Peter said. "I want to see if they find Damien's body."

"Of course they will find his body," Danielle said quietly. "How could they not?"

"Anyway, I'll be away for a few hours. Do try to sleep."

"Damien answered me," she said. "He seemed to want to come."

"I know, Danielle, I know. Now please rest if you can. You need it."

She looked at him, hollow-eyed, and he left.

The scene at the cenote was as Peter expected. Police had cordoned off the area and a military team was coordinating the search of the well. One man in scuba gear was being lowered down the well, with two others controlling the descent from above. Peter watched them raise a bag that looked like it might contain the Minister of Armament's head. As he was waiting for Damien's body to come out, Peter was surprised to see a small man standing to one side, and recognized him as the old man he had met when Damien had escaped Gutteriez's cave.

Peter approached him. "Do you remember we met once at the Usumacinta River and talked about the Special Being?"

"Oh yes, I remember."

They were both watching the well, and observed the scuba diver climbing out.

"Well, I don't speak Spanish. Would you please ask them if they've found the body of Nah T'subi'?"

"It doesn't look like it."

Three of the soldiers who had been working by the well were heading in their direction.

"If not, would you please ask them if Nah T'subi's body could have been carried away by a stream at the base of the cenote, or have disappeared some other way?" Peter asked.

The old man turned to the three young soldiers and asked them Peter's questions. They confirmed that only the Minister's head had been found, not Nah T'subi's body, and explained that there was no way out but up, which was why the bottom of the deep hole still held bones from ancient Mayan and Toltec human sacrifices. Asked where

DAMIEN

they thought Nah T'subi's body might be, they shrugged and moved on.

Peter looked at the old man and said, "I have a feeling that it is no accident that you were there at Nah T'subi's last escape, and you are here now."

"I saw him emerge from this cenote an hour before dawn." said the old man, calmly.

"But how is that possible? It must be more than fifty feet to the bottom. How could he survive such a fall?"

"Simply because the well contains at least twenty feet of water."

"But those walls are sheer. And he must have banged himself up on them, going down. Did you help him climb out?"

"Ah," said the little man, "that I have not the strength to do."

"Someone else?"

"No. He did it on his own. I have done some mountain climbing in my time. I can see only one way he could have done this, and it would have taken enormous strength."

The old man stretched his arms and legs wide, "He would have had to push his hands and feet into the walls of the well, like so, suspending his body in the centre, and inch his way upward."

"That sounds impossible."

"For an ordinary man, yes, I think so." The old man fell quiet, then, "Even Nah T'subi' had to rest in the shadow of the well when he made it to the top. Fortunately the guard had fallen asleep."

"Did he see you?"

"Oh yes, and we had quite a talk."

"About what?"

"About his mission. He seems to believe that violence is necessary. He said big changes require it, and I guess, if you think of the American War of Independence, the Civil War, the French Revolution, or the Russian Revolution of 1917, led by men like Lenin and Stalin, he's probably right."

"Stalin was a mass murderer."

"Yet it was Stalin's leadership which won the war against Hitler. Because he was a mass murderer he could execute the kulaks and force hundreds of thousands of people to leave their farmlands and travel far beyond the Urals to build industrial cities, with factories that made powerful artillery, modern fighter planes, and above all, the superb T34 tank that proved its superiority at Kursk in 1943. And then think of ancient Greece or Rome, and men like Julius Caesar, who were made through violence."

"And unmade."

"Only after several hundred years. The point is: he has found himself and believes he has a vital mission. He's no longer the boy he was."

"But he's serving the drug lords! How do you turn that into an important mission?"

"Quite right, and I made the same point. He said drug money will be used to topple the governments of Mexico, the Central American states, and large parts of South America, leading to a new way of life."

Peter was reminded of Britain's use of the opium trade to weaken the Chinese government in the nineteenth century, but still he could only shake his head. "Damien's out of his mind."

"Or using the tools available to achieve a greater end," the old man said. "Don't forget he is a Special Being."

"What exactly do you mean by Special Being?"

"I'd rather not get into that."

"Why?"

"Because it'll sound like nonsense to you."

"Try me."

DAMIEN

The old man shook his head. "You'll have to keep a very open mind."

"I can do that."

"You see, as an astronomer I have looked through high-powered telescopes—some of the best in the world—at unimaginable realities. I've seen the deaths of stars, and not only stars, star systems, even whole galaxies like our Milky Way swallowed by other incomprehensibly huge galaxies. And new galaxies and stars are formed from these gigantic convulsions. Watching all this, I came to realize that what we call intelligence or consciousness is an integral feature of the universe. It is not separate from physical existence, it is… part of it. To imagine that we are the only intelligent beings inhabiting this universe is simply childish."

"Excuse me," Peter said, "but what has all this to do with Damien?"

"That this linking of modern human and jaguar genes has opened him to the source of great power without sacrificing intelligence."

"But humans are also animals. We still have our animal genes, don't we?"

"But most of those are not functioning. In the course of our evolution we've become centered on certain genes which have enabled us to become human beings, focused on what we value as rational processes."

"Nothing wrong with that, is there?"

"Except that we've distorted reality to achieve this narrow use of rationality and tried to impose it on nature. But in your Damien, latent gene linkages have been reactivated, which makes him literally a New Being, connected physically to the universe in a way that you and I have lost."

"Which makes him also very dangerous."

"Very—but to whom?

ABOUT OSCAR DONALD ERICKSON

Award-winning author Oscar Donald Erickson was a professional script writer for television, film and radio. He has also produced novels, short stories, poems, plays, and essays, many of which can be found on his website, oderickson. com. Before turning to full-time writing Oscar taught English at the University of British Columbia and the British Columbia Institute of Technology.

He divides his time between homes on Bowen Island and in Vancouver, and enjoys travelling to research his novels.

Printed in Canada